Praise for *The Uncertain Places*

"*The Uncertain Places* continued to surprise me on almost every page—and, as a writer, filled me with raw, disgraceful envy: Boy, I wish I'd thought of that one..."
—Peter S. Beagle

"Has it really been nine years since *The Alchemist's Door*, Lisa Goldstein's last book under her own byline? It's been a long wait, but *The Uncertain Places* is one of those delightful books that are worth the wait. It combines all the things that I like best about Goldstein's work: great, believable characters; a well-defined setting (this time it's 1970s Berkeley); and subtle magic that plays by the rules."
—Charles de Lint, *Fantasy & Science Fiction*

"Goldstein's complex and ingenious plot transplants the forest realm of European folktale, where witches grant wishes with strings attached and you'd better be careful which frog you kiss, into the sun-drenched hills of Northern California in the 1970s—and beyond."
—Ursula K. Le Guin

"This entrancing book perfectly captures the subconscious logic of fairy tales—you'll find yourself believing it all, and wishing you could go to these places yourself, with all their wonders and perils."
—Tim Powers

"It's fitting that a spider is the symbol of the elf-struck family in this book, because Lisa Goldstein's prose is more than a little like a spider's web: so deceptively simple that you could take it for granted until the angle of light changes and its full beauty is suddenly revealed...a tale as tangling, tricksy, and enchanted as the Fair Folk themselves."
—Tad Williams

"From Lisa Goldstein, one of our most subtle and enduring writers, comes this exquisite interweaving of fairy tale and modern life. *The Uncertain Places* demonstrates that love and the stuff of legends are sometimes indistinguishable and share the same dark bed."
—Lucius Shepard

"A gripping story that twists with compelling dream-logic; Goldstein's fairy tale family radiate believable unreality, and the faerie realm contained herein evinces the perfect mix of terror and attraction. Start reading this at your peril; once I did, I couldn't stop until I was done."
—Cory Doctorow

"It's an engaging look at Northern California in the '70s by way of the Brothers Grimm...a shrewd and satisfying venture down the crooked paths and unpredictable byways of the Otherworld."
—Patricia A. McKillip

"It's all about family values: ancient legacies, young love, dumb luck, and home cooking. And no one understands better than Lisa Goldstein that terror is a dish best served cold."
—Terry Bisson

Praise for Lisa Goldstein

"She has given us the kind of magic and adventure that once upon a time made us look for secret panels in the halls of wardrobes, or brush our teeth with a book held in front of our eyes, because we couldn't bear to put it down."
—*The New Yorker*

"Lisa Goldstein is the perfect, born storyteller. Her story pulls you in and wraps you round and it is hard to think of anything else until it is over."
—Diana Wynne Jones

"Lisa Goldstein's work deserves to be celebrated along with that of Alice Walker and Shirley Jackson."
—Lucius Shepard

"[Lisa Goldstein] never writes the same type of story twice, and she never disappoints."
—Mark Graham, *Denver Rocky Mountain News*

THE UNCERTAIN PLACES

The Uncertain Places

Cover design and illustration by Ann Monn
Interior design by Elizabeth Story

Tachyon Publications
1459 18th Street #139
San Francisco, CA 94107
415.285.5615

smart science fiction & fantasy
www.tachyonpublications.com

Series Editor: Jacob Weisman
Editor: Jill Roberts

ISBN 13: 978-1-61696-014-8
ISBN 10: 1-61696-014-0

First Edition: 2011

Printed in the United States of America by Worzalla

9 8 7 6 5 4 3 2 1

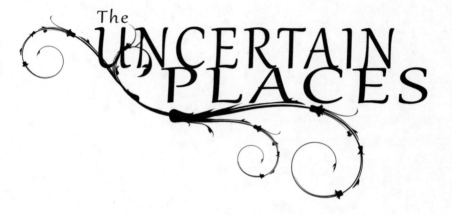

The UNCERTAIN PLACES

A NOVEL BY AMERICAN BOOK AWARD-WINNER

LISA GOLDSTEIN

Tachyon Publications / San Francisco

Acknowledgements

If I could arrange for the San Francisco Opera Company to gather under my agent's window and burst into a chorus of "Thank you, Russell Galen," it still wouldn't repay my debt to him for everything he did with this book. I'm very grateful for all his hard work.

Other people I need to thank are: Michaela Roessner, David Cleary, Lori Ann White, Darrend Brown, Larry Goldstein, Nancy Weidlin, Janet Voet, Nick DiChario, Lucius Shepard, Tim and Serena Powers, Ursula Le Guin (for, among other things, information about Napa), Rick Kleffel (who told me about the perfect book at the perfect time: *When the Rivers Ran Red: An Amazing Story of Courage and Triumph in America's Wine Country*), Tim and Karen Hildebrandt at Spectator Books, Bobbie Vierra at the St. Helena Public Library, and of course Jill Roberts and Jacob Weisman, the managing editor and publisher of Tachyon Publications respectively.

And special thanks to Doug Asherman, for his encouragement and patience and good humor, and for just generally being wonderful.

1

IT WAS BEN AVERY who introduced me to Livvy, Livvy and her haunted family. This was in 1971, when Ben and I were sophomores in college. A lifetime ago, another world, but it seems like I can still remember all of it, every motion, every color, every note of music. For one thing, it was the year that I fell in love. But for another, I don't think that anyone who experienced what I did that year could possibly forget it.

Ben had gone to Berkeley early in September, before classes started, to find an apartment for us. He'd seen Livvy's sister Maddie in a play and they'd started dating, and when I got to Berkeley he couldn't talk about anything else. Now we were going to visit her family up in Napa Valley, in the wine country, for a couple of days.

Back then Ben drove a humpbacked 1966 Volvo, a car that seemed ancient even though it was only five years old. It smelled of mold and rust and oil, and to this day, whenever I find myself in a car like that, I feel young and ready for anything, any wild scheme that Ben or I would propose. The car went through a constant cycle of electrical problems—either the generator didn't work, or the regulator, or the battery—and on this trip, as on so many others, the battery warning light flickered on and off, a dull red like the baleful eye of Mordor.

We got on the freeway and headed out of Berkeley, then passed through the neighboring suburbs. As we crossed the Carquinez Bridge Ben started telling me about the last time he'd taken the car in, and the Swedish mechanic who told him the problem was with the "yenerator." He did a goofy imitation of the mechanic, who I was sure was nothing like Ben portrayed him, but I barely paid attention. I was thinking about my upcoming classes, and about this sister of Maddie's he wanted me to meet.

"Tell me again why I'm coming with you," I said, interrupting him in the middle of the story.

"You'll like them," Ben said. "They're fun. Come on, Will, have I ever disappointed you?"

"Disappointed, no," I said. "Frustrated, enraged, terrified—"

"Terrified? When were you ever terrified?"

"That time you took your mom's car out for a drive—"

"Every kid does that—"

"You were twelve."

"Yeah. Well."

"And you haven't gotten much better since then. Slow down. Ah, God, you're not going to try to pass that car, are you?"

The Volvo rattled over into the oncoming lane for a terrifying moment, and then Ben swore and moved back. "Where did all these cars come from all of a sudden?" he said. "It's like they grow them around here or something, along with the grapes."

"A bumper crop," I said.

"Give me a brake," he said, not missing a beat.

"Don't be fuelish."

"Have I ever steered you wrong?"

"Yes. Yes, you have," I said, returning to my first theme. "My very first day at your house, when you gave me that chili pepper and told me it was a yellow strawberry—"

"They're fun, I told you," he said. He could usually keep up with me like this; it came of knowing each other since kindergarten. "You'll like them. And Maddie has a sister—"

"Not as pretty, you said."

"Well, I would say that, wouldn't I? Maddie's beautiful, and talented, and creative, and Livvy's..."

"A pale shadow."

"No. No, they're different, that's all. Livvy's a chemistry major."

"Chemistry? What have you gotten me into here? We'll talk about the chromium molecule or something. *Is* chromium a molecule? I don't even know. Stick close to me, Ben."

"Can't. Maddie and I have plans."

"Oh, great."

The sun was setting, throwing long shadows across the road. We'd reached the farmlands by this time, and I could see cows grazing in the fields on either side of us, and long rows of grapevines.

We left the freeway and started up a twisting mountain road. Trees stood along either side, just starting to turn autumn red. A truck carrying a load of grapes crawled in front of us, then finally turned down a driveway and was hidden by the trees.

"Look, you'll like it," Ben said. "It's this huge farmhouse, that they've added to every generation—you get lost just looking for the bathroom. And acres of vineyards, and their own wine label...Livvy plans the dinner around the wine. Last time she made—"

"Livvy cooks?"

"Yeah, didn't I tell you? She's a terrific cook. Interested now?"

"She cooks in the kitchen, right, not over her Bunsen burners? Adding chromium to the meatloaf? Because I think I have a chromium allergy or something..."

"Ah," Ben said. "Here we are."

He twisted the wheel hard and we headed down an unpaved road. The road had a brief argument with the car, shaking it back and forth; then finally they seemed to resolve their differences and we continued on. A few minutes later he parked, and I looked out.

The house we'd come to looked as if Hansel and Gretel's witch had taken a correspondence course in architecture. The front was the Craftsman style so common in California, with deep eaves, a wide porch, a gabled roof, a couple of stone chimneys. Behind that, though, was another house, attached halfway along its front to the first; this one was Victorian, with curlicues and gewgaws and a round, pointed turret with a weathervane on top. Stepped back behind that was yet another front, timbered and plastered like a Tudor cottage. Balconies stuck out at weird angles, and stairs went up and down connecting them, and small windows peered out wherever there was room for them. Somewhere in the midst of all of this a cathedral tower lifted high above the other buildings, looking as bewildered and out of place as a man who had lost his glasses.

The front door opened and two dogs ran out, barking. Then a girl who looked about thirteen came out onto the porch and hurried after them.

I turned to Ben angrily, wondering if this was one of his jokes—though it seemed a lot more mean-spirited than they usually were.

"Oh no," he said. "No no no. That's Rose, the third sister. The rest of them should be around here somewhere."

We left the car and got our duffle bags out of the back seat. The front door opened again and Maddie stepped down to meet us.

I'd met Maddie before, of course, with Ben; I'd even gone to see her in her play. It was true, as Ben said, that she was beautiful, but after a while you saw that a lot of her beauty came from the way she presented herself. She was dramatic, vividly present, with long hair the color of polished mahogany, and brown eyes that seemed lit from within, like a lantern behind smoked glass. Her teeth stuck out slightly, the result, she'd said, of refusing to wear her retainer when she was younger. At first glance she seemed tall; then you'd realize, with a start of surprise, that she was actually less than average height, that it was all an illusion caused by her long legs and the graceful way she carried herself.

"Ben!" she said, hugging him. She gave me a hug next, much shorter. "I'm so glad you could make it. Livvy, this is Ben's friend Will Taylor."

I turned, startled. I hadn't seen Livvy come out. She looked a bit like Maddie, but darker, with black hair tied in a thick braid down her back and nearly black eyes. And she seemed different from her sister in other ways too—more self-contained, self-sufficient, as if she carried an important secret. Maddie was always open; she would say anything to anybody. In contrast Livvy seemed exotic, mysterious.

Maddie pulled her shawl around her. It had bright blocks of color, red and yellow and green, from Mexico or South America somewhere. "It's cold out here," she said. "Let's go inside."

"That's my shawl," Livvy said.

"I'm just borrowing it," Maddie said.

"The way you borrowed my boots. And my embroidered blouse. And—"

"Here—you can have it back."

"No, no, you take it. I just want to say goodbye. Goodbye, dear shawl, it was good knowing you for the little time we had together."

Livvy reached out for the shawl. Maddie slipped away and ran for the porch, laughing.

By the time Ben and I caught up with them Maddie was holding the door open for us, and we went inside. The living room was in the Craftsman style too, huge and dark, with wide plank floors and wooden rafters. One wall held a fireplace big enough for Ben to have parked the Volvo in. A small fire burned inside it, seeming to shiver within the vast space. Around the fireplace was a flowery pattern of jade-green and gold tiles, with writing in black Gothic letters just under the mantelpiece. There were built-in bookcases to either side, the shelves crammed with books, some standing, some lying down or leaning diagonally against their fellows. The smell of garlic and roasting meat wafted out from somewhere within the house.

"You can leave your bags here," Maddie said. We set them down near the door, under a line of pegs that held coats and scarves and dog leashes, and then followed Maddie past some overstuffed couches and chairs.

There was a fireplace in the dining room, too, and another built-in cabinet, the kind most people would put their best china in, although Maddie's family seemed to use it as another bookcase. A wooden table ran the length of the room, with benches on either side.

The table was mostly set, but Livvy came out of the kitchen carrying some napkins and silverware. "Do you need any help?" Maddie asked.

"Great timing, as usual, Maddie," Livvy said. "No, I'm pretty much done here."

Maddie straightened a few napkins. A heavy terracotta pot stood in the middle of the table, with a pine tree in it half as tall as I was, and I went over to pick it up.

"No, leave that there," Maddie said, and Livvy said at the same time, "No, that's okay where it is."

I set it down, and Livvy carefully moved it back a few inches. "I thought it would get in the way," I said.

Maddie and Livvy looked at each other. "Our mother would have a fit if anyone moved it," Maddie said.

"Okay," I said. I wondered, uneasily, what other family customs I would violate in the next few hours.

Suddenly I realized I didn't even know their last name. "What's the mother's name?" I whispered to Ben.

"Sylvie."

"I can't call her Sylvie, can I? Sylvie what?"

"Sure you can. Sylvie Feierabend."

What the hell, I thought. "What kind of name is Fire Robin?" Ben had told me the family were hippies, but I wasn't expecting one of those pretentious pseudo-Indian names.

"It's Feierabend's name, sir." This was one of the phrases we passed back and forth, the way other people quoted baseball statistics. It's from *Catch-22*—someone says it whenever he's introduced to Yossarian.

Usually it made me laugh, but right now I was too nervous. Still, I realized I hadn't heard the name right. "Fire...whatsis?"

"Feier," Ben said. "Abend."

"What does it mean?"

"It means quitting time in German," Livvy said, coming out with more napkins and stuff. "Getting off work. Festive evening."

"Really? How'd you get a name like that?"

"Maybe we had a really lazy ancestor," Livvy said, heading back to the kitchen.

Rose came in, followed by her dogs, and then Mrs. Feierabend. The mother had dark hair, streaked with gray and piled on top of her head, and dark eyes behind black-framed glasses. She was plumper than her daughters, and she looked tired, a bit vague about everything, as if she'd suddenly found herself having dinner with no idea of how she'd gotten there. That could have been because of the glasses, though; the thick lenses made her eyes look distant, blurred, like fish in an aquarium.

We sat down to eat, and I have to admit that the food was everything Ben said it would be. Terrific pork chops, homemade bread, bean salad, pasta with pumpkin sauce instead of tomato, three or four kinds of wine—and this was long before nouvelle cuisine, this was just Livvy making up a dinner out of whatever she'd bought that day.

"How long have you been here, Mrs. Feierabend?" I asked. She was sitting across from me, and I could only catch glimpses of her face through the pine needles. At this point I wasn't going to move the tree, though, not for anything.

"Here? Oh, I got here a few minutes ago, didn't I, Livvy?"

Livvy and Maddie looked at each other, trying not to laugh. "No, I meant—how long has the vineyard been here? When did your family start making wine?"

"It belongs to my husband's family, really. They came to the United States, oh, sixty years ago, something like that. Seventy."

"Rose knows," Maddie said.

"Rose supposes she knowses," Livvy said. It sounded like something they repeated a lot, a private family nursery rhyme.

"I *do* know," Rose said. "The Feierabends came here in 1888, from Germany." She turned to me and said, very serious, "I'm writing a history of the vineyard."

I wondered where Mr. Feierabend was, but it didn't seem like something I could ask. Yet another thing Ben hadn't told me. I felt as if I'd been dropped over enemy territory without a map. Hell, without a parachute.

"This is a wonderful dinner, Livvy," Mrs. Feierabend said.

That seemed a safe enough subject. I turned to Livvy, who sat next to me, and said, "It's delicious. Where did you learn to cook like this?"

"We just started experimenting," Livvy said. "Maddie and I, when we were kids."

"So you cook too?" I asked Maddie.

"Not really," Livvy said. "Mostly she just played around with the spices."

Maddie laughed. "I liked their names," she said. "They sounded so exotic—tarragon, turmeric, cardamom. I put in anything that sounded good."

"She made sweet hamburgers one night," Livvy said. "What was in that one? Cinnamon?"

"I don't remember. I wrote a poem about it, though. About all the names of the spices."

"Can I read it?" Ben asked.

"Of course not. I was twelve."

"Do you still write poems?" I asked.

"Oh, Maddie's a complete Renaissance woman," Ben said, looking at her admiringly. "Actress, writer, dancer... What else?"

"She used to recite poetry when she was ten," Livvy said.

I'd felt the rivalry between the sisters all evening, and I thought this was just one more example of it, Livvy making fun of her sister's younger self. But to my surprise Maddie pushed her hair back and looked out at us, her face serious. "'The moon was a ghostly galleon tossed upon cloudy seas,'" she said. "'The road was a ribbon of moonlight over the purple moor—'"

"'And the highwayman came riding—riding—riding,'" Livvy joined in. "'Up to the old inn door.'"

"You left out one of the 'riding's."

"He put too many in," Livvy said. They laughed.

"Will and I are thinking about writing a movie," Ben said. "It's called *Theater Closed for Repairs*."

We'd told this joke before, of course. It was part of the routines we did, our two-man band. People either got it or told us we were idiots. This time Livvy and Maddie laughed, though Mrs. Feierabend looked a little confused.

I started to relax, to eat without worrying about making conversation. "Pass the chromium," I said to Ben, and he grinned and sent over one of the wine bottles.

Rose went off somewhere after dinner. Ben took a joint out of his shirt pocket and lit it. All through high school and college Ben had had the ability to smoke dope without attracting any attention, a sort of superpower that had served him well on many occasions. This time, though, I couldn't see how he could possibly get away with it.

"Hey, man," I whispered urgently, nodding at Mrs. Feierabend. The smell—a combination of burnt rope and skunk—drifted out over the table.

"It's okay," Ben said. He sucked in the smoke and held it, then passed the joint to Maddie. When she was done she passed it to her mother, and I watched, faintly scandalized, as Mrs. Feierabend toked as if she'd done it all her life.

I don't remember much of the rest of the evening. The room grew dark, and Livvy set out silver candlesticks along the table and lit the candles. We talked about the horrible war in Vietnam, and the elections the next year, which we hoped would get rid of Nixon. We talked about the draft lottery, and how Ben and I had both, miraculously, gotten high numbers and so avoided the draft. We got hungry again, and Livvy went back to the kitchen for second and third helpings. Maddie told us about her latest audition, which was for an experimental play about Joan of Arc.

Finally Mrs. Feierabend stretched and said she was going to bed.

"Where's Will going to sleep?" Livvy asked.

Mrs. Feierabend blinked. "I thought he was with you, dear," she said.

I was too stoned to feel embarrassed, though I sensed I would have been, under other conditions. I thought Livvy blushed, but it might have been the candlelight. "We could put him in the Moaning Bedroom," she said.

"The Moaning Bedroom?" I said. "I don't know if I like the sound of that."

"She doesn't really moan very often," Livvy said. "No one's heard her for a while now."

"Who doesn't?"

"Our ghost." Livvy smiled at me, then seemed to see something in my expression. "Okay, what about Aunt Alva's room?"

"Is Aunt Alva another ghost?"

"I don't think so. I'm not sure who she was, to tell you the truth. Some German ancestor or another. Rose knows." She looked around blearily, then seemed to remember Rose had gone.

"Okay," I said.

Livvy and I stood and went back out into the living room. I got my duffle bag and followed her down a hall and up a grand polished staircase. Black-and-white photographs hung on the wall over the stairs, groups of unsmiling people in old-fashioned clothes, those German ancestors probably. We went down another hall, stopped at a closet to gather sheets and blankets, took another turn, and then Livvy opened a door and motioned me inside.

We made up the bed together, first the sheets and two pillows, none of which matched, then a heavy goose-down comforter, and finally a threadbare quilt covered with patchwork stars. "The bathroom's down this way," she said, heading back to the door.

I memorized the twists and turns to the bathroom, remembering what Ben had said about getting lost. "Good night," she said.

"Good night," I said. "Thanks for dinner."

I got up in the middle of the night, needing to pee. After the warmth of the comforter the air in the hallway seemed arctic. I traced the steps carefully to the bathroom—turn to the left, three doors down on the right—stood for a long time in front of the toilet, getting rid of all the wine I'd drunk, and then headed back. The way back looked different somehow, and after a while I found myself in what seemed like another house altogether, one with carpeted floors and flowered wallpaper. Moonlight shone in through the windows, and I remembered uneasily that I hadn't seen any windows on my way out.

Something stood ahead of me in the hallway, a tall apparition with glowing red eyes. I screamed. A door opened, and light streamed out into the hall.

A cat jumped down from a table and ran off. I leaned against the wall, breathing heavily. A few working neurons in my brain shouted "Cat! Cat!" to the rest of my body, which ignored them and continued to panic. My palms were damp; I wiped them on the jeans I'd worn to bed.

"What is it?" someone said.

It was Livvy, coming out of the open door. "Sorry," I said, finally starting to calm down. "It was just a cat. I didn't know you had cats."

"A few," Livvy said. "Along with the dogs."

She looked at me with those dark eyes a while longer, saying nothing. Her hair was unbraided, and she was wearing a loose white nightgown that fell to her ankles. Her feet were bare. I had the feeling that I could walk up to her, kiss her, take her into her room, and that she would welcome it. I was very aware of Ben and Maddie in their own room, somewhere in the house. We stood still for a long moment, and then one of us said, "Good night," and the other repeated it: "Good night."

I found my room easily after that. I opened the door and went in, cursing my cowardice. But what had I seen, after all? What if I had been wrong?

The next morning I used the shower, an ancient contraption made out of pipes and valves and pressure gauges; it looked like a cross between medical equipment and a place to hang your coat. Then I got dressed and went downstairs.

The long table was already set for breakfast, with cereal and rolls and half-full pitchers of milk and orange juice. Dirty plates and cups lay scattered across the table; I was probably the last one up.

I looked around for coffee, and found a nearly full pot on the sideboard. I poured myself a cup and sat down, feeling the silence of the house gather around me. So Ben was keeping to his plan of spending the weekend with Maddie, I thought, and I would be left to my own devices. I couldn't say I blamed him.

I picked up a blue bowl painted with bright red and yellow flowers. None of the dishes matched, I noticed; they all seemed to have come from different sets. I had been too nervous to see that at dinner. There was even a cup of nearly transparent porcelain, which I vowed to stay away from; it would be just my luck, after last night, to break it.

Livvy came in and started to stack the dirty dishes. "Sorry about last night," I said, pouring out some cereal. "Hope I didn't wake you up."

"Don't worry about it," Livvy said.

"Oh, God—I screamed like a girl, is that what you're saying?"

She laughed. "No, really—it's all right." She picked up a final bowl and headed for the kitchen. "Is there anything you want to do today?"

"We could see the vineyards, I guess."

"Well, they're down on the flatlands—we'd have to drive there. But we could take a walk. Let me just finish here."

I ate breakfast while she washed up, and then we headed outside. The land around here seemed very changeable, going from dry yellow grass to shady trees and then back to grass again.

"Here—let's take the Moon Bridge. This way," Livvy said.

With that name I expected something curved and fanciful, but the bridge turned out to be broad and flat, with a stream below that had dried to a trickle. "Why is it called that?" I asked, but she didn't know.

Still, we talked easily, as if the embarrassing moment of last night had never happened. She told me about studying chemistry, sometimes being the only woman in the class, about living off campus with roommates—and I got a promise that we would see each other in Berkeley, that we would exchange phone numbers.

We followed a path under a stand of trees, almost a small wood. Birds chirped all around us. I was telling her about being a psych major, and trying not to sound too boring, when I heard some people talking up ahead of us. "Quiet," someone said, or I thought they said. "They're coming."

A flurry of wings sounded, and birds flew up all around us. I went on ahead of Livvy and came out of the trees. There was no one there.

"What was that?" I asked, heading back toward her.

"What?" she said.

"There were some people here."

She frowned. "I didn't hear anything."

"You sure?"

"The acoustics are pretty weird in here. You can hear all kinds of strange things."

It probably wasn't important. I let it go, too focused on Livvy.

One other odd thing happened, though I didn't make too much of it at the time. We went back to the house, and Livvy took me into the kitchen to make that day's bread. The kitchen looked as old as everything else, the floor and counters made out of chipped black and white tiles. There was a wooden table in the middle, a smaller sibling of the one in the dining room. The stove was one of those ancient white monsters up on four legs, with two ovens, a griddle, and a shelf above the burners with an overhead light. A frayed rag doll sat on the shelf, next to salt and pepper shakers, and looked out at us with one button eye.

Livvy mixed the dough, then scattered flour along the table and started to knead it. "This is the most relaxing thing I know," she said. "If I was a psychiatrist I'd tell my all patients to make some bread if they felt unhappy. Here—you want to try it?"

She tore off a lump of dough and gave it to me. Our fingers brushed as I took it, and a small, secret burst of fireworks went off inside me. I started to push the dough flat, but it was more difficult than it looked.

"Use the heels of your hands," she said. She wiped her face with the back of her hand, leaving a smudge of flour on her cheek. "Work your wrists."

We kneaded the bread side by side for a while. "She's getting ready to drop him, you know," Livvy said suddenly. "You might want to warn him."

"What?" I said, startled.

"Maddie. She doesn't keep men around very long. She manages to get rid of them quietly, though, without any fuss. Almost as if she loses them and can't remember where she put them."

It was only then that I heard footsteps in the dining room, and I realized that whoever it was must have heard the last part of the conversation. A moment later Ben and Maddie and Mrs. Feierabend came into the kitchen.

"Were you talking about me?" Maddie asked. "I heard my name."

"Of course," Livvy said, not looking at all embarrassed. "About all the men you've broken up with."

"Livvy," Mrs. Feierabend murmured. "That isn't very nice."

"I might be keeping this one, though," Maddie said, putting her arm around Ben.

"Maybe she just had to kiss a lot of frogs to find her prince," Ben said.

Everyone fell silent—a shocked silence, as though Ben had said something dreadful, broken some taboo. Then Maddie laughed. "Livvy's more like that other fairy tale, 'The Frog King,'" she said. "She throws them against the wall to see if they'll turn into princes."

"Maddie!" Mrs. Feierabend said. Her vagueness disappeared suddenly, like a movie snapping into focus. "Stop it!"

"All right," Maddie said. "Sorry, Sylvie."

"That's ridiculous," Livvy said. She turned to me. "Don't listen to her."

This was the moment, I think, that I realized that there was a lot about the family I didn't understand. It wasn't just private jokes and phrases, like Ben and I had. It was something deeper, something they didn't share with anyone.

I didn't care, though. I was already charmed, as Ben had said I would be. I was half in love with this batty, disorganized family, so different from my own—Livvy's cooking, and Maddie's poetry, and all the mismatched sheets and dishes. I even liked it that they called their mother by her first name, something I would never have dared to do with my own parents. So there were mysteries here—so what? I was intrigued by Livvy, wanted to know more about her. I wondered what it meant that Livvy cared what I thought about her. At this point there was really only one mystery I wanted to solve—what would Livvy be like in bed?

We left early the next day, to spend Sunday back in Berkeley studying. Ben kissed Maddie one last time in the living room and, for something to do, somewhere to look, I tried to read the black spiky letters on the fireplace. "Spinne am abend," it said, German, probably. Abend was evening, Livvy had said; feierabend meant festive evening. So—"Spinner in evening"?

"Spider in the evening," Ben said, coming up behind me.

"What?" I said. "When did you learn German?"

"Rose told me. She doesn't know why it says that, though—none of them do." We went outside and got into the Volvo. "You ever hear of anything like that? A nursery rhyme or something?"

"Itsy bitsy spider?" I suggested.

Ben looked at me, disgusted. We said nothing while he turned the ignition, each of us praying in our own way that the battery hadn't died. The car started, and we cheered. Ben pulled out the choke to give it more gas—I'd never seen a car with a choke before, and was never to see one again—and wrestled the car out onto the road.

"So?" he said, once we'd gone past the rough patch of road. "What did you think?"

"I wasn't adequately briefed, man," I said. "There's a lot you forgot to tell me."

"Like what?"

"Like where's the father? Are he and Sylvie divorced?"

"I don't know. I don't even think they know. He disappeared a few years ago, I think."

"Disappeared?"

"Yeah. Sylvie had a hard time around then—she sort of collapsed."

"Collapsed?" I was aware I was repeating everything he said, that we sounded like a call-and-response for some bizarre religious sect. "What do you mean?"

"A breakdown or something. Remember when Livvy said that she and Maddie had started cooking? They had to—Sylvie couldn't do anything for a while. She's still not over it, not completely."

I felt briefly ashamed. People had started talking about Women's Lib around that time, and I thought I was all for it, and yet I hadn't realized how much work Livvy had done that weekend. I'd just sat back and enjoyed it, oblivious as a lord. My only excuse was that I was used to it; my mother had cooked for us every evening, and then cleared the table and washed up afterward.

"So the three of them do all the housework?" I asked. "Along with school, and—and Maddie's acting?"

"No, it's not as bad as that. They have someone who cleans for them, I think. The vineyard does pretty well, I guess."

"But how? The father's gone, and Sylvie can't be running it—"

"I'm not really sure—they have people to run it, probably. Maddie once told me that the family's been lucky, that everything they do goes well. That's why she thinks her acting career will take off."

That sounded pretty freaky to me, but I wasn't going to say so to Ben. "What do you think?" I asked. "About her acting?"

"Well, she's good. I mean, you saw her." He sighed. "I don't know, man. It's a hard business."

"And what about that weird reaction yesterday, when Maddie said something about the Frog King?"

"What weird reaction?"

"When we were in the kitchen, remember? Everyone looked shocked. Even Sylvie woke up for a minute there."

"They were probably just mad at Livvy, for saying Maddie's going to break up with me. She's jealous of Maddie—you probably noticed."

"Yeah, but Maddie's jealous of Livvy too."

"There's something going on with those two, that's for sure. Probably best not to get into it. So anyway. How did it go with Livvy?"

"Well, she gave me her phone number."

"All riiight!" Ben said, and punched his fist into the air.

2

READING THIS OVER, I see I've concentrated so much on the Feierabends that I never even described Ben and me. I'm tall and skinny, with a tall, skinny nose; my hair is straight and brown, and back then I wore it long like everyone else. I have no idea what color my eyes are—they're brown or gray or green, depending on when I look at them—so mostly I just say hazel and everyone's happy.

Ben's as tall as me but stockier, with long wavy sandy-colored hair. He shaves once a week, on Sunday, because, he says, he likes looking in the mirror and seeing a different face every day.

I was thinking more about what I looked like just then, working my way up to calling Livvy and asking her out. I was nervous, though not so much about what she'd say; she had made it pretty clear she wanted to go out with me. But there was something about the farmhouse, something different, and the mad thought had occurred to me that what we'd had, whatever it was, couldn't survive outside it. Finally I called her on Wednesday, and we made arrangements to see each other that weekend.

I borrowed Ben's car to pick her up. She lived in a huge crumbling house on Dwight Avenue, with posters papered over the cracks in the walls and plants climbing up over the windows—almost, it seemed, as if she was trying to replicate the relaxed disorder of the house in Napa.

I didn't notice a lot of my surroundings, though. I was too busy trying to take her in. Her hair was loose, unbraided, and fell to her shoulders. She wore a green embroidered blouse, from Mexico I thought, and a green velvet skirt that reached to her ankles, and silver bracelets on each arm. She picked up her shawl and put it on.

"You got your shawl back from Maddie, I see," I said.

"Oh, no," she said, laughing, drawing it closer. "This is more of a loan. Maddie gets what she wants, sooner or later."

I let her pick the restaurant—she knew a lot more about food than I did, after all—and she suggested a place on Telegraph Avenue. She yelled goodbye to her roommates, none of whom I saw that first time, and we drove off.

Telegraph in those years was like a caravan, a carnival. I parked, and we threaded our way through palm readers, drug dealers, jugglers, exiled poets, religious acolytes in saffron robes. A girl with a cat on a leash came toward us, then a man shouting about being followed by helicopters. Music played from radios and storefronts. Every third person was on some drug or another, oblivious to his or her surroundings. It smelled like patchouli and marijuana and unwashed bodies, and sometimes, after a demonstration, of teargas.

Finally we reached the restaurant. We sat down, and I realized I needn't have worried; we began to talk as easily as we had in Napa, as if no time at all had passed.

It didn't hurt that I apologized for not helping her out that weekend. "I didn't realize how hard you were working until later," I said.

She looked startled, and I wondered if I'd violated another taboo, strayed into yet another one of those areas the family avoided. "What did I say?" I asked.

"I've never heard a guy say that before. That he wanted to help."

"Hey, I'm all for that stuff. Women making as much money as men, men doing housework."

"Really? How many times have you done the dishes after a meal?"

I thought about my mother. No, best not to mention that. "Me and Ben don't actually wash the dishes *after* a meal. More like before—someone says, Hey, all the dishes are dirty, and someone else says, Well, why don't you wash them, and then the first person says, I washed them the last time..."

She laughed.

After dinner we decided to go to the Berkeley Rose Gardens. She'd seen them before, though I'd only heard of them—as a place to make out, though I didn't tell her that.

We drove around the campus and up Euclid Avenue, then parked and sat on a bench looking out at the terraces carved into the hillside. A lot of the rose bushes had been cut back for fall, but there were still rows and rows of flowers spread out before us. The sun began to set over the bay and other people joined us, standing or sitting and talking quietly, watching as intently as if they were at a play.

Color after color spread out across the sky: yellow, apricot, gold, bronze, like another garden overhead. We talked about everything: favorite books, favorite movies, food, our classes. At one point I found myself telling her why I wanted to be a psychologist.

"So there we were, in her room, and I saw that she'd taken out a cigarette lighter and was lighting a pile of paper on fire. And I said, 'What the hell are you doing?' and she said, very calmly, 'Lighting this paper on fire.'

"And I'd had no idea she was going to do that. I'd been going out with her for a month, and she'd never given me a clue."

I stopped. Was I really talking about an ex-girlfriend on a first date? Not a good idea, Will. Still, Livvy was smiling at me, waiting for me to go on. She had a way of smiling without opening her mouth, and along with her high cheekbones and her nearly almond-shaped eyes, she looked—well, not like the Mona Lisa, more as if da Vinci would have painted her instead, if he'd known her back then.

"Anyway, I wanted to know why she'd done that, wanted to understand," I went on. "So I took a psych class and I liked it, and then took a bunch more."

I'd had another reason for taking that psych class, but there was no way I'd tell Livvy this part. Beatrice hadn't been the only crazy woman I'd gone out with. Was there something wrong with me, was I somehow drawn to these people? Was Livvy, was her family...

But she was still looking at me with that smile, and I managed to change the subject by asking her what her family had been up to. She told me about Maddie, who had spent Sunday looking frantically through their library for something about Joan of Arc, and Rose, whose new project was learning how to spin yarn from dog fur.

"Dog fur?" I asked. "No, wait—you have your own *library*?"

She looked a little embarrassed. It was unfashionable to be rich in Berkeley in those days; everyone wore torn jeans and T-shirts and pretended to be working class.

"It's just a room filled with books," Livvy said. I refrained from saying, as I would have said to Ben, that yes, that was the definition of a library. "Mostly dictionaries and German history, stuff like that."

"Why doesn't she use the library on campus?"

"She doesn't go to Berkeley. She went to a city college for a semester, but she dropped out."

Everyone I knew went to Berkeley; it was faintly shocking to find someone who didn't even go to college. "She's that sure she'll make it as an actress? That's right—Ben said she thinks your family's lucky, that she'll succeed no matter what she does. What do you think? Is she crazy, or do you think she'll pull it off?"

"Well, she's pretty serious about it," Livvy said. "What about your family? What are they like?"

"Pretty dull, especially compared to yours. I have two brothers but they're a lot older than I am, so I hardly ever see them. My father's a bookkeeper." I didn't want to sound *too* dull, though, so I hurried on. "When I was a kid I spent most of my time at Ben's house."

"So what's his family like?"

"Not that great, right now. His parents were really messed up by the sixties. They got married in college, and they settled down, and his father became some kind of bureaucrat at the Capitol Building. They'd never had a chance to experiment much, and then all of a sudden there's all this talk about free love and dropping out. I think it made them crazy that they missed it. They're going to get divorced, probably."

"Wow. What does Ben think?"

She was so easy to talk to. I told her about growing up in Sacramento, each of us feeling that real life was happening somewhere else, without us, and about how we had decided in the fifth grade to escape to Berkeley together.

The sun sank into the bay, and Livvy kissed the palm of her hand to it. Everyone else applauded: a very Berkeley moment.

"Hey," I said. "Quitting time. Feierabend."

She laughed. I could barely see her face in the darkness. I fixed on one point, a smudge of nose, and leaned over and kissed her. She kissed back. The other people were getting up and leaving, talking softly, but we barely noticed them.

It was cold when we left, and fully dark, the sky so black and velvety you could have painted a picture of Elvis on it. I invited her back to my place but she said no, she had to get up early. It was only later that I realized she had never really answered my question. Did she, like Maddie, think that her family had some secret source of luck, some inside track, or was this just Maddie's delusion?

The weeks that followed were probably the happiest time of my life. We went to movies, to concerts, we tried out new restaurants with Ben and Maddie. The four of us stayed up late and talked about those things you only ever discuss in college—Is everything fated, or is there free will? Is what I see as green the same thing that you see as green?

Every day seemed exciting, from the moment I woke up to when I fell into bed. I was tired all the time, from trying to cram too much into one day, but it was a good tiredness, it lent a sharp, hallucinatory quality to whatever I did. I even did well in my classes. I felt open to everything, eager to take in anything the world wanted to give me.

And I was smart enough to know that I was happy, to understand that I had won some kind of cosmic lottery. My only mistake was thinking that it would never end. Why should it, after all? We would graduate, I would marry Livvy and Ben would marry Maddie; we'd live next door to each other and write "Itsy bitsy spider" on our fireplaces.

Well, I was nineteen. That's my excuse. Nineteen-year-olds don't know anything.

Maddie got an audition in Los Angeles. The day she was due to come back I found a banner that said "Aloha" and some plastic leis, and I told Livvy and Ben to wear Hawaiian shirts, and the three of us stood waiting at the Oakland Airport to welcome her to Hawaii.

She saw us as she came off the plane and nodded, as if to say, Of *course* we would do something like this. "Aloha!" Ben said, and slipped a lei over her head.

Everyone around us laughed; a few people even applauded. No one looked annoyed, as had been the case with some of my other youthful exploits. The world seemed to conspire to wish us well.

"Aloha!" Maddie said. She reached out to hug all of us, nearly knocking the bottle of champagne Ben had brought out of his hand. "It went fantastic—I got the part, I know I did!"

Ben took her suitcase in his other hand. Maddie talked about the audition all the way back to the car, and then as we drove away from the airport. I couldn't make any sense of what the play she'd tried out for was about, but it didn't matter. A small secret exaltation was growing within me. Livvy and I hadn't slept together yet, but this time she would have to at least spend the night in our apartment. Ben had the only car, and he'd be busy with Maddie.

We reached the apartment and went inside. Livvy and I sat together on the couch. Ben went to the kitchen to get some glasses and then sat in our only chair, and Maddie dropped gracefully to the carpet beside him, her legs crossed. "So if you get this part—" Ben said, inching the cork out of the champagne bottle.

"When," Maddie said.

"When do rehearsals start?"

"In a few weeks."

The cork popped loudly. Suddenly I saw what was happening. Maddie would be away for rehearsals, and for the play itself. And then maybe she would go on to something else, more plays, a part on television, a movie. Los Angeles was full of opportunities.

It didn't matter, though; I was sure of it. We four were lucky, protected. We had aligned ourselves with the grain of the universe; whatever happened to us would be for the best.

"You could transfer to be with her," I said. "Go to UCLA."

Ben looked at Maddie. Maddie said nothing. Livvy glanced at me, a look intent with meaning, but I turned away from her quickly. Silence filled the room like water; any minute we would drown in it.

I had to say something. "Miss Feierabend, what would you say is the secret of your success?" I said, pretending to speak into a microphone. "Do you have any words for your adoring fans?"

I held my closed fist out to Maddie. "You'd better be adoring, you fans," she said. "I didn't spend all this time in Famous Movie Star School to have just any kind of fans."

"That's good, 'cause we went to Adoring Fan School," I said.

"Was this an accredited Adoring Fan School, or one of those fly-by-night places?"

"Absolutely the best. We learned Humble Abasement, and Spontaneous Applause, and Asking Politely for an Autograph..."

I was running out of things to say, an unusual occurrence for me. I looked over at Ben. He had finished a glass of champagne and was pouring himself another one. I reached for the bottle and filled the other glasses. "To us," I said.

"To success," Maddie said. "My name in lights."

"That's a lot of lights," I said. "Madeleine Feierabend. Or are you going to change your name?"

"Not a chance. I'm gonna make them use every one of those lights."

We drank. Only Maddie spoke, telling us what the director had said about her voice, her gestures. Finally Ben and Maddie said good night and went off to Ben's bedroom.

I looked at Livvy. We stood and headed toward my room, as if it were the most natural thing in the world, something we did every night. At the same time, though, my heart was pounding, and everything around me seemed heightened, as sharp as crystal.

We fell onto the bed and undressed each other slowly. I slipped her silver bracelets off each hand, and after I set them down on the nightstand I opened the drawer, as casually as I could, and took out the rubber I had so carefully prepared beforehand.

"It's okay," she whispered. "I'm wearing my diaphragm."

"Really?" I said. "Hey, I love you."

I'd meant it lightly, that I approved of her foresight, and yet when I said it I realized it wasn't light at all. She didn't answer, though, and we pretended that I had never said anything.

3

BEN AND I SAID NOTHING about Maddie in the days that followed. In the entire time we'd known each other, three-quarters of our life on earth, we'd almost never talked about emotion, love, any of that sticky stuff. Once when we were in the second grade I'd come across him sitting behind the buildings at school, curled into himself and sobbing as quietly as he could. The class bully had beaten him up; the skin on his face was red and shiny from being shoved against the asphalt playground. I put my arm around him, and after a while I began to cry too, and we sat there for a while, sobbing and looking around nervously, knowing our lives would be over if anyone found us together like this.

And we never discussed it, not even at our most drunk or stoned. Sometimes I wondered if I had only imagined it, but then I remembered the feeling of the sun on my head, the hot tarry smell of the asphalt, the thin bones of Ben's shoulders.

We'd planned to go to the farmhouse that weekend, and as the time grew closer Ben became more cheerful. Finally, late on Friday afternoon, the four of us piled into his car, Ben and Maddie in front and Livvy and I in the back.

Ben had the radio tuned to the rock station KSAN, and as we headed off the song "Lil' Red Riding Hood" came on, Sam the Sham howling "Awwwooohhh" at the chorus. "God, I hate this song," Maddie said.

"Why?" Ben asked.

"Too sexist?" I asked, from my new perspective as a liberated man.

She didn't answer, just reached over and turned the radio off. "Why don't we sing instead?" she said. "That's what we used to do on long trips—remember, Livvy?"

She started on Joni Mitchell's "Carey, Get Out Your Cane," wavering off pitch a few times—surprisingly, since I thought she'd turn out to be a good singer along with all her other talents. Then Livvy joined in, and for a while they sounded eerily beautiful together, the way members of the same family sometimes do. Livvy sang "Dear Prudence," and Ben did Janis Joplin's "Oh Lord, Won't You Buy Me a Mercedes Benz."

When it was my turn I sang "Everyone Says I Love You" from *Horse Feathers*, a Marx Brothers movie Ben and I loved. I wasn't sappy enough to do Zeppo's part, the straight romantic lead; instead I sang Chico's nonsense verses, where flies and mosquitoes, cows and bulls and Christopher Columbus all sing about their love.

Livvy had brought bags and ice chests of food along, and when we got to the farmhouse I helped her unload them and carry them inside. In the kitchen I asked her if I could help, but she said that everything was ready and just needed a half an hour to warm up.

I wandered around the house for a while, then headed back to the living room. This time I saw a bowl of oatmeal and a glass of milk on a table near the stairs, but I wasn't going to ask about it, not for anything. I started into the dining room—and turned quickly, sure I'd seen something move behind me.

Now I noticed a short, stout man, crouched in the corner of the living room. He'd unscrewed one of the electrical outlets and was lining up the various pieces in front of him.

He turned around to look at me. His face was almost completely covered in fuzz, from which his nose stood out like a rock; he looked something like a cross between a bush and a hedgehog. He wore a green coat and trousers and a flowered vest, not exactly the clothes you'd choose for electrical work, and his hair had a green tinge too, though that might have been the light.

Sylvie came in from somewhere. "Will!" she said. "You've met our neighbor, I see."

The neighbor turned back to his work. "He's going to help Lem open a restaurant," Sylvie said.

This was another trait of the family's; they seemed to think you knew the same people they did, that you would pick up on all their references. At the same time, though, they seemed determined not to tell you anything. It was off-putting, exasperating, and if it wasn't for Livvy, there were times when I might have given up and gone home.

"Who's Lem?" I asked.

"Our cousin. Uncle, really. No, wait—my husband's cousin. That's right, isn't it?"

The neighbor nodded.

"What kind of restaurant?" I asked.

Livvy bustled out of the kitchen and set a bowl of grapes on the living room table, and at the same time Ben and Maddie came into the room. "Oh, for God's sake," Maddie said, sounding disgusted.

"What?" Livvy said.

"The grapes."

"I told you—they're our grapes," Livvy said. "You can boycott other people's grapes as much as you like."

"They shouldn't even be picking grapes. They're supposed to be on strike."

I looked at Maddie, amazed. I'd known that Cesar Chavez had called for a grape boycott, of course, but I'd never heard of anyone demanding that their own employees go on strike.

"Yeah, well, they pick our grapes because we pay them better than anyone else," Livvy said. "We pay them more than Chavez is even asking for. So why shouldn't they keep working?"

"Because of solidarity. They should stand with their brothers."

"You gonna go out and tell them that? Stand out there with a picket sign?"

"Maybe I will."

Livvy laughed. Maddie laughed too, a little, and I saw that they had only been half serious. She seemed to realize she had radical ground to make up because she said, "Are you going to the Moratorium Day rally?"

"I don't know," Livvy said. "I'll have to see what my schedule is like."

"Right, your schedule. And I suppose people in Vietnam will stop dying until you get your schedule straightened out."

"Stop hassling me, Maddie. I'll see what I can do."

"You can march with us if you want. I'll be with the Young Socialist Alliance—"

"Wait a minute," I said. "You're a Trotskyite?"

"Trotskyist," Maddie said. "Yeah, what about it?"

I knew she had radical politics, but I'd had no idea. To me Trotskyists were like Cubs fans—their team was never going to win, but you had to admire their loyalty.

Livvy headed back to the kitchen. Maddie followed her, and Ben followed Maddie, and Sylvie had gone somewhere, and I was all alone again. I turned to the electrician. "So are you a cook too?"

He shook his head. For a horrible moment I wondered if he couldn't talk, but then he said, "I help."

"Help what?"

"The family."

"How do you know them?"

"Oh, we've known each other for a long time, our family and theirs. Years and years."

"Is your family from the Old Country too?"

He laughed, as if I'd said something clever. "The Old Country, yes. The Oldest Country."

"Dinner's ready!" Livvy called.

I gave up and headed into the dining room, where Maddie was pointedly singing the farmworkers' anthem, "De Colores." From then on everything went nearly the same as our last visit, a terrific meal, good wine, interesting conversation. I noticed that there was no pine tree on the table this time, but that was another thing I wasn't going to ask about.

After dinner we got ready to go to bed, a little earlier this time since I was looking forward to sleeping with Livvy in her own room. "Wait a minute, dear," Sylvie said to Livvy. "Where's Will going to sleep?"

"He's with me," Livvy said.

One of those confused looks wandered onto Sylvie's face and stayed there just a moment too long; her eyes grew vague and her mouth opened. Then she shrugged and laughed, as if to say, Oh, you girls are always having your fun with me.

Livvy had a brass bed, sounding, to my ears anyway, as loud as its namesake, the brass section of an orchestra. Livvy assured me that no one could hear us. "Let's check that out," I said, and rolled over to kiss her.

*

That night I dreamed I was being chased by the family's huge white stove. I ran, terrified, but the stove kept gaining on me, its burners clattering, its doors opening and closing like mouths.

I woke suddenly, feeling Livvy's bedroom reassemble itself around me in the dark, then sat up. The bed played the first few notes of "Seventy-six Trombones," and I stayed there awhile to make sure I hadn't woken Livvy.

I knew where the bathroom was by this time, and I padded outside and down the hall. I used the toilet, remembered to put the seat back down, and headed back.

Two eyes glittered down the hall in front of me. I slowed but kept walking; no damn cat was going to frighten me this time. Then someone whispered in the dark, and the next thing I knew I was in one of the empty bedrooms, my heart playing jump rope inside my chest.

I peered out the door. Some light was coming through the windows now, and I saw two shapes walk into a room across the hall. One was tall and very thin, the other stout and much shorter, only about five feet tall.

I moved as silently as I could and looked into the room. One, the stout one, had his back to the other, dusting something.

The tall man spoke. "Have you swept the floors?" he asked.

The other man didn't stop working to answer. "I have, sir."

"And washed the dishes?"

"I have, sir."

"And scrubbed the bathrooms?"

"I have, sir."

"Very good," the tall man said.

I cleared my throat. The stout man jumped and turned around, scattering dust. His duster was made out of peacock feathers, I saw. The other man came about slowly, ponderously, like an ocean liner.

"What are you doing here?" I asked.

"We're the cleaners," the tall man said.

"In those clothes?" They were dressed in black, like pallbearers from the last century, with gloves and top hats, and coats with long tails. The taller man carried a cane. "In the middle of the night?"

"We like working at night," he said. His face was narrow and very pale, his eyes dark, with darker shadows beneath them. There was something almost sneering about his hat, which was taller than any hat I'd ever seen.

"Does the family know you're here?" I asked.

"Of course." He turned to the other man. "Come," he said, and they moved into the room across the hall.

I watched them go, then went back to Livvy's bedroom. I was feeling very tired now, as though there was nothing unusual about finding two men cleaning in the middle of the night. "Livvy," I said. "Livvy, there's some people in your house."

She murmured and turned over. I felt bad for waking her, but I couldn't just let those men go wandering around. I shook her. "Livvy."

"What?"

"I just ran into some men out in the hall. They said they were the cleaners."

"Uh-huh."

"Are they?"

She opened her eyes. "Are they what? Cleaners? Yeah. They come to clean for us at night."

"Why?"

"I don't know. They like it." Her eyes closed again.

I thought of something. "Is that why you put out the oatmeal and stuff? For them to eat?"

She didn't say anything; she'd gone to sleep again. I got into bed next to her, feeling exhausted. The next thing I knew I was waking up. I stuck my head up and saw a clock on Livvy's nightstand, the kind with a round face and two bells like earmuffs. It was seven thirty.

Livvy rolled over, snoring softly. I wanted to talk to her, ask her about the men I'd seen, but I couldn't bring myself to wake her up again. And already it was starting to feel like a dream, like something that had happened a long time ago and far away.

I stood up carefully and went to the window. The sun was rising, and I could see a balcony or veranda or whatever you call it out there, stretching around this side of the house.

I wandered aimlessly around the room, ending up at a bookcase by the far wall. Livvy had the books everyone was reading in those days—Vonnegut, *Dune*, *One Flew Over the Cuckoo's Nest*—a row of chemistry textbooks, and then, on the bottom shelf, some Mrs. Piggle-Wiggle books. I grinned at that, thinking about how I was going to tease her, and then, on second thought, decided that it probably wasn't a good idea.

The children's books struck some association in my mind, and I realized, finally, what last night reminded me of. A children's book, a fairy tale, a story about people who were forced to do someone else's bidding. I remembered how I'd thought of Hansel and Gretel when I'd first seen the Feierabends' house, and how Ben had said something about kissing a frog prince. And I remembered too how strange they had all acted, as if Ben had said something as unmentionable as sex.

There were no fairy tales on Livvy's bookshelves, not that that proved anything by itself. I pulled out *Mrs. Piggle-Wiggle's Magic* and sat down to read it by the window. She was quite a woman, apparently, was Mrs. P.-W. She had built her house upside-down, with lamps sprouting out of the floors and low walls to step over in the doorways. No wonder Livvy had liked these books.

"Hey," Livvy said sleepily.

I put the book back and sat next to her on the bed. "Do you remember what I told you last night?" I asked.

She thought a moment and then said, "Yeah. You met those people."

"Those people?"

"That's what we call them," she said, laughing. "You know—'I don't think Those People cleaned the bathroom last week.'" I heard the capital letters this time.

"The strangest things happen when I go walking around your house," I said. I hesitated, then took a gamble. "Next time I go to the bathroom I'm leaving a trail of breadcrumbs. Like Hansel and Gretel."

She turned away from me, then used the same motion to push herself out of bed. "Everyone's going to be up soon," she said. "I should probably start breakfast."

Was that the time I saw the crows, and met the man in the woods? No, I went into the woods the day Maddie and Ben had their argument, so it had to have been later.

A week or so after this, then, we went up to Napa again. Saturday morning I helped Livvy make breakfast, pancakes with apples and sunflower seeds, then sat down to eat.

Rose sat next to me. I realized that I hadn't paid much attention to her on these visits, that nobody did, really, that she seemed to enjoy going off on her own or with her dogs. She was plumper than her sisters, and her hair was lighter, a darkish blonde. She had the same light brown eyes as Maddie, though.

I asked her about knitting with dog fur, and she started telling me about her dogs, their possible ancestry and where she'd gotten them. All three of them lay near the table, hoping for scraps, their tongues, the pink color of bubblegum, hanging down from their mouths. Obviously I'd been wrong about Rose; all it took was one question from me to get her talking.

"I'm going to make some dinners for my mother when we're done here," Livvy said to me after breakfast. "You can come watch, but it probably won't be very exciting."

"Okay," I said. "I'll just go exploring."

I half-expected some objection, Livvy telling me I could go into every room but one, like Bluebeard (and there were those fairy tales again), but she just said, "Great. It'll take me about three hours—come and get me then."

"Okay," I said, and headed for the front door.

"Wait a minute," Rose said, running after me. "Here."

She took a knitted scarf from the row of pegs near the door and handed it to me. It was dark brown, the color of the imported mustard Livvy had served the night before.

"Thanks," I said. It was ridiculously ugly, but I felt touched nonetheless. "Did you make this out of dog fur?"

She nodded and ran back into the house. I slung the scarf around my neck, feeling the itchy fur against my skin, and went outside.

I took a path away from the Moon Bridge and the trail Livvy and I had followed earlier. I found an old garage divided into four bays, with Rorschach blobs of oil stains on the floor, and then another outbuilding with an old broken padlock on the front door and nothing inside. There was a tall, round hill beyond that, and I set off toward it.

It was October, before the rains had started, and the grass and foxtails along the road had dried to straw. I skirted the hill and began to see trees, first alone and then in clumps, and finally I came to a wood. A sharp breeze blew, and I pulled the scarf closer around my neck.

The path continued on through the trees, and I kept going; it was wide enough that I didn't worry about getting lost. The forest seemed grander than anything I'd seen so far in Napa, and the trees were bigger too, their leaves turning red and copper and gold. I could smell the drying leaves, and underneath it a faint scent of cool mold.

Were these oaks? I'd grown up in a city and had never learned a lot about trees, and I wondered how much Livvy knew, and if she could teach me. Probably—it seemed a piece with her all her cooking and baking and housework. Everything seemed wonderful to me in those days, and I thought how far out it was that my girlfriend's family owned their own forest, for God's sake. We could come here in summer, and she would tell me the names of the trees, and we would lie down together on the forest floor...

I heard voices near me, on the other side of a stand of trees, and for some reason I stopped to listen instead of going forward. "What do you think of the Young Masters, then?" one of them said.

"The first seems a good choice," another voice said. "The second—I'm not sure about the second. He senses things. He has dreams."

They made strange noises as they spoke, clacks and ticks, as if a clock had learned how to talk. "Does he know about the bargain, do you think?" the first voice said.

"Some keep to the bargain even when they know," a third voice said. "And some keep to it in ignorance."

"Rose knows."

"Rose supposes she knowses."

There was a kind of metallic stuttering laughter then, like knives falling to the floor.

"And so? Will he keep to the bargain, whether he knows or no?"

"We'll test him, then. See if he holds fast. Show him his side of the bargain, then look to see if he says yea or nay."

"Test him, then wait and watch."

"Watch and wait."

I couldn't take it anymore; I had to know who these madmen were. I pushed my way through the trees but I couldn't see anyone. Were they farther on?

I heard a loud raucous caw, and then another, and then a flock of birds lifted from the trees into the air. Crows, black and shining. Had they...? No. No, of course not.

I hurried on, looking frantically for a group of people. Normal people, standing around, having a normal conversation. Even an insane conversation, like the one I'd just overheard. Crows didn't talk—that was one thing I knew for sure.

I broke through another group of trees, but there was no one there either. I kept going, running now, glancing back and forth as I went.

Trees seemed to crowd around me, to circle me, coming forward and bowing and stepping back. I heard nothing but my breath, sawing in and out, and somewhere, far away, the sound of one crow calling to another. I felt a panic stronger than anything I'd ever known before, something elemental, a desire to run screaming through the forest. I was aware that I'd left the path far behind, but it didn't seem to matter.

I hit something and fell down. I stood, panting, and realized a moment later that I had run into someone and knocked him to the ground.

"Oh, God," I said. "Oh, God, you're hurt. Here, can you stand up?"

It was the neighbor who had fixed the electricity, the man with the fuzzy face. No, wait—it was someone who looked like him, a brother or cousin. This one was fatter, for one thing, his face rounder, and he wore a green coat and jeans. Light fell on him through the trees, turning his hair a greenish-brown. Forest colors: it was no wonder I hadn't seen him.

I held out my hand. The man took it and sat up cautiously, then stood. "Are you all right?" I asked.

"I believe so," he said. He had a very deep voice for such a small man.

He'd torn his jeans somehow, and there was blood on his leg, a shocking red against the green. "You're bleeding," I said.

He looked at his leg and sat down suddenly on a log. "Here," I said. I took off the scarf Rose had given me and wrapped it around the wound, tying it tight. "Is that better?"

He got up again and tried his leg carefully. "I—yes," he said. "Yes, that's a good deal better. Thank you."

"Don't thank me, man. I was the one who knocked you over."

"I do thank you, nevertheless."

I realized that I had run off the path a long time ago, that I had no idea how to get out of the forest. "Do you—do you know how to get out of here?" I asked.

"Indeed I do. Do you see those trees over there?"

I nodded.

"Go past them and you will find the path. Turn left, and the path will lead you out."

"Thanks," I said. "Thanks a lot."

"You're quite welcome."

He bowed and walked away. I had a lot more questions for him—Where had he come from? How was he related to the electrician? Did he know any talking crows?—but I was also eager to get out of this place.

I followed his directions and found the path, and a short while later I reached the edge of the forest. The land here looked unfamiliar, and I realized that I'd come out of the trees at a different spot from where I'd gone in. For a moment I felt that horrible panic again, and then I saw the high tower of the house in the distance and ran toward it.

I burst into the house and hurried toward the warmth of the kitchen. Livvy was still there, frying bacon over the stove. "You'll never believe this," I said.

"What?" She turned and looked at me with her mysterious smile.

My heart melted like syrup whenever she did that, and for a moment I couldn't talk. Finally I said, "I went for a walk in the forest. And I heard this weird conversation, these people talking about God knows what, a bargain, keeping to the bargain, and Young Masters—I could hear the capital letters when they talked. And then I went to look for them, and all I saw were some birds. Crows."

She frowned. "What do you mean? You couldn't find them?"

It didn't sound very interesting, put like that, didn't capture the strangeness of it. "Or they turned into crows," I said, laughing unconvincingly.

She didn't say anything. "I heard something like it the first time I was here, when we were out walking," I went on. "And you said the acoustics were funny in the woods."

"Well, they are. Probably you heard someone from half a mile away."

"Yeah, but I went in the other direction this time. This was different, a different forest."

She turned back to the stove. "I should have warned you about that. There are all kinds of weird people living there, violent people, some of them. Thieves, ex-mental patients."

"I did meet someone. Remember that guy who was working in the living room, the neighbor? I met his brother, or someone... Do you know him?"

"I don't know. I might have seen him around."

"What about a bargain, the bargain? Did you ever hear of anything like that?"

"No, sorry."

She wasn't telling me the whole truth, I knew that much. But I couldn't accuse her; she was my girlfriend, the woman I loved. We had never even had an argument yet.

I tried again. "They said something about Rose, that she knows about it—"

Someone screamed. Livvy dropped her fork and ran from the kitchen, and I followed.

"Woooo!" someone shouted. "Woooo-hoooo!"

We hurried into the living room. Maddie stood in an alcove under the main stairway, holding a telephone receiver. "I got it!" Maddie said. "I got the part!" The receiver buzzed; she seemed to realize she was still holding it and hung it up. "I got the part. They just called me."

"That's great!" I said.

"Far out," Livvy said.

Just then Ben came up. "Did you hear?" Maddie asked him.

"I think the whole valley heard," Ben said. "They might have heard you in Berkeley."

"Well, let's see some enthusiasm here. What did I send you to Adoring Fan School for, anyway?"

"It's terrific. Obviously." He tried to smile; it looked wrong on his face. "So when are you leaving?"

"Leaving?" She didn't seem to have thought about it until that moment. "As soon as I can. Tomorrow."

"Do you want me to come visit? Or I could blow off my classes, go down with you—"

"Oh, God. I have to pack, and get a ticket—"

"Wait a minute. Do you want me to visit or not?"

"I can't think about that now. Livvy, can I borrow—"

"So—what?" Ben said. "Are we breaking up?"

I looked at Livvy, and without saying anything we retreated back to the kitchen. It was a private argument, obviously.

We could still hear them in the kitchen, though, their voices getting louder and louder. Ben said something about "selfish," and then Maddie said, "Oh, come on, Ben, you could at least try to be happy for me."

"Poor Ben," I said.

"Poor Ben," Livvy said.

Poor Ben decided to drive back that day, leaving me with a dilemma: I could go with him, or Livvy and I could make our own way back on Sunday, which meant spending half a day on buses. BART, the underground system, had been scheduled to open by then, but had been subject to a hundred delays.

I stayed with Livvy, of course. I was still at that stage where I wanted to spend all my time with her. And I knew that driving home with Ben would be awkward, that he would speed wildly and either rail against Maddie or drive in furious silence.

After he left I tried asking Livvy again about the forest. "Look—don't go in there, okay?" she said. "It's dangerous, like I said. And could you do me a favor? Don't tell Sylvie or Rose what you heard. Sylvie's afraid of burglars."

4

I GOT BACK LATE Sunday evening. The house was dark, and Ben was sitting on the couch with the television on. Four or five empty bottles were ranged in front of him on the floor, like a little beer graveyard.

"How'd it go?" he asked.

"Okay. Good."

I waited uncomfortably for some kind of tirade, but it didn't come. Instead he shook his head and said, "They're a trip, those Feierabend sisters. Livvy knew Maddie would break up with me all along, didn't she? How did she know? Did you ever ask her?"

I shook my head.

"They'll go out with us, sure, but no one's ever going to come between them," he said. "Well, you'll see."

"See what?"

"I don't know. Something. They're hiding something. Don't you think?"

"Well, sure." I thought about my visit to the forest. Livvy had made me promise not to tell Sylvie or Rose about it, but she hadn't said anything about Ben. Probably she wouldn't want me to tell Ben either, but hell, he was my friend. And she'd been so secretive, and Ben deserved something after Maddie had broken up with him...

"Did you ever go into the forest near the house?" I asked.

"No—Maddie never wanted to. Why?"

I told him what I'd seen and heard, the crows and the strange little man. He listened closely, even getting up to turn the television off. And he didn't laugh once, not even when I said I hadn't seen anyone talking, only the crows.

"Weird, man," he said when I'd finished. "So what do you think those crows were talking about?"

"About us, actually. We're the Young Masters."

"Then they're behind the times, aren't they? I'm not going back there."

"Well, this was before Maddie broke up with you. They liked you, I think—they thought you'd be a good choice. I'm the one who sees things."

"That's right, you do. Like those strange men cleaning the house. I never saw anything like that, and I've been to the house more times than you."

"I think—" I stopped, trying to figure out how to put it into words. "It's like something out of a story, isn't it? Someone keeping the house clean while they sleep? And did you ever notice that the family changes the subject when you bring up fairy tales?"

"Huh."

"What?"

"Nothing. Just that you're probably right. I wonder what it means." He stretched. "It's late—I'm going to bed."

Suddenly I realized that I was exhausted too. It had been a very long day. "G'night," I said.

Something bothered me, some part of what Ben had said. If Livvy had been right about Maddie, then could the reverse be true? Was Livvy about to throw me against the wall, as Maddie had said?

No. No, we were solid, a couple. I was sure of it.

Life went on more or less as usual. I missed Maddie more than I thought I would; she was funny, one of the few people who'd been able to keep up with Ben and me when we were in the middle of some foolishness. Livvy never tried; she was more of an audience. I certainly didn't mind that, though. Everyone needs an audience, someone to laugh at their jokes.

The next weekend Livvy borrowed a car from one of her roommates and we went up to the farmhouse, and once again I explored the house while she cooked. I found the library, which was in the Victorian part of the house; it had high bookcases along all four walls, a fireplace with a carved wooden mantel, comfortable chairs, a table in the center with green-shaded lamps. A copper rail ran along the bookcases, probably for a rolling ladder, but that was gone now, replaced with an ordinary folding ladder from a hardware store. A lot of the books were in German, with long forbidding-looking titles; the English ones seemed to be whatever anyone was reading at the time, serious history mixed in with ancient bestsellers.

The Victorian turret was completely empty, but the tall cathedral tower had window seats under slit-like windows, and old toys littered across the floor. There were a lot of plastic bows and arrows, the arrows tipped with suction cups, and I imagined the young hellions Livvy and Maddie must have been, age eight and nine, kneeling on the seats and shooting down on anyone unfortunate enough to be walking past.

I couldn't open the doors to the Tudor section of the house; the front door was locked, the other entrances boarded over from the inside. I asked Sylvie about it during dinner.

"Well..." she said. She hesitated, and I thought that at last I would hear some of the family's secrets, stories about strange noises, levitating furniture, mad ancestors locked away behind bars.

"Well," she said again, "it was just too expensive to heat."

I nearly burst out laughing, though I managed to contain myself for Livvy's sake. I have to tell Ben about this, I thought; Ben kept asking me about Livvy, and I never knew what to say.

The next Sunday evening I stood waiting for Livvy at a restaurant on Telegraph Avenue. It was Halloween, and the usual costumes passed by, ghosts and pirates and witches. This being Berkeley, though, there were also political statements, people wearing Richard Nixon and Spiro Agnew masks or dressed like Ho Chi Minh or Che Guevara, and one horrible-looking woman who looked like she'd been burned by napalm. And of course the crazies came out in force, dancing and mumbling and howling at the moon.

Livvy was fifteen minutes late, then half an hour. It got darker and colder; parties started around me, people drinking and playing drums and passing around dope, calling to friends and walking out in traffic to greet someone across the street. A bottle smashed against the pavement, and I heard a siren coming closer.

I kept seeing Livvy everywhere: every woman who wasn't in a costume, and even a few who were, seemed to dress like her. It was as if they'd all found the same giant costume box and taken out things at random—scarves and boots and bangles, patchwork and fringe, embroidery and tie-dye, stars and suns and moons. A lot of them even looked like her, with straight black hair parted in the middle, so that I grew excited and downcast by turns. I realized I had divided people into two categories, Livvy and not Livvy. It didn't seem an unreasonable way to look at the world.

Fifteen more minutes passed. I was starting to get some strange looks, though I was by no means the oddest sight on Telegraph. Two people tried to sell me drugs, and one person wanted to buy some.

A small woman came toward me. She wore what looked like padding on her butt and stomach; she had a gray bun up on her head and wore round steel-colored glasses. At first I thought she was in costume, someone's grandma, though it didn't seem terribly inspired.

Then she turned toward me, giving me a look of concentrated malevolence. Before I knew it I'd backed into a doorway, my heart pounding loudly. After a while I roused myself and looked out into the street, but the woman was gone. I still felt anxious, though, and very paranoid—as if there was something or someone out there, something evil, watching me.

I waited another fifteen minutes. My paranoia grew to include Livvy: Why hadn't she shown up? Was this her way of breaking up with me? Finally I gave up and went home to call her.

"Oh, hi, Will," she said when she answered the phone. She sounded tired. "What's up?"

"Well, we had a date tonight," I said, trying not to sound too accusing.

"Oh. That's right. I forgot."

"You forgot?"

"Yeah. I feel strange—I'm not feeling myself today."

"Who do you feel like?" I asked.

I realized I'd made a mistake before the words were out of my mouth. "It's not funny," she said. "I didn't sleep very much last night—I kept having these horrible dreams."

"Sorry. I'm sorry. What kind of dreams?"

"Awful dreams. I think—I think it's starting. I'm worried, Will."

"What's starting?"

She didn't say anything. "Maybe you should see a doctor," I said. "If you're worried about something."

"No, I'm just...just tired."

"Look, you have to take care of yourself. You can't go around taking care of everyone else like some earth mother..."

"Like *what*?"

"Like an earth mother." I felt stupid now. That was the way I saw her, but I never should have said anything. "You know, with all your cooking and gardening and stuff."

She laughed; even her laughter sounded tired. "Gardening? I never did any gardening in my life. And I cook because it's like chemistry, putting different ingredients together. I'm about as far away from an earth mother as you can get."

Now I remembered going to the forest, thinking she could tell me about the trees. Okay, so I'd made a mistake. She didn't have to take such a sarcastic tone.

"Sorry," I said. Why was I apologizing so much? She was the one who'd forgotten about our date. "Look, I'll call you tomorrow. Get some sleep."

"Okay. Bye."

One of her roommates answered the phone when I called the next day. I hardly ever talked to this woman, a foreign student who didn't seem to speak English. I'm sorry to say, in fact, that I didn't even know what country she came from, and when I talked to Livvy I used to call it Freedonia, the imaginary country in the Marx Brothers' *Duck Soup*. "Can I talk to Livvy, please?" I said.

"Livvy sleep," she said.

Livvy sleep? It was three o'clock. Well, maybe this was good news; maybe she needed a rest after a night of bad dreams.

"Could you tell her that Will called, please?" I said.

"Okay."

I called Livvy again that night, but the same roommate answered and said she was still asleep. With each phone call my anxiety had grown, and by the next day my worry had driven out everything else. I had classes until afternoon, but as soon as they ended I found a phone booth and called her.

I got the same roommate again. I was beginning to hate the poor woman, and I didn't even know her. "Livvy sleep," she said.

Livvy's house was fairly close to campus, and I decided to walk there. I felt like two people as I went, full of optimism and foreboding in turns. One part of me was sure it was all a mistake, that the roommate had misunderstood or forgotten to deliver my message yesterday. The other part kept wondering why Livvy hadn't called, if she was too sick even to come to the phone.

The roommate opened the door when I got there. I brushed past her, too impatient to try to make myself understood, and hurried to Livvy's room. Livvy lay on her bed, her face toward the wall.

I walked as quietly as I could toward the bed. "Livvy," I whispered.

She turned toward me. Her eyes opened, but there was no recognition in them; they were like two zeroes, staring at nothing. "Hello, Livvy," I said. A strand of her hair fell over her face, and I brushed it away carefully.

She didn't say anything. Did she have a fever? I put my hand against her forehead, but it felt normal.

"How do you feel?" I asked.

She stirred, but still said nothing. Fairy tales, I thought. I leaned over and kissed her.

"A wild night, and a terrible one," she said. Her voice was hoarse, as though she hadn't spoken for a long time. "The cries of the horses, the screams of the riders..."

It sounded like a drug trip, acid, maybe. I'd never heard of an acid trip lasting this long, though. Something was terribly wrong. "What do you mean?" I asked.

"I saw a spider, a few mornings ago," she said.

I looked at the roommate, who was standing by the door. "How long has she been like this?" I asked.

"Yesterday and today Livvy sleep," she said.

"Was she sleeping? Or was she talking, like this, with her eyes open?"

The roommate shrugged. I hurried out of the room, found the phone, and called the farmhouse. My fingers were shaking as I dialed.

Sylvie answered. I sagged with relief, delighted to finally talk to someone who didn't speak Freedonian, and an adult besides. "Sylvie!" I said. "Hi, it's Will. I think there's—I think Livvy's sick."

"Sick?" Sylvie said. "Oh, my God, Will. What do you mean? How sick? What's wrong with her?"

Her voice fluttered; she sounded as helpless as she always did. I knew then that although I thought of her as an adult she wouldn't be able to help me, that I was still on my own. It was a terrible feeling, like finding out the floor wasn't solid after all.

"She's, well, she's babbling," I said. "Talking nonsense. And she's been sleeping a lot, too—she slept about two days."

"Oh, God, Will. Look—I have to call Maddie, ask her what to do."

"Maddie? Why? She's in Los Angeles, she won't be able to help."

"No, not Maddie, you're right—"

"Should I take her to a doctor?"

"We have a doctor here. That's it, that's what we'll do. Could you bring her up here? To the farmhouse?"

"Sure," I said. I had no idea how I'd manage it; I'd have to borrow Ben's car, and he had no reason to like the Feierabends. But it was an emergency—he'd understand. He'd have to understand.

"Okay," I said, and hung up.

I ran out of the house. Then I remembered that today might be one of the days Ben worked on campus, in the cafeteria. I hesitated, my brain pulled in a hundred different directions at once. Finally I ran back to the phone and called our apartment, and when he didn't answer I headed toward campus.

I pushed my way through the circus on Telegraph Avenue, past the panhandlers and political activists, the bikers and Tarot readers and guitar players. I hurried into the cafeteria, and there, to my great relief, stood Ben, talking to someone with his back to me.

I went up to the counter. The other man turned. I got a quick impression of an older man, somewhat plump. "Will!" Ben said. He looked startled to see me; then he grinned and indicated the man standing in front of him. "You have to meet this guy. This is Professor Rothapfel, from the German department."

"Ben, listen—"

"He's an expert on German folklore, on fairy tales. He has some theories about the Feier—"

"Listen, it's an emergency. Livvy's sick—I have to take her up to Napa, to the farmhouse. Can I borrow your car?"

"Sure," Ben said. "Sure, but—I'm coming with you."

"What? Why?"

"I want to see the house again. I miss it. And Maddie won't be there."

I sighed. "Okay, whatever you want. Only let's hurry."

I still have dreams about that day. I can't find Ben, or I find him but we can't find the car, or we're driving the car but we realize we've forgotten Livvy. In one dream we make it halfway to Napa, and then we have to turn around to pick up a hat rack.

The reality was almost as nerve-racking. It felt like we spent a year driving through traffic to Livvy's house, two years looking for a parking space. Finally we parked, and Ben and I went into the house to get her. She seemed the same, her eyes open but staring at nothing.

"Come on, Livvy," I said. "We have to go."

I got an arm under her and eased her up, and between us we managed to carry her outside. She was as limp as a sack of laundry. I maneuvered her into the back seat of Ben's car, and she immediately lay down again. I got in with her and put her head in my lap.

We drove away. No one said anything for a while. When we left the freeway I heard Livvy mutter something, and I bent closer to hear her. "What?" I said.

Her voice grew stronger. "Up the hill and down the hill and round about and back again," she said.

"What's she saying?" Ben said.

"I don't know," I said.

She repeated it, louder this time. "It sounds like a nursery rhyme," Ben said. "You know, you really should talk to Dr. Rothapfel—he's an expert on the Brothers Grimm. Did you know—"

"I'm not really interested right now, Ben," I said.

"Right. Okay, I'll tell you later."

Finally we reached the farmhouse. Sylvie and Rose were waiting outside for us, the dogs pacing restlessly around them as if they sensed something was wrong. I expected Sylvie to help me with Livvy, but she just stood there, her hand to her mouth, her eyes wide. Her hair had come loose from its usual bun and hung around her shoulders.

Ben and I got Livvy out of the car, up the steps to the farmhouse, and then inside. We headed toward the stairs to her bedroom, but Sylvie nodded to one of the couches in the living room and said, "No, just set her down here."

"You sure?" I said. "We could take her upstairs."

"No, it's okay."

"Are you going to take her to the doctor?"

"The doctor's coming here."

"Great," I said, feeling relief for the first time that day.

The farmhouse had always been such a welcoming place; I think on some level Ben and I expected to be invited to dinner and to sleep over. Sylvie just stared at Livvy and said nothing, though, and I realized that we certainly couldn't expect anything, not at a time like this.

"Could I—" Ben said. "It was a pretty long trip—could I use the bathroom?"

Sylvie nodded, still looking at Livvy.

I told Sylvie about Livvy's symptoms, even mentioned, because the doctor might want to know it, the possibility that Livvy might have taken some drug. She nodded again, but I don't think she'd heard a word of it.

"You know what's funny?" Rose said. "I never expected it to be her. I always thought it would be me."

Sylvie's head jerked up sharply. "Rose!" she said.

"What do you mean?" I asked.

Rose looked at her mother. "Nothing," she said. "I didn't mean anything."

She did, of course. I was tired of secrets, tired of not understanding things; I wanted to scream at Rose and Sylvie to tell me what was going on. But I couldn't say anything, not while Livvy lay in front of us like this, drifting in and out of consciousness.

Somewhere in the house a clock rang the hours, five o'clock. I wondered where Ben was, if he'd gotten lost. "I'm sure she'll be all right," I said awkwardly.

Finally Ben came downstairs. "Okay," he said. "Let's go."

"Bye," I said. "Good luck."

"Thanks," Rose said.

My heart went out to her. One sister had gone, the other was ill, and her mother hid from the world in a cloud of vagueness. Rose was far too young to have to go through this alone.

"Let me know what the doctor says," I said, and we left.

We got into the car, but Ben made no move to start the engine. Instead he pulled out something from under his coat. It was a faded brown accordion folder, tied with a red string that wound around two circular tabs like an infinity symbol.

"What's that?" I said.

"It's from their library. Dr. Rothapfel said—"

"You stole it? You stole it from their library?"

"Well, yeah. I thought you wanted to know what's going on."

"Not if it means stealing things. I can't believe you did that."

"Look. They're never going to tell us anything, right? The only way we'll ever learn what's happening here is if we find it out for ourselves. And maybe this'll help Livvy."

He knew me too well; with that last sentence all my scruples vanished. He started to unwind the string.

"Let's get out of here first," I said. "The doctor's coming, remember? You don't want them to find us still in their driveway."

"Just a minute."

He opened the folder and took out a pile of paper. The top page was in German, in that spiky handwriting that looks like a seismograph after a minor earthquake.

He riffled through the rest of the pages. "Shit," he said. "They're all in German."

He put them back in the folder and threw the folder into the back seat. "I'll get Dr. Rothapfel to translate it," he said.

He started the car and we drove off. "Why do you care?" I asked. "And why are you talking to Dr. Rothapfel about all this? How did you meet him, anyway?"

He was silent a moment. Finally he said, "I just want to know what's going on. What they're hiding from us."

He wasn't telling me the whole truth, I could tell. "You're hoping to get Maddie back," I said.

This time he was silent for so long I thought he hadn't heard me. "Yeah," he said. "Yeah, I am. I miss them, the whole family. It's weird, you know, that you're the one going to visit them on the weekends now. Talking to them, eating their dinners, sleeping with their ghosts. I was the one that found them."

I couldn't concentrate on Ben's problems for very long. "Do you think she'll be all right?" I asked.

"Sure," he said. "Sure she will."

Dr. Rothapfel took a week to translate the pages, and during that time I did very little but think of Livvy. I called the farmhouse every day, and every day either Sylvie or Rose would tell me that there had been no change, that Livvy was still sleeping, sometimes delirious. Sometimes they'd get her awake enough to eat, but afterward she would go right back to sleep. I asked if I could visit, but Sylvie said she preferred I didn't, that she would let me know if anything changed.

I spent a lot of time wondering if I had ever really known Livvy, or if I'd made her up out of a mysterious smile and a few home-cooked meals. She wasn't the nurturing earth mother I'd thought she was, that was for sure; she was a chemist, a scientist who approached her cooking as logically as everything else. A culinary Mr. Spock.

And what about her sarcasm? She could be unmerciful with Maddie, I'd seen that, but I'd never expected her to turn that scorn on me. How did she even feel about me? I'd told her I loved her, once, and we'd passed it off as a joke. What if she thought of me as just someone to spend time with, pleasant enough, someone who would do until a better alternative came along? The song I'd sung in the car the last time Ben and I visited the farmhouse together, "Everyone Says I Love You," kept running through my mind, only this time it was Groucho's version, full of bitterness and ridicule. Love just invites trouble, he says, and I was starting to think he was right.

I even began to wonder if Sylvie was lying to me, if Livvy had woken up and was doing fine but for some reason didn't want to see me. Maddie had been right, I'd think, Livvy had smashed me against the wall. Only I hadn't turned out to be a prince; I was still just a frog. A hundred times I would decide to visit, to force them to let me see her. Then I would tell myself that I was being paranoid, and I would try to wait patiently until evening, when I could call Sylvie again.

Then one day Ben came home and told me we had an appointment with Dr. Rothapfel. Rothapfel had finished translating the papers.

5

I HAD A CLASS the afternoon of the appointment, but I decided to skip it. I wasn't doing very well in my classes, though I hadn't stopped studying. I just couldn't seem to grasp things, or remember them.

We got into Ben's car, but instead of driving to the university Ben turned toward the freeway. "Where are we going?" I asked.

"To his house," Ben said. "He didn't want to keep all those papers on campus."

I'd had no idea Ben knew this guy well enough to visit him at home. I wondered how many times he'd been there and what they'd talked about, but I wasn't curious enough to ask.

We got off the freeway in El Cerrito, a suburb of Berkeley. Ben stopped the car on a street of nearly identical houses, all of them small and new with well-kept lawns. The car parked in front of us had a bumper sticker that said "POWs Never Have A Nice Day."

Dr. Rothapfel met us at the door and ushered us inside. He had a round head, with close-cropped balding hair and wire-rim glasses, and a brown mustache that looked like a scrub brush.

The furniture in the living room looked like a garage sale at the Winter Palace, everything in white and gold: white carpet, white sofa and chairs with gold legs, white tables with gold scalloped edges. What looked like little diaphragms cupped the furniture legs, protecting the white carpet. The folder lay on one of the tables.

We sat down. "Ah, Ben," he said. "Wonderful stuff you've brought me, truly marvelous. So the rumors were true after all."

"What rumors?" I asked.

"And to think they were living in Napa all this time," he went on. "Since—when did you say?"

"The late eighteen hundreds," Ben said.

"Yes. Yes, that would fit."

"What would fit?" I asked. "What are you talking about?"

Light glinted off Rothapfel's glasses as he turned to me. "What do you know about the Brothers Grimm?" he asked.

"Nothing. They traveled around Germany, didn't they, collecting fairy tales?"

"That's what most people would say, if you asked them. And yet it isn't true. The Brothers Grimm—Jacob and Wilhelm—they hardly traveled at all. Most of the people who told them stories lived in the same town they did. And we think of them as talking to illiterate peasant women, to the proletariat, and yet most of their informants were middle class or even aristocrats, were friends of theirs."

I didn't see what this had to do with anything. I was trying to think of a polite way to say so when Rothapfel went on. "The fairy tales went through seven editions—the brothers kept arranging and re-arranging them, rewriting them, even. Some of the early tales were lost and then found again, found fairly recently. But there's always been a rumor, a hint, that one of the tales is still missing. That it was censored, maybe. The brothers censored a good many of the tales they heard, did you know that? All those evil stepmothers—they were really evil mothers, but the Grimms thought that would be too frightening for children. There's been a lot of speculation about this missing tale, what it contains. The stories we have are about incest and cannibalism and parents killing children, so we thought, well, what could be so horrible that the Grimms kept it out of their collection?"

"And what Ben brought you—that's the missing tale?"

"Oh, better than that. It's the tale, and the correspondence. It tells us why the tale went missing."

"How did you know the Feierabends had it, though?"

"Never mind about that," Ben said impatiently. "I'll tell you later. What's it about?"

"Here." Rothapfel opened the folder and passed him some typewritten sheets of paper.

I read over his shoulder. The first page was headed "21 September, 1808—The Bondmaid. Told by Klara Feierabend."

"A long time ago there lived a poor woodsman. One day he was walking in the forest when a man came out of the trees and hailed him. 'Good day,' the man said. 'And how are you doing today?'

"'Very poorly,' the woodsman said. 'My family and I have not eaten for three days, and if I do not find food for them soon I fear we will all die.'

"'I can help you,' the man said. 'But you must promise to give me the first thing you see when you return home today.'

"'Certainly,' the woodsman said. 'But how can you help me?'

"'Go home and see.'

"The woodsman hurried out of the forest. His heart was light for the first time in many days. He thought to look at the tree growing beside his house when he returned home, and so fulfill his bargain with the man that way. But as he walked up the road to his house his daughter came outside and hailed him.

"'Good day, Father,' she said. 'Have you had any luck in the forest today?'

"The woodsman groaned aloud. But at the same time his wife ran outside and called to him. 'Husband, come look! Every chest we have is filled with gold!'

"The woodsman went inside and saw that it was true. He reached into a chest and pulled out a handful of gold coins, and the chest filled again to the top. His wife laughed and grabbed more gold, and yet more, and every time she took the gold from the chest it filled itself again.

"'Why are you frowning, Husband?' the wife said. 'Look, our troubles are over!'

"The woodsman said nothing for a long time. Finally he took his wife aside and told her about the man he had met, and the bargain they had made. 'What does it matter if we give him our daughter, Husband?' the wife said. 'We would have starved, all of us, if you hadn't met this man in the forest. At least this way two of us will survive. And perhaps the man will not treat our daughter so very badly.'

"The days passed, and the woodsman expected the man at every moment. But he did not come, and the woodsman thought for a while that he was safe, that the man had forgotten them. Then one morning his daughter did not wake up, and nothing he or his wife could do would rouse her.

"The daughter slept for days, for weeks. The woodsman went to the forest every day to look for the man he had met, but he never found him, and meanwhile the daughter slept on.

"Finally one day, a year after the daughter had fallen asleep, the woodsman found the man again. 'You must help me,' he said. 'My daughter will not wake up.'

"'You promised me the first thing you saw,' the man said. 'That was our bargain.'

"'I did not know it would be my daughter,' the woodsman said.

"'That doesn't matter,' the man said. 'A bargain is a bargain.'

"'But why do you want her? Why does she have to sleep like this?'

"'Every night we fight a great battle,' the man said. 'And every night she helps us. It seems to you that she sleeps, but she is with us, aiding us. Without her we would be lost.'

"'How long will she sleep? For the rest of her life?'

"'Do you want to take back your bargain? Do you want to be as you once were, a poor woodsman?'

"The woodsman now lived in a grand house in the center of town. His wife wore a new dress every day, with ropes of pearls and jewels at her neck, and she ate fine food every evening at dinner. She would be angry with him if she lost it all, if they became poor once again.

"'No,' he said. 'No, I stand by the bargain we made. But is there nothing I can do for my daughter?'

"'There is one thing,' the man said. 'We can change the bargain slightly.'

"'How?' the woodsman said eagerly.

"'I can make it so that your daughter sleeps for only seven years. But in return you must promise me your descendants, a daughter in every generation, a bondmaid to us. Each of them will sleep for seven years, and in exchange their families will prosper to the ends of their days.'

"'Very well,' the woodsman said. And so it has been from that day to this."

Ben and I finished reading at the same time. "An interesting tale, isn't it?" Dr. Rothapfel said. "Usually the stories end, as they say, 'happily ever after.'

And yet in this one the family is still in thrall to the man in the forest..."

I wasn't listening. I looked at Ben, feeling horror creep over me. "Seven *years*?" I said, aghast. "Livvy's going to sleep for seven years?"

"You think to take the tale literally, then?" Rothapfel said.

I glanced at him suspiciously. "What did you tell him?" I asked Ben. "How much does he know about the Feierabends?"

"Everything," Ben said. "Everything I know, anyway."

"Goddammit, Ben. You know they don't talk to people—"

"So? They never said anything to me about keeping their secrets. And if it's all so secret, why did this woman, Klara Feierabend, tell Wilhelm the whole story?"

"Ah," Rothapfel said. "There's some correspondence in the folder that explains it."

He pulled out some more typewritten sheets of paper and handed them to us. The first few pages seemed to be a letter.

"Amelie," it said. "I need your help—something terrible has happened. I had to go away for a while, and I asked Grandmother to look after Dortchen. And when I came back, Grandmother met me at the door and asked me why Dortchen had to spend so many years asleep.

"Well, at first I thought she'd gone senile. She knows about the bargain as well as I do. I started to repeat the story, the one they tell us all as children, but she interrupted me and said that of course she remembered it, her own sister had been the bondmaid when she was a child. But she'd realized, she said, that it was unfair, that we couldn't expect such things from our children.

"I told her that she had benefited from the bargain as much as any of us, and that in any case it couldn't be changed. Then she smiled, like a child that had gotten into some mischief, and said that she'd already changed it. I asked her what she'd done, truly angry now. At first she wouldn't tell me, but finally I threatened her until she confessed.

"It seems that there are two men here in town, brothers, who are collecting children's stories. Grandmother went to their house and told them the story of the bargain. She was tired of keeping secrets, she said, and perhaps if she told the world someone would know how to break the bargain.

"I don't know if this is true, but we can't afford to let the story out into the world. Cousin Amelie, you have to get it back right away, even if that means asking our friends to help you. I would do it myself, but I am busy with Dortchen, and with watching Grandmother so she doesn't do any more damage. The brothers' names are Jacob and Wilhelm Grimm, and they live right here in Kassel."

The letter was unsigned. The next page had only two sentences. "It's done, Cousin. Here's the story."

None of us said anything when we'd finished. "Would that work?" I said finally. "If we told someone about the bargain?"

"How, though?" Ben said. "Everyone read the Brothers Grimm back then, but no one would pay attention to a story like that today. You'd have to, I don't know, make a movie about it or something."

"Well, we have to do something. They changed the bargain once—we can do it again." I remembered my first question to Ben. "How did you know the Feierabends had this story, anyway?"

"Well, it's like you said—they never talk about fairy tales. So what are they hiding?"

"I simply asked Ben to keep an eye out for a lost tale," Rothapfel said. "And it proved to be easier than I thought." He turned the folder toward me. On the cover, in faint pen-strokes, was the word "Märchen." "Fairy tales, in German," he said.

"How'd you find it so quickly, though?" I asked.

"Oh, I'd been in that library before," Ben said. "I was pretty sure it would be in one of the drawers in that table."

"Is there anything else in that folder?" I asked.

"I don't think so," Dr. Rothapfel said. He fished inside for a moment. "No, wait, here's something." He brought out a small piece of paper, folded lengthwise. Someone had written on it, in English, "Bondmaid: In folklore, a girl or woman who falls asleep for seven years, in exchange for which her family prospers..."

I brushed it aside. "What are we going to do, though?" I asked. "How do we wake Livvy up?"

"Ah, but do they want her woken up?" Dr. Rothapfel asked. "The bargain has gone on since the early eighteen hundreds, and almost certainly before that. And whoever wrote the letter wanted it to continue."

"But the grandmother didn't," I said. "And probably other people fought against it too, over the years."

"You should talk to the family, though," Ben said. "See what they want."

"And what if they want Livvy to go on sleeping? Maddie gets to be a successful actress, and Sylvie keeps living off the vineyard, and Rose—Rose gets whatever she wants... No, the hell with them. I'm going to break the bargain, and they can take whatever comes."

"How?" Ben asked.

I sighed. "I don't know." Suddenly I remembered the crows talking in the forest. "Rose. Rose knows. I'm going back to the farmhouse, to talk to her."

By then it was late afternoon, and a miserable cold rain was falling. I'd intended to wait until morning but Ben wanted to leave right away, and of course it was his car. We didn't call to say we were coming; Sylvie would have only told us not to.

We got into the car and headed toward the freeway, and I remembered my earlier question. "How did you meet this Rothapfel guy, anyway?" I asked.

He didn't say anything; instead he turned his signal on and carefully switched lanes. "I took a class from him," he said finally. "In mythology."

"How do you know where he lives, though?"

"Well, we started meeting at his house, back around January or February. Talking about the stuff we'd studied in class."

Nearly a year ago, I thought. "You never told me about that."

"Yeah. Well."

There was more he wasn't telling me, something I thought he was embarrassed to mention. I knew him, though, knew our friendship. I waited, saying nothing.

"He told us about these stories he'd heard," Ben said. "About something called the glückskind, fortune's child, people who were supposed to be lucky all their lives. He wasn't the only one who was into this—there's this whole group of people, exchanging information, studying folklore... They had these lists, families that, well, that fit the profile, that there were rumors about, and the Feierabends were one of them. Like there was some kind of disease, something that attacked the grapevines in the last century, but all their grapes stayed healthy. And their vineyards kept going during Prohibition, even when no one was buying grapes or making wine, when everyone else was shutting down. And then I saw that someone named Feierabend—that Maddie—was going to be in a play, so I went to see it—"

"Wait—wait a minute. You saw Maddie *after* you heard about this—this buckskin, or whatever it was?"

"Glückskind. Yeah."

"But why?"

"Why do you think? I wanted their damn luck. If it was true, if I could, I don't know, get close to them—"

"So all this time—is that why you went out with Maddie?"

"Well, yeah, at first. But I liked her, I really did. It wasn't about that once I got to know her."

"And when you introduced me to Livvy—was that because you saw that Maddie was about to dump you? So you'd still get to see them, or hear about them from me?"

"No. No, man—I thought you'd like her. That was all there was to it, I swear."

Did I believe that? I thought I did. Still, I was surprised by how much I hadn't known about him. I'd had no idea he'd been so dissatisfied with his life, so unhappy. Had he really gone to a play just on the chance that he'd get to know one of these lucky people? And what about the meetings at Professor Rothapfel's? I couldn't remember him ever leaving for one, or coming back.

"Here's what I don't get, though," Ben said. "They made the bargain, right, they got their good fortune. Wouldn't you expect, I don't know, some kind of mansion, or—or Maddie gets to be a big Hollywood star, or one of them becomes president? But here they are, living quietly in that old house..."

"I don't know," I said. "That's not the vibe I get from them. I mean, maybe that's all they want."

"Hmmm," Ben said.

And what did Ben want? I thought I'd known, but apparently I hadn't understood the simplest thing about my oldest friend.

We said nothing for the rest of the trip, each of us wrapped up in our own thoughts. The windshield wipers dragged back and forth, their rhythm starting up an idiotic rhyme in my head—"Rose knows, said the crows." I thought about how the family seemed to attract stories and nursery rhymes. And when we went up a rise in the road I remembered Livvy muttering, "Up the hill and down the hill..."

There had been a terrible storm the night before, loud with thunder, and the dirt roads near the farmhouse were slick with mud, forcing Ben to fight with the car even more than usual. As we pulled up to the house and got out of the car we glanced at each other nervously, and I had the feeling that if either one of us had suggested turning back we would have done it. Finally Ben said, "Okay—let's do this thing," and we marched up the porch and knocked on the door.

Sylvie answered. "What—what are you doing here?" she asked.

"We want to see Livvy," I said.

"She's still asleep."

Sylvie started to close the door, but I put my foot in the doorway like some kind of gimcrack salesman. "Where is she?" I asked.

"Upstairs."

I pushed past her into the living room. Maddie was coming down the stairway. Ben had followed me in, and he and Maddie stopped and stared at each other.

"What are you doing here?" he asked.

"I live here," Maddie said. I remembered the Moratorium Day protest had been last Saturday; I hadn't really paid a lot of attention. "What about you?"

"We're worried about Livvy," he said. "I care about your family, believe it or not."

"There's nothing you can do for her."

"We just want to see her," I said, trying to stave off an argument. I headed toward the stairs, but at that moment a dog appeared out of nowhere and cut me off, growling.

Rose hurried after it. "Storm!" she said. "No!"

Storm stopped, looked at Rose, looked back at me, then growled again, deep in its throat. "Storm, come," Rose said.

The growl trailed off, and Storm headed toward Rose. Now I saw that the dog was walking on only three legs, with one of its front paws held up near its chest.

"Sorry," Rose said. "She just showed up on the porch last night. I think she hurt her paw in the storm."

"It's okay," I said. I took a few more steps, but now it was Maddie, still standing at the foot of the stairs, who was blocking my way.

"It's better if you don't see her," she said.

"Why? What happened?"

"Nothing happened. She's just still asleep. Like I said, there's nothing you can do."

"So you're just going to let her sleep? For seven years?"

I'd meant to surprise them with my knowledge of the bargain, but I was startled at the vehemence of their reaction. Sylvie moaned and sat down on a couch. Maddie put her hand to her mouth. Even the dog growled, and Rose scratched her behind the ears.

"How—where—" Sylvie said.

"It doesn't matter," I said. "I know about the bargain, and I'm going to break it. All you have to do is tell me how."

"How did you find out?"

"Tell me how to break it first."

"You can't. There's no way. Don't you think we've tried, over the years?"

"You changed it once. The first"—I stumbled over the word—"the first bondmaid was supposed to sleep for the rest of her life, wasn't she? And someone, some ancestor, changed that to seven years."

"Where did you hear that?" Maddie asked.

"I read it," Ben said. "In the library."

"Ah, you speak German, then?" Maddie said sarcastically.

"He stole the story," Sylvie said suddenly, her vague expression sharpened to an intense glare. "He was up there a long time, the day they brought Livvy here. I bet he stole it then, and got it translated."

"And you still expect to see Livvy, after that?" Maddie said. "You steal, you lie to us, you take advantage of us, and you still think you can come back here like nothing's happened?"

I'd grown angrier and angrier through all of this, and finally I couldn't hold back any longer. "*We're* taking advantage?" I said. "You're the ones who are letting Livvy sleep—letting her sleep for *seven years*—just so you can keep living your comfortable lives. So you can stay rich and fat, keep your house and your precious library, so you can make it as an actress. You don't think you got that part on your own, do you?"

"I told you—we can't do anything," Sylvie said.

"You're lying," I said.

"No—"

"You're not telling the whole truth, then. The crows said—I heard some crows in the forest, one of the times I was here, and they said that Rose knows about this." I turned to her. "You're writing a history of the family, you said. So tell me how to get Livvy out of this bargain."

Rose had been backing away, until she was practically hidden by Storm. "I don't know," she said in a small voice. "No one's ever done it. It's been going on for a long time—"

"How long?" Ben asked.

I nearly growled at him, like Storm. What difference did it make? "Since the mid-1600s, we think," she said. "Maybe longer."

Over three centuries. I sat down on the couch across from Sylvie, feeling defeated. How did I think I was going to save Livvy, when I knew so little about the family's history? Well, at least I'd get some answers, while they were in such a talkative mood. "How did it start?" I asked.

"We don't know," Rose said. "Probably it was something like the fairy tale—someone asked us, and we agreed."

"All right then—why do the bondmaids have to sleep for seven years? And don't say you don't know—some of them must have talked about it after they woke up."

Rose looked at Sylvie. Sylvie looked at Maddie. Maddie stared at me, still angry, I think, at what I'd said about her acting. Finally Sylvie said, "They don't remember a lot of it. They fight, I think—they're fighting a war. And they dance. They're—"

"They *dance*?" I said.

Sylvie nodded. "I think—whatever they're doing, I think it tires them out. They sleep because they're so tired."

I remembered Livvy saying something about horses and riders. Was she fighting someone, or something? "Do they—can they die in this war?"

"I don't know." Sylvie must have seen something in my expression, because she went on. "I heard—my husband told me they sometimes die in their sleep. He thought—his family thought—they might have died in some battle or other." She hesitated, then went on. "That's why he left us, you know. Hilbert. Because he had three daughters, and his cousins only had sons, and he knew one of his children was going to be taken. He couldn't stand it, watching them grow up, wondering which one it was going to be."

Somewhere in the middle of all of this I registered that the father's name was Hilbert, poor guy. I tried to focus, to remember what else Livvy had said in her sleep. Had she been trying to give me clues? I heard the stupid rhyme again, and the beat of the windshield wipers.

"Livvy said something, a poem—up the hill and down the hill—"

Rose shook her head. "It's just a nursery rhyme," she said.

"No it isn't."

"Yes it is. Don't you remember, from when you were a kid? Like this." She went up to Maddie and clasped her hands, and they recited together. "Up the hill"—their arms swung out and up to the side—"and down the hill"—their arms swung to the other side—"and roundabout"—they turned back to back, still holding hands—"and back again"—and they came around to face each other.

"I never heard it before." I looked at Ben. "How about you?"

He shook his head.

"It must be something your family says," I said.

"So what?" Rose said.

"So it might mean something."

"Oh, that's ridiculous," Sylvie said. "How can it possibly—"

"Livvy and I always thought it had something to do with the hill near the forest," Maddie said suddenly.

"Like what?" I said.

"Like if you go up the hill, and then down, and then around, well, something might happen. We tried it a few times when we were kids, but nothing did."

"Maybe nothing happened because no one was asleep then," I said. "Because they hadn't taken their bondmaid yet. Maybe if we do it now—"

"What?" Sylvie asked. "Walk around a hill?"

I heard an echo of Livvy's sarcastic tone in her voice. "Why don't you want me to do it, Sylvie?" I asked. "Because I might break the bargain? You might have to go out into the real world, learn what it's like to struggle along with everyone else?"

"Look, Will, why don't you just wait? Seven years—it's not that long a time. Livvy will wake up, and you can get married, and then you'll be part of the bargain too. It's not a bad life. You'll be rich, and, and comfortable, like you said—"

A tear fell down her face, though she made no other sound. I was too angry to feel bad about hurting her. "You would do that to your daughter?" I asked. "Take away seven years of her life? And I bet they aren't the same when they wake up, those bondmaids. How can they be? Or do you think she'll just go back to school and then get a job, like everyone else?"

She put her head in her hands and sobbed. Now I did feel bad. "You—I don't—but they—I don't like to think about it, but I do see, Will—"

I think this was the closest she ever came to admitting that the bargain was a bad one, the sacrifice too great to ask. Like she said, though, she didn't think about it much. Still, I took her words, garbled as they were, to mean she agreed with me. "All right," I said. "I'm going to try that hill."

Everyone followed me out, dogs and all. Storm made a questioning sound deep in her throat, torn between growling at me and obeying Rose's commands.

I hadn't realized how late it had gotten. The mountains in the west had already cut the sun in half, and the light was growing fainter all the time. The rain had stopped, but it was still chilly, far too cold for fall. Clouds swam across the sky.

I buttoned my coat and we headed toward the forest. The hill appeared as a black shape in front of us, a triangular doorway.

I began to climb. The path was muddy from the rain, and barely visible in the fading light. I reached the top and headed down the other side, once slipping and nearly falling in the mud. Ben was following me, and Maddie, and that wretched dog.

I came to the bottom and looked around. "Now what?" I said, mostly to myself.

"Now you go around," Maddie said.

"Which way?"

Maddie shrugged.

I went to the right and circled the hill. Did "back again" mean that I had to go around it again, this time in the other direction, or climb over it? Over it, I thought, and started back up.

"No, this way," Maddie called, heading around the hill.

I ignored her. My way suddenly seemed right to me. Ben followed her, and the dog seemed to lose interest and wandered off.

I reached the bottom of the hill. Nothing happened, and I felt an intense disappointment. I'd believed in the rhyme more than I'd let myself know.

It was almost completely dark now. I called out for Ben, and Maddie, but no one answered. Someone near me cleared his throat.

I leapt like a pole vaulter. When I regained my composure I saw a man standing next to me, dressed in green. I peered at him and made out the short, bearded man I'd met in the forest.

"Here," he said. He held out the scarf I'd given him. "This will help you."

I didn't see how, but I took it anyway. "Thank you," I said, and wrapped it around my neck.

A door in the hillside stood open.

6

THE DOOR HAD PROBABLY opened when I finished my walk, I thought, but without the scarf I hadn't been able to see it. I looked inside and saw candles, what seemed like hundreds of them, setting the place alight. Faint music drifted toward me, a complex, beautiful melody.

I went through the door and into the hill. There were trees inside, the candles shining from within their branches. A space stood open between the trees, the floor tiled with green and gold squares, and in this space men and women were dancing.

They were all sorts: some like the man I'd seen in the forest, small and bearded; some with wings; some with heads like animals, with sharp narrow faces and pointed ears and long shaggy hair. They danced an old-fashioned dance, two lines on either side with couples taking turns to sweep down the middle. They wore clothes in rich, ancient colors, maroon, forest green, dark gold.

I stood and watched them awhile, my heart pounding as fast as the dance. A few of them turned to look at me, but with curiosity, nothing more. There were animals among them too, I noticed: a hedgehog lay curled up underneath a chair, and a cat slunk across the tiles, a chicken leg clasped in its mouth. A face peered at me from within the trees.

The short man had followed me in. "What are they doing?" I asked.

"They're celebrating."

"Celebrating what?"

Now I noticed a dais at the end of the room, and a bench on top of it. A woman sat on the bench, and another woman lay sleeping on it, her head in the first woman's lap. Her hair fell to the floor, long and black.

"Livvy!" I shouted.

"Hush," the man said.

I ignored him and headed toward Livvy. He reached out and grabbed me by the arm. "They don't mind you watching," he said. "But they'll throw you out if you interfere."

"If *I* interfere?" I said. "They stole her away from me. They stole her, and they're going to keep her for seven years. I have to get her back."

I tried to jerk away but he held fast, surprisingly strong for such a short man. "They won't let you touch her."

The music stopped. A tall man in leather clothes left the dancers and came up to the dais and bowed. The woman sitting on the bench looked up, and at that moment I realized she was the same person I'd seen on Telegraph Avenue, with the gray bun and steel-colored glasses.

I shuddered and fell back, hoping she wouldn't see me. She smiled at the man—even her smile seemed filled with malice—and they both shook Livvy and tugged at her, trying to rouse her.

"No," Livvy said. Everyone was silent, watching her, and I could hear her voice from across the room. "No, let me sleep, please."

The woman on the bench laughed, a sound that ran up along my nerves and made me shiver with dread. Some of the others laughed along with her. "No, my dear, my dearest dear one," the woman said. "We can't let you sleep, oh my goodness no."

Livvy sat up. The man took her hand and pulled her to her feet, then dragged her out to the dance floor.

The music struck up again, and everyone started to dance. Livvy lagged a step behind, her head down, pulled along by her partner. There was something like a shackle on her wrist, a heavy hinged bracelet made of dark silver; the candlelight shivered over it as she moved.

I struggled to get free. "Look what they're doing to her!" I said.

"I know," the man said. "It's necessary."

"Necessary! For who?"

Livvy stumbled. A few of the dancers murmured, and one or two even laughed.

That did it. I pulled away and ran toward her. "Livvy!" I said.

The music stopped abruptly. The light from the candles shot upward and then went out. I stood in the middle of a cold, dark place, a cave, with a gray outline showing me the door to the outside.

I groped my way toward it, and found myself standing by the side of the hill. I turned, but the door was gone. It was the middle of the night; a silver half-moon shone down, enough to light my way to the farmhouse. I staggered along the path and nearly fell through the front door.

"Will!" someone said. "Where were you?"

"I was—I saw—"

"Here, sit down," Ben said.

I sat on one of the couches, and the others took the couch and chairs around me. I wanted to tell them what I'd seen, but I didn't have the words, I'd never experienced anything like it. "There were these people dancing, and candles, candles in trees, and music, I've never heard anything like it—" Suddenly I realized I couldn't remember the music. It had been beautiful; I had the feeling I'd try to recall it for the rest of my life.

"That's the other realm," Sylvie said.

"What?" Ben said. "What do you mean?"

"It's another realm, a—a place. Something like fairy tales, but not really—people tell fairy tales to try to understand it. How did you get there, though? You're not part of the family."

I laughed. I felt drunk, or crazy, or both at once. "I helped a man in the forest once. I gave him my scarf, and when he gave it back it was magicked somehow... Isn't that what happens in fairy tales? The intrepid son meets someone on his travels, and helps him out... No, never mind that. There was this horrible woman there, like a—a witch, and Livvy was lying on her lap, and they wanted her to dance, but she was too tired. And I tried to reach her, but the whole place vanished."

Sylvie nodded. "I told you—they won't let you take her."

"Yes, they will. I'm going to find out how, and then I'm going back." I thought about what I'd seen, trying to hold onto it as it faded. "Why were they dancing, though? The bearded man—the man I helped—said they were celebrating."

"I don't know," Sylvie said.

"Maybe they won a battle," Ben said. "Sylvie said they were fighting someone."

"Who, though?" I asked.

Sylvie shrugged. "I don't know."

A clock somewhere rang the hours, seeming to go on forever. "God, what time is it?" I asked, realizing only then how exhausted I felt. "It sounds like midnight."

"Oh, that clock's never worked right," Sylvie said. "Not since I came here."

"Well, do you know what time it is?" I asked.

No one did. That seemed typical; the family seemed to live their lives by some other time. I never wore a watch either, though, so I couldn't very well complain.

Ben looked as tired as I felt, too tired to drive home. To my surprise, though, he stood and said goodbye to Sylvie and Rose, then, very quickly, to Maddie.

I'd wanted to see Livvy, but I didn't think I could impose on their patience any longer. Anyway, I was sure I'd be back. I said my goodbyes too, told Sylvie I would call her, and followed Ben out.

It had started raining again while we'd been inside. "Are you sure you're okay to drive?" I asked Ben.

"Don't worry," he said.

He stopped before we got to the car. "Oh, shit," he said. The car's headlights were still on, weak and wavering in the rain. They had probably overloaded the fragile electrical system; there was no way it would start now.

"What do we do now?" I asked. "Call a tow truck? Or throw ourselves on their mercy?"

"Do they have enough mercy, do you think?"

I couldn't face waiting for a tow truck. "Sylvie might," I said.

Ben shut off the car's lights and tried the ignition a few times, but of course nothing happened. We turned around and knocked on the door again and explained our predicament. I'd been right, thank the god of stranded travelers; Sylvie opened the door wider and let us back inside.

"You'll have to get your own blankets and things, though," she said. "I'm going to bed."

Maddie said nothing, just looked at Ben briefly with a hint of Livvy's enigmatic expression. Ben and I climbed the stairs. I headed down the hall to Livvy's room and went inside.

She lay still, her eyes open and moving, seeing something besides the room around her. Was she still at the dance? How could she be there, and here in this room too? I knew she could, though, knew that what I'd seen was real.

I brushed her hair away from her face. "Don't worry, Livvy—I'll come and get you soon."

I'd had some thought of sleeping with her, of holding her, but in the end I decided it wasn't a good idea. She was somewhere else; we wouldn't be together, not in the way I wanted.

I went into the nearest empty room. It held a bare mattress, with no sheets or blankets, but I was too tired to look for the closet Livvy had shown me. I fell down on top of the bed and wrapped my coat around me.

I woke up in the middle of the night, roused by a noise. At first I thought it was one of the cats, or that the cleaners had come back. Then I made out a soft sobbing, the sound of someone so brokenhearted as to be beyond help. I got up and went to Livvy's bedroom, but though she moved restlessly every so often she made no noise.

I headed back to my room and went to bed. The sobbing came again, and went on and on. I fell asleep and woke again, and sometime during the night I realized I had found the Moaning Bedroom.

I woke up for the last time early the next morning and lay in bed awhile, thinking about what I'd seen. I never for a moment thought it was a dream; I believed it all, had partly believed it even as far back as the crows in the forest. This was 1971, remember, the tail end of the sixties, when people had had stranger beliefs—that you could levitate the Pentagon by reciting Tibetan chants, for example. Even if it had been later, one of the more rational decades that followed, I wouldn't have been all that surprised. The Feierabends had always seemed to live partly somewhere else, in some other world.

I was going to fight back, though, even if the rest of the family wouldn't. And the first thing I had to do was find out more about the bargain, talk to other members of the family.

I got up and headed downstairs as quietly as I could, keeping an eye out for the dogs. I went into the telephone alcove under the stairs and opened the top drawer, looking for an address book.

The drawer was filled with the kind of junk that accumulates over the years—candles and stamps and a tray with "Fairy Soap—The Oval Cake 5¢" on it, postcards and tarnished napkin rings and a foreign coin with a hole in the middle. I rummaged around and finally found the book I was looking for.

There were no Feierabends under "F," which I thought was odd, until I realized that Sylvie was more likely to call someone by their first name. I turned to "H" and found Hilbert. He lived in Oakland, though I didn't recognize the street. I scribbled the address and phone number down on a piece of paper and stuffed it in my jeans pocket.

I did feel bad for the family, first Ben and then me invading their privacy, stealing information we had no right to. Not bad enough, though, that I would throw away the address and forget about it. Livvy's father had to know more about the bargain than Sylvie or any of their daughters; after all, he, unlike his wife, had been born a Feierabend.

What about other relatives? That cousin who was opening a restaurant—what was his name? I couldn't remember. And there were probably others—the family had come here in 1888, after all. I riffled through the address book, but I only got a few pages in when I heard someone come down the stairs.

I hurried to the kitchen and got some cereal from one of the cupboards, trying to look like I'd been there all along. Ben joined me, then Sylvie and Rose. Sylvie knew a garage mechanic in the flatlands, she said, someone who could drive up and jump-start the Volvo, and she went to the telephone alcove to call the garage.

After breakfast I went outside and walked to the hill. I paced over and around it, back and forth, in every combination I could think of. Nothing happened, though I had made sure to wear the scarf. They wouldn't let me in again, not after what I'd done the night before.

I heard a car driving up the road and headed back to the house. The others were already out on the front porch, and I stood there with them as the tow truck pulled up.

I'd been vaguely surprised to see Sylvie functioning so well in the real world, actually knowing someone useful like a mechanic. Then I saw him climb down from the cab of the truck, so short he had to jump to reach the ground, and I understood the connection. He looked like the neighbor, and like the man in the forest, with the same fuzzy face and faintly green hair. Like them he wore green clothes, though his were stained overalls and a T-shirt. And he was different in other ways, thinner, with half-moon spectacles somewhere in all that fur. He mumbled something to Sylvie before lifting the hood and attaching his jumper cables.

I ran down the porch stairs, calling out questions to him even before I reached him. How could I get back under the hill? What was happening to Livvy? How could I free her?

"They don't want you there," he said, still looking under the hood.

"Why not? You're here to help the family, aren't you? You and your—your brothers, or whatever they are. So help us get Livvy back."

"Try it now," he said.

For a moment I thought he was telling me to go back to the hill and try again. Then I realized he was talking to Ben. Ben got inside the Volvo and turned the key.

The car made a deep groaning noise, like a large animal being disturbed in its sleep. He tried again. The engine whined a bit but Ben stayed firm, and finally it caught.

"Come on, Will," Ben called.

The mechanic wound the cables around his forearm. I looked around, trying to think of one last question, but finally I got in the car.

Ben said nothing until we were out on the winding road. "Well, the library was a bust this time," he said.

"What?" I said.

"I couldn't find anything in the library."

"What—you went back there?"

"Of course I did. You didn't think I really forgot to turn off the headlights, did you?"

"I—well, yeah. Yeah, I did."

"I had to make sure we got invited to stay over. Then I got up early and looked around in the library."

I felt annoyed, though I had no moral justification whatsoever; what I had done was just as bad. We were partners in crime now, I thought. I might as well share what I knew.

"Well, I got the father's address," I said.

He laughed, delighted. "Far out," he said. "I bet the old bastard knows a lot of things. When are we going to see him?"

I'd planned to visit Mr. Feierabend by myself. My annoyance grew, tipped over into anger. Why did Ben always insist on coming along? Was he still looking for the family's luck, trying to get back into their good graces?

I remembered him going out into the rain and seeing the car's headlights on; he'd seemed genuinely upset, a brilliant bit of acting, worthy of Maddie. And I remembered the secret he'd been hiding from me until just recently, what he'd known about the Feierabends.

Well, but what about me? I wasn't going to get any merit badges for honesty either.

"After Thanksgiving, I guess," I said. Ben and I were visiting our families in Sacramento over the Thanksgiving vacation.

"Great," he said. "Man, I wonder what Livvy would have done for Thanksgiving. She could make even turkey taste good."

"Don't, man," I said. I didn't want to talk anymore. I closed my eyes and pretended to be asleep for the rest of the trip home.

7

AND HERE WE WERE AGAIN, heading off in Ben's car. This time we were climbing the winding streets of the Oakland hills to Mr. Feierabend's house; Ben was driving, and I had an unwieldy map spread out over my lap. Although the hills were only a few miles from campus I had never been here, never even realized this ritzy enclave existed so close to the students and panhandlers of Berkeley.

Most of the houses were set away from the road, behind trees or down a gentle slope, but I caught glimpses of brick walls and pillared porches, of weathered wood facades with huge windows overlooking the bay. It smelled of pine and eucalyptus, like the astringent mixture my mother used to put on my chest when I had a cold. Fat brown squirrels ran across the trees and telephone lines.

The Feierabends seemed to like living on hills, I thought. But on this trip I felt none of the excitement and anticipation that sparked through me whenever I visited the family. For the past week or so my thoughts had circled endlessly: What if she never woke up? What if she woke but was utterly changed? What if she—but I couldn't admit the most terrible possibility to myself, even then.

It was even worse because I'd just gotten back from visiting my parents in Sacramento. Ben and I had seen old friends; some of them were back from their own colleges, some had never left and had found jobs in construction or a plant nursery. Everything went on just as it had before I'd met Livvy; it was horribly easy to see what life would look like without her.

"He's done well for himself, old Hilbert," Ben said. "I wonder if he still gets the family's good luck even though he left them."

I didn't care about the man's luck. I disliked him for leaving his family, but I was willing to put even that aside if he could help me.

Ben kept talking, this time about his parents and their continuing slide toward divorce. "So then my mother says 'Thank God' about something, I don't remember what, and my father says 'Thank Buddha.'"

I was so sunk in unhappiness that it took me a while to get the point of this story. "What do you mean? Your father's a Buddhist?"

"Well, I don't know. I mean Buddhists don't say 'Thank Buddha,' do they? I think he wants to be something different, something besides a bureaucrat, but he has no idea how to go about it. He even started growing his hair long. It's goddamn embarrassing—he looks like Ben Franklin."

I mumbled something about fathers, thinking about Mr. Feierabend. "Hey, wasn't that our street?" Ben said. He swung the steering wheel around and pulled into a driveway, then backed out and headed down the hill. "Some navigator you are. You're fired. Take this man out and have him shot."

It was another quote from *Catch-22*. I smiled weakly, grateful for Ben's attempts to cheer me up. I directed him right at the street we'd passed, and then left at the next corner. "There it is," I said, spotting the address on a mailbox. There were no curbs in this exclusive part of town, and no sidewalks; Ben pulled over next to an uneven line of trees.

We walked up some brick stairs. I stood in front of the door awhile, nervous, until Ben reached across me and rang the doorbell. A muffled chime sounded inside the house, and then a man opened the door. He was plump and disheveled, and his shirt had come loose from his pants. With his untidy brown hair and light brown eyes he looked a bit like Rose.

He kept his head down, his chin pressed against his chest. His chins, I should say—he had quite a few of them. He gazed up at us, waiting.

"Um, Mr. Feierabend?" I said.

"What can I do for you?" he said. He had a surprisingly deep voice, as if his words welled up from some distant place within him.

"I'm, um, Will Taylor," I said. "This is Ben Avery. I'm a friend of your daughter's. Livvy's boyfriend. She's fallen asleep."

"Ah," he said. "I see."

He walked away from the door. Ben and I looked at each other and shrugged. Did he mean for us to follow him? Even if he hadn't, I was coming inside.

We crossed a foyer tiled in stone. The living room looked a bit like the one at the farmhouse, dark, with wooden floors and rafters, bookshelves and comfortable-looking chairs. But it seemed deserted, as if no one lived there: no coats and scarves, no books and magazines scattered over the tables.

"Sit down, sit down," Mr. Feierabend said, squinting up to look at us. "Can I get you anything? Wine, tea?"

"Sure," I said. "Tea." If we were drinking something we'd be able to stay awhile.

He shuffled off into another room. Ben and I sat and looked around us, saying nothing. There were more bookshelves than I'd seen at first, lining each of the walls. A bird cage with a rounded top stood on a table in the corner, draped in cloth; it looked like a tombstone.

Mr. Feierabend came back, holding a tray with tea things. "Cream and sugar?" he asked, setting the tray down. "Or lemon, if you like."

"I want to talk to you about Livvy," I said impatiently. "About breaking the bargain."

"Yes, yes, of course. What would you like in your tea?"

"Nothing, thanks," I said.

We spent a geological age getting the tea ready. Finally he sat down and said, "Livvy," and then, "O-liv-i-a." I'd never heard her full name spoken before. "How did you meet her?"

"Ben introduced us," I said impatiently.

"And where did Ben—"

"Look," I said. I started to get angry, a welcome feeling; it drowned out my unhappiness. "This isn't a social visit. You left them, okay? You have no right to ask about Livvy, about any of them. All I want to know is how to break the bargain."

My voice had gotten louder and louder. The noise started the bird squawking, and I felt a spike of terror even in the middle of my tirade. I knew that sound: it was a crow's call.

"I can't answer you, I'm afraid," he said.

"Can't or won't?"

"Did you try talking to those little men, the dwarves? They send them to serve us, to serve our family, as part of the bargain."

"Why would they help me? You said it yourself—they're part of the bargain. They're not going to turn against their masters."

"Masters, well. I don't know if they have masters, exactly. Did you know that some of the ancient Scandinavian dwarves had the same names as the dwarves in Disney's *Snow White*? Toki, which means foolish, and Varr, shy one, and Duri, sleepy... I have a book here somewhere—"

He stood and went to one of the bookshelves, tucking his shirttail in absently. "I don't care," I said. "Unless those Scandinavian dwarves can help Livvy somehow."

"Well, anything might help, you know," he said. He was still turned away from me, looking at his books. "It's good to know things, to keep on learning..."

"Not if it lets you hide from reality. Is that what you do here—you learn stuff?" He didn't answer. "It must be nice—not having a job, being able to do anything you want. No wonder you won't help me with Livvy. You still get the family's luck, and you don't even have to watch your daughter sleep for seven years."

He turned back to us. "I thought I broke the bargain, actually. I thought I'd saved the family when I left them. I signed over the winery to Sylvie, gave up everything I had—"

"Yeah, I can see that. You're really living in poverty here."

"Well, I got married again, to a woman who turned out to be the heir to a fortune. I swear to you I had no idea about her money when I married her. Then her father died, and—" He waved at the living room, and the house beyond it. "We're getting divorced, but—here's the funny thing—she insists on giving me half the money." He looked up at me, his neck cricking. "They give us health and riches, sometimes love. They never promised us happiness."

"Who? Who gives you these things?"

"The other realm. Didn't Sylvie explain it to you? I told her the story before we got married, the fairy tale, but I don't think she believed it."

"She believed it. She just managed not to think about it."

"Yes, yes, very good. That's Sylvie exactly."

He was distracting me again. "So now that Livvy's asleep—now that it turns out you didn't break the bargain after all—are you going to go back to them? Live with Sylvie and the family again?"

"Do you honestly think Sylvie would have me? After what happened to Livvy?"

"She might if we get Livvy out of there. If we ended the bargain once and for all."

He paced the floor. His shirt seemed, magically, to come loose from his pants again. He turned to Ben. "And who are you? What's your business here?"

"That doesn't matter—" I said, but Ben said at the same time, "I used to go out with Maddie."

"Livvy *and* Maddie," Mr. Feierabend said. "You're brave men, both of you." He looked briefly at each of us. "I wonder—you know, we've had some extraordinary people in our family. I sometimes wonder if that's because of the bargain too, if it's because of our closeness to the other realm. Would Maddie and Livvy be who they are, if we hadn't made the bargain? Or would they be duller, more ordinary, Maddie less dramatic, Livvy just an average student... You've benefited from the bargain too, you see. What if you woke her up and all the enchantment fell away, if you found yourself with an ordinary woman on your hands?"

"Stop changing the subject!" I said. Ben looked at me, startled; I don't think he'd ever seen me this angry. Hell, I hadn't either. "Tell me how to stop this, once and for all."

"You can't. I've tried—you can see how I've tried. They won't let us. They're older than us, and far cleverer."

He went to the birdcage and pulled off the cloth. The cage was huge, an Arabian palace of domes and arches and filigreed wire. It was filled with all sorts of bird knickknacks, bells and beads and mirrors and food trays. A crow, black as a coffee bean, cocked its head and looked out at us from between the bars.

"Tell them," Mr. Feierabend said.

"Only a dishonorable man seeks to break a promise, once it's made," the crow said. It sounded like the crows I'd heard in the forest, its beak clacking, breaking words like birdseed. "And only a fool speaks his plans to his enemy. We've marked you, now—we'll know if you work against us."

Suddenly I felt terrified. What was I doing, going up against this ancient world? I looked at Ben for reassurance, but his expression hadn't changed; all along, he'd seemed to accept this place we'd found ourselves in easier than I had. "Enemy?" I asked Mr. Feierabend. "Is that what you are? What can they do to us?"

"Not me, no," he said. He indicated the crow with his chin. "But he will be, if you keep on like this."

"Well, why—why the hell do you keep him around, then? What is he, some kind of spy?"

"Yes, exactly. A spy. He came with the bargain, he and the other crows. To make sure we keep to the terms. I took him with me when I left—Sylvie always hated him."

"Why didn't you just kill him?" I asked. The bird gave me a look of sheer malevolence.

"Because something terrible would happen if I did. To me, maybe, but more likely to Sylvie or one of the girls." He must have seen something in my expression, because he went on: "They send us protectors too, of course. Those dwarves I mentioned. You've seen them, haven't you?"

I nodded. "What about the other things I saw? There was a pine tree on the table the first time I came over—"

"The rituals, yes. They're supposed to protect us as well. I don't know if they work or if they're just superstition, but we've never dared to give them up. The pine tree, you know, stays green all winter, unlike the deciduous trees, and I suppose indicates life, or growth—"

"Protect you from what?" I asked. "What do they want?"

"Well, I don't know, really. My father always thought they were fighting a war. That they needed us to help them fight."

The crow chirped, a melodic sound, nothing like its usual rasp. It seemed to be listening hard.

"Or maybe it's just that we give them something they can't get anywhere else," he went on. "They live a long time, we think—either that or they aren't alive at all, not in the same way we are. Our lives are exciting to them in some way, maybe because they're so short, so vivid, just a spark compared to theirs. And we give them meaning, though the stories we tell about them. There aren't any stories about them apart from us, you see. We tell the stories, but they are Story."

He was losing me. "Why is it always a girl—a woman?" I asked.

"Look at the fairy tales. The girls are always the ones who fall asleep—Sleeping Beauty, Snow White. The boys are the ones who rescue them."

"Well, but it would work just as well the other way. The boys go to sleep, and the girls rescue them."

The bird shifted on its perch. "That's right—this new feminist movement," Mr. Feierabend said. "Though it's not new, of course, just like so many of these fads today. Look at the suffragettes in the early 1900s—" He must have seen my expression, because he hurried back to his original subject. "You have to remember that the times were a lot different back then. Girls were supposed to be modest, obedient, busy cooking or sewing or churning butter. The Grimms even changed a few of the tales to make sure people got the point. Snow White, for example—in the original story she didn't do any work for the dwarves at all. They added that later. Maybe they believe all that, in the other realm—that girls are easier to deal with."

"They never met Maddie, I guess," Ben said.

"Or Livvy," I said.

Mr. Feierabend looked away. He hadn't seen his children in years, I realized, didn't know how terrific they'd turned out. Well, too bad, I thought. He shouldn't have left them in the first place.

"Was that something else you researched?" I asked. "The Grimms?"

"Yes, of course. I looked at anything that might give me an answer, help me save my family. The Grimms didn't just collect fairy tales, you know. That wasn't even their primary focus. They studied mythology, legal precedents, etymology—they worked on a German dictionary, for example, got as far as 'Frucht,' the word for fruit."

"Is that significant?" I asked, not bothering to hide my skepticism. "Fruit?"

"Well, I don't know. Anything might be. The word 'bondmaid,' for example—some interesting things there. It didn't make it into the *Oxford English Dictionary*, strangely enough—they had to stick it in the supplement. And it's very old, older than a lot of the other words in the dictionary—"

The bird moved again. "Sorry," Mr. Feierabend said, shaking his head.

I thought of another question. "What about other relatives? How can I find them?"

"Relatives, yes. Let's see. My father's still alive, and my uncle Peter—well, we live a long time, part of the bargain. And some cousins, too, and second cousins, or would that be first cousins once removed?"

"Could you give me their addresses?"

"I could give you my father's. The rest of them—I'm afraid I lost touch with them when I moved. Sylvie might know."

She didn't, of course, or said she didn't. I had asked her. Hilbert walked away from the cage and perched on the arm of one of the chairs. "Would you like some more tea?"

My tea cup was empty, I saw with surprise. And we were finished here as well; I doubted he would tell me anything else. "No, thank you."

"Are you sure? Or would you like to use my bathroom? Tycho Brahe, you know, the astronomer, he died because he was too shy to ask if he could relieve himself at a banquet. His bladder burst, poor man. He had a copper nose, too, lost his real nose in a duel—" He stopped. "Sorry," he said again. "I wanted to be a teacher, actually—I wasn't really suited to growing grapes."

We stood. "All right," I said. "Your last chance. How do I rescue Livvy?"

"I'm afraid you can't. Look at me—I gave up everything I had, and they took her anyway. You'll just have to wait the seven years."

I didn't say anything. He misinterpreted my silence and went on. "I wouldn't blame you if you didn't, though. Seven years is a long time, and you're young yet..."

Yeah, you know all about giving up, I thought. "Well, we should go," I said. "Can I have your father's address?"

He went farther into the house and came back with a piece of paper. He handed it to me and I thanked him.

"Wait," he said. "You didn't tell me how they are. What are they doing?"

I nearly didn't say anything. He could write them if he wanted to know, or call. He was looking directly at me, though, for the first time in our visit, and I could see the naked need in his expression. "Livvy is—was—studying chemistry, at UC Berkeley. Maddie's in Hollywood, in a play. Rose is writing a history of the family, she says. And Sylvie—Sylvie can't cope, not with Livvy or anything else."

"Ah," he said.

"Give them a call sometime," I said.

"Maybe. Maybe I will."

I doubted it. He walked Ben and me to the front door, and we left.

"My God," Ben said as we drove away. "What a toad. He tries to get around the bargain by not speaking to them, and then when that doesn't work he doesn't speak to them anyway."

"Cognitive dissonance," I said.

"There speaks the psych major," he said. "Give a few fancy words to something, and you think you know all about it. What the hell does that mean?"

"It means having two contradictory thoughts in your head at the same time. He thinks he's saving them, on the one hand, but on the other hand he knows he's escaped, and he feels guilty about it. It explains Sylvie too—she thinks about her good fortune, and she puts everything else in another part of her mind and tries to forget about it."

"It doesn't explain anything. How can people live like that, with a split personality?"

"And I suppose you know all about it, from whatever your major is this week? What is it now—Finno-Ugric studies?"

"Very funny. English literature."

"That's a new one, isn't it?" In the year and some months we'd been at Berkeley he'd had at least four majors—sociology, art history, theater, and now English. He would have to declare a major soon and stick with it; for a while, before Livvy fell asleep, I'd been looking forward to seeing what he came up with.

"I told you about it," he said.

Probably he had, and I hadn't paid attention. "So what does English literature tell you about the Feierabends?"

"It tells me he's a toad. Mr. Toad of Toad Hall. How can he leave them like that?"

"People do all kinds of strange things."

"Is that what they teach you in those psychology classes? People do strange things? That's a scientific formulation, is it?"

"Oh, shut up," I said, but good-naturedly. He was trying to cheer me up, I knew. And in fact I did feel better, not because of his silliness but from talking to Mr. Feierabend. The father had researched the bargain, had studied fairy tales and epics and family history, all sorts of things. And he had found something, I thought, something he couldn't tell me in front of that horrible crow.

I asked Ben to drop me off on campus, then went to the library and checked out a book of Grimms' fairy tales. I finished it a few days later and tried to follow up on the other hints Mr. Feierabend had dropped, reading about Scandinavian mythology and women in the nineteenth century, even Walt Disney and Tycho Brahe. These seemed to be false trails, as he'd said; perhaps I was wrong, perhaps the bird had wanted him to mislead me. But I didn't think so. I thought that somewhere in all his talk he had left a clue, had dropped a scattering of breadcrumbs for me to follow.

I was thinking about this one day as I went through the library, down a long room lined with books. Light shone through a window at the end, outlining a tall figure standing in front of the books about fairy tales. As I came closer I saw that he was wearing a top hat and black coat and carrying a cane, and I realized that I'd last seen him at the farmhouse, giving orders to the cleaner. One of Those People.

He took a book from the shelves and dropped it into a pocket. His pocket stayed flat, as if he'd made the book disappear, and suddenly I was certain that he'd taken the very book I'd wanted. "Hey," I said.

The man turned. He looked taller and more frightening in daylight, his black hair stringy and disordered, his eyes sunken, a red glow deep within them. "Didn't he warn you not to interfere?" he asked.

"What? Who?"

"You know who. That man who helped you, in front of the hill, though he should have known better."

My hands were shaking now, and I thrust them into the pockets of my jeans so they wouldn't give me away. The fact that he was here, in an ordinary place like a library, seemed somehow worse than anything else about him, as if he'd stepped out of my nightmares. He could show up anywhere, in my classes, in a restaurant, at my apartment...

I forced myself to answer him. "I'm not going to let you have Livvy," I said.

He laughed. He had too many teeth, as thin and sharp as needles. "Yes, you will. You'll let us and you'll be grateful for it, like the rest of the family. They don't try to stop us, and do you know why? Because they know what we can do."

"I—I don't care."

"Do you remember that man, the one you saw cleaning the house for the family? He defied us too, a long time ago. He belongs to us now—and he will for fifty years."

I couldn't think of anything to say. He saw that and he laughed again, showing those dreadful teeth. "Go home," he said. "Go home and wait for her to wake up."

He walked away. "No," I said, though I knew he couldn't hear me. "No, I won't."

I looked over the shelves, determined to continue my research, but I couldn't find any of the books I wanted.

I stayed away from the library the next day, too afraid of what I might find there. Instead I called Hilbert's father, a man named Henry who lived in New York. No one answered the phone, and I spent that day calling every couple of hours, growing to hate the monotonous sound of the ringing bell. Hilbert had given me Henry's address along with the phone number and I wrote to him, but I didn't expect a reply. I had the feeling that the family had ranged themselves against me, in a conspiracy to keep me ignorant of their history.

Finally I couldn't stand it anymore, and I gathered my courage and went back to the library. I stayed in sight of other people, never venturing out to the shelves I wanted if there was no one there. I sometimes waited hours for another library patron to come along, once a whole afternoon, but that was easier than having to face that man, That Person, alone.

The first day I couldn't get to the shelves, I started studying for my classes again, and I kept on with it when I ran out of other books. A few weeks later we had finals, and I did well, much better than I thought I would.

The library closed over Christmas vacation. The days were dark and chilly now, colder at the coast than I was used to in Sacramento, and it seemed to rain constantly. I stayed inside, sitting and reading by my small space heater, the room smelling of burnt dust and old books that hadn't been opened for years.

After a few days of this I couldn't stand my own company any longer. I wrapped myself up in my coat and scarf, Rose's scarf that had been magicked and then unmagicked again, and took the bus to Telegraph Avenue.

It was drizzling on Telegraph, but despite that it was still crowded with shoppers, and with street vendors selling wind chimes, beaded headbands, tie-dyed socks, Tarot readings. Christmas lights had gone up, and there were still a few tattered signs saying "Beat Stanford!" though the Stanford game had been a few weeks ago. Even I knew that, though I couldn't say who had won.

After the solitude of my room everything seemed too bright, and far too loud—shouts and conversations and music, cars honking out on Telegraph. I walked slowly, trying to get used to the sight of people again.

I stopped at a table displaying silver jewelry, thinking about the rows of bracelets I'd seen Livvy wear. Then I remembered the shackle around her arm in the other realm, and I turned away.

Still, I thought, I should get Livvy something for Christmas. I should be more optimistic, should at least act as if I expected her to wake up before then, though to be honest I had started to lose hope, to understand what I was up against. I continued on, working my way through the throng.

A top hat moved toward me, high above the crowd. I turned and pushed to get away, but the crush of people held me tight.

I looked back, out over the people coming toward me. The hat was gone. Had I imagined it? Then I glanced down and saw the man again, just a few feet away from me. Even worse, he was with the woman I'd seen in the other realm, the witch.

I turned again, forcing my way through the press of people. "Fifty years," the man said behind me.

"Think of it, my little boykin," the woman said. "Fifty years."

They laughed together, a sound that, if I think about it now, still sends shivers down my spine. I hurried home, forgetting any idea I'd had of buying presents.

The day before Christmas I took the bus to Sacramento and visited my parents for two days. I stayed in my old room and tried to read while I was there, amazing them with how hard I worked.

And then finally, on New Year's Eve, the last night of 1971, I remembered something.

Ben had gone to a party given by someone we'd met when we were living in the dorms last year. I'd been invited too, but I hadn't been interested, determined to get through the books I'd checked out.

A few hours later I found myself struggling through a dense thicket of sentences, sharp words sticking out like thorns. I looked up for a moment and stared off into space. I thought about words, and then something Mr. Feierabend said came back to me. The word "bondmaid," he'd said, hadn't made it into the *Oxford English Dictionary*. And there'd been a piece of paper, something about a bondmaid, in the folder Ben had stolen.

Ben had gotten a copy of the *Oxford English Dictionary*, a "compact" edition in two huge volumes, when he'd become an English major. I went to his room and looked up bondmaid. Mr. Feierabend had been right; it wasn't there.

But so what? What did that prove? I turned to the preface. The A-B section had been finished in 1888, it said. The editors had added a Supplement for words that had come into use after the dictionary was published, and I looked at that.

There it was: "Bondmaid. A slave girl." The examples they gave were from 1526, 1535, 1552. I glanced at the words around it; they'd all come from the late 1800s and the 1900s. So why wasn't bondmaid in the main dictionary, along with all the other old words?

And what about that slip of paper? By this time I'd completely forgotten what it said. Did Ben still have the folder or had Professor Rothapfel kept it?

I looked around Ben's room. The folder was in plain sight, on top of a brick-and-board bookshelf. I picked it up. Someone cheered loudly from outside, and for one crazy moment I thought they were cheering for me, for all my hard work and ingenuity. Then fireworks went off, and more people cheered, and someone shouted, "Happy New Year!"

Right. New Year's. I emptied the folder on Ben's desk and found the piece of paper. "Bondmaid," it said. "In folklore, a girl or woman who falls asleep for seven years, in exchange for which her family prospers. **1665** J. Woodhouse, *Spiderweb and Candlelight*, 125. The Elf made him this Bargain, that his Daughter would be a Bondmaid to the Fair Folk, in exchange for which he and his Family would live for ay in pleasure and comfort."

I felt excited, renewed. My search had paid off. There it was, in black and white; someone else had known about the bondmaids, and had written it down. All I had to do was find the book, *Spiderweb and Candlelight.*

The library wouldn't be open tomorrow—no, today, New Year's Day. I paced back and forth in Ben's small room. The Feierabends' library would be open, though, and if anyone had the book it would be them.

I put away the dictionary and stuffed the papers back into the folder, though I kept the note with the definition. More fireworks burst outside, and a siren went off. I went back to my room and wrote a letter to the Oxford University Press, asking them why they hadn't included the word "bondmaid" in the main dictionary. It was a long shot, I knew, but I felt filled with energy and optimism, unable to sleep. Happy New Year.

8

BEN HAD A HANGOVER the next day, his face a pale poisonous green, but he still wanted to come with me. To my relief, though, he agreed to let me drive. Before we left I got some frozen dinners out of the refrigerator; I'd been worrying about how Sylvie and Rose managed without Livvy.

Sylvie didn't exactly welcome me when she opened the door, just nodded and took my offerings and stepped aside. "We'd like to use your library, if that's okay," I said.

She nodded again and we headed for the stairs. On the way there I looked into the dining room and saw that the long table had been set with the family's mismatched cups and plates. I felt a sharp wrench: they were having a New Year's Day celebration and hadn't invited me. I told myself firmly not to be stupid. Why the hell should they, after all?

Ben wandered over to the table and I followed, too curious to worry if we were being rude. There were three places, which meant that Maddie was here. Either that, or... But no, they would have told me if she was well enough to come downstairs.

Each place setting had three knives. I looked at Sylvie, puzzled. She pulled out her hair pins and pinned up her bun again, stalling for time, I thought. Then she said, "One knife for each of the three fates, who cut the thread of our lives. It's supposed to be done every new year, to show we remember them."

I nodded, remembering what Mr. Feierabend had said. Was this superstition, or did it really help keep the other realm at bay? Still, I couldn't help feeling pleased that Sylvie was finally trusting me with the family's secrets.

We headed for the stairs. I looked around for the unwelcoming dog I'd met the last time, but I didn't see it anywhere. "What happened to that dog you had?" I asked Rose. "What was its name? Killer?"

She looked stricken. "Storm ran away," she said. "A few weeks after I got her."

"Oh. I'm sorry."

"Her paw had healed by then, at least. That's something, anyway."

We went up the stairs to the second floor. I looked in on Livvy's bedroom as we passed, but of course there was no change. The Moaning Bedroom next to it was silent. The hallway made a sharp left, then a right, to match up with the second part of the house, and we came to the library.

It took us about half an hour to find *Spiderweb and Candlelight.* I called out to Ben and pulled it down, then turned to page 125, fumbling in my eagerness.

The book was divided into short sections, some only a paragraph or two. They seemed to be anecdotes, stories a man named John Woodhouse had heard and written down. The one on page 125 was called "A Bargain."

"A Friend who went into Germanie told me of a curious Tale he had heard there. A Man walking through the woods came upon a little Creature, an Elf or a Sprite. The Elf made him this Bargain, that his Daughter would be a Bondmaid to the Fair Folk, in exchange for which he and his Family would live for ay in pleasure and comfort. But when his Daughter fell asleep, and the Man learned that she would sleep for seven years, he repented of the Bargain he had made. He consulted a Wise Woman, who advised him thus: that he should go to the Fairie Mound and say, Rick Rack Ruck, and his Daughter would be returned to him, hale and whole. The Man did so, and his Daughter came forth from the Mound. But from within he heard the Creature shouting angrily, saying, You have forfeited the Bargain, you and your Family, and you shall have ill Fortune all the days of your Lives. And my Friend heard that afterward the Elf sought to make this same Bargain with another Family, and that there were many who put themselves forth as Candidates, wishing good Fortune for themselves and their Families."

Ben was reading over my shoulder. "Look," I said. I was whispering, barely able to speak in my excitement.

"Rick rack ruck?" Ben said, grinning.

"Never mind that," I said. "Let's go."

I hurried downstairs, past the family sitting at the dining table, then ran outside. "Wait!" Ben shouted.

I kept going. I reached the hill and stopped, panting.

"Listen," Ben said, catching up with me. "Wait a minute. The book said that the family had ill fortune after they rescued the daughter, remember? Something bad could happen to them, to Maddie or Sylvie."

"What could be worse than sleeping for seven years?"

"Lots of things. Sickness, poverty, even death. Look, at least ask Sylvie if she wants you to do this. It's not up to you, they're not your family—"

"Livvy's my family."

"Just think about it. You could make it worse. Talk to Sylvie, or—or Rose—"

I turned away from him and faced the hill. "Rick rack ruck!" I said.

Nothing happened. I stared at it, willing it to open. Something rumbled, and a shadow appeared on the hillside. The shadow grew darker, larger; a part of the hill was opening outward.

I hurried toward it. "Wait!" Ben shouted behind me.

The door opened wider, and I squeezed through the gap. It was cold inside, and stale-smelling, as if it had been sealed for centuries. I looked around, but the light was already shrinking down to a sliver; the door was closing again. Then the rumbling stopped, and I stood in total darkness.

Suddenly light shot up all around me. I saw dozens of candles, lighting the inside of the hill. But instead of the tiled hall and the dancers, the trees and the bench where Livvy had slept, there was only a cave. Cold, white walls surrounded me, and stalactites dripped from the ceiling.

Someone stepped forward, a tall figure, black against the light. He drew closer and I saw that it was the man with the top hat. My heart pounded.

"We warned you," he said. "Several times. Fifty years, we said."

The cave disappeared. I was in a room somewhere, dressed in a black coat and trousers, a duster made out of peacock feathers tucked into my belt. "Have you dusted the furniture?" the man asked, his voice coming from behind me.

"What?" I said.

Something hard struck the side of my head. Pain jarred through me, and tears filled my eyes. I couldn't see, couldn't think.

"Have you dusted the furniture?" he asked. I turned to look at him. He held up a heavy cane, bound with a brass ferrule at the tip.

"I don't—"

He raised the cane higher. His question came again, his tone even, unchanged.

"No, I—"

The cane whipped through the air and hit me again, striking my back this time. "Stop!" I said. "Stop, please! I don't know what you want from me."

"Of course you do. You saw the man working for us in the farmhouse—you know what to do. Come, I'm growing impatient." He didn't sound impatient, though; his voice was as cool and dry as before.

"No," I said. "I'm not going to—"

His cane struck me again, and I fell. I got to my feet and went after him, hitting out at random. I couldn't connect with anything, though; he seemed to move out of the way just before my blows landed.

I stopped. Tears ran down my face, from the pain, I hoped, and not because I was crying. There was no help for it, I saw, no escape. I would have to do what he said, at least for the moment.

I tried desperately to remember what I'd seen that night at the farmhouse. "I have, sir"—that's what the other man had said, the stout one. I hadn't dusted yet, though. I took out my duster and started working on the table in front of me.

I finished the table and looked around at the room. It held a couch and a few chairs, an end table, a television. I had no idea where I was; I'd never seen any of it before in my life.

"Have you dusted the furniture?" the man asked.

I dusted the chair, then the rest of the room. The horrible question came again.

I forced myself to answer. "I have, sir."

I saw the cane coming, but it struck me before I could move. I fell against the chair, opened my mouth to say something, closed it again. I looked frantically around the room. The lamp. The lamp and the ashtray on the end table—I hadn't done them yet. I stood and headed toward them.

We went on to another room, and then another. I got into the rhythm of working, enough so that I could begin to think again. It was night, I realized, though somehow I could see clearly enough to do my work.

"Have you washed the dishes?" a voice said behind me.

I looked down, saw that the dishes were done. "I have, sir," I said.

So this was what life had been like for that other man, I thought, the one I'd seen working in Livvy's house. Those People, Livvy had called them, laughing. And I'd thought they were funny too, the men who cleaned her house in the middle of the night, typical of her eccentric family.

Now, though, I knew what that man was. He was Rumpelstiltskin or something like him, a creature who worked for a family until he was set free. I had never seen it from the other side before. What had he done to deserve his fate? What was his story, and how had it gotten tangled up with mine and Livvy's?

Whoever he was, though, I vowed that his tale would be different from mine. There was no way I would spend fifty years here.

I managed not to get hit the rest of that night. I fell asleep somewhere, and when I woke up I found myself in another house, a mop in my hands, looking down at the tiled floor of a bathroom.

That Person's voice came from behind me. "Have you cleaned the floors?"

I ran the mop over the tiles, then realized in a kind of panic that the mop was dry. I looked around, found some cleanser, and poured it over the floor. Then, before I could think about it, I turned and swung the mop as forcefully as I could.

The man whacked my arm with his cane, hard enough to make me let go of the mop. "Have you cleaned the floors?" he asked.

I picked up the mop and bent to work.

The days passed, each one much like the day before it. I worked, dusting and washing, mopping and polishing. I ate the food the household set out for me, oatmeal or cheese or apples. I hadn't given up the idea of getting free, but there seemed no way to escape the man and his cane. In one house I tried heading toward the front door, all my attention focused behind me—and sure enough, That Person loomed at my back, his cane raised, a grim expression on his face. In another place I locked myself inside a bathroom and opened the tiny window I found there—and he appeared inside the bathroom behind me. His cane began to haunt me; even the thought of it was enough to make my muscles tense.

Every so often I would wake to find myself on a boat, crossing a river. A dark-cloaked ferryman stood in front of me, silent, his pole stroking through the water. I understood that I was in the other realm, being taken from one place to another. Once I tried to speak to the ferryman but I fell asleep again, then woke in another house with another task before me.

One day I sank into a chair, exhausted beyond anything I had ever felt in my life. I looked behind me, guiltily, but That Person was gone, or at least I couldn't see him. How long had I been working like this? What was Ben doing right now, or Sylvie and Maddie, or my parents? Did any of them miss me?

Despair overcame me. It was hopeless, useless. I would keep on like this for fifty years. Livvy would wake to find me gone, would meet someone else and get married. Her story would go on, while mine had already ended.

I remembered my determination to escape, but it seemed like something from a long time ago, a dream or a book I'd read once. I forced myself to stand up and walk through the house. The first room I came to held a man and a woman asleep in their bed. I went on, going into three more bedrooms, each with a sleeping child.

Who were these people, and what had they done to deserve their good fortune? And what about all those other houses I'd cleaned? Whose stories had I stumbled into?

I headed back to the first bedroom and reached out to shake the man, to wake him up. A cane smacked down on my shoulder. "Have you swept the floors?" That Person asked behind me.

"No!" I said. I was screaming as loud as I could, not even sure what I was saying, just trying to wake up the couple in the bed. "No, I haven't swept your precious floors! Clean them yourself if you want to, just leave me alone!"

The man opened his eyes. "What is it?" he asked sleepily.

"It's Those People, dear," the woman said.

"That's right, just Those People," I said. "Just me, trapped here, cleaning your shitty house..."

They closed their eyes. "They can't help you," That Person said. "We put a glamour on them, to keep them from interfering. Though they might not help even if they could. Everyone likes a clean house."

"Who are they?" I asked. Despite his words, I felt pleased that he'd finally said something besides his eternal questions. I hadn't realized how much I missed someone to talk to. "Why do I have to clean their house? Did they make a bargain, like Livvy's family?"

He didn't answer me, just said, "Have you swept the floors?"

"What's your name?" I asked.

"Have you swept the floors?"

"No. No, and you know I haven't—"

He raised his cane, and I left the bedroom as quickly as I could, looking for a broom.

My despair had lifted slightly, though. Something had happened, something different from the everlasting cleaning. For the first time I remembered all those fairy tales I'd read, the stories and folklore. Maybe I could outwit them after all.

The next night I looked around for That Person, and when I didn't see him I woke up a man I found sleeping in one of the beds. "Hey," I said.

"What?" the man said, coming awake slowly.

"I like your coat," I said. "Can I have it?"

"Very clever," That Person said behind me.

I spun around. He raised his cane, and I flinched.

"Yes, very good," he said. "It's true—once they give you a gift besides food you're free to go. They won't give you anything, though. I told you, we put a glamour on them."

"You can't blame me for trying."

"Indeed I can." He took a step toward me, his cane still lifted, and I shrank back. "Have you dusted the furniture?"

I took out my feather duster and left the room, trying not to show him my fear.

I didn't try anything for a while after that. I felt more awake, though, more alert. I looked around at my surroundings while I worked; I read people's mail and scanned their shelves, opened drawers and filing cabinets, peered inside their refrigerators and studied the art on their walls.

I learned that I worked for all kinds of people, a stockbroker, a garage mechanic, a concert musician, a teacher. One of the houses I cleaned, I discovered, belonged to a woman who cleaned houses herself, an irony I didn't appreciate at the time. I tried to stay awake, to see how I got to the ferry-boat and how I left it, but I never managed it.

I read newspapers, and discovered that it had only been three weeks since I'd begun this horrible work. At first I didn't believe it; it had seemed like decades. How would I ever make it through fifty years?

Finally I had the glimmering of a plan. I took it slowly; I turned the plan over and over like a diamond, looking for flaws in any of its facets. I considered the people I worked for, one by one, and picked out the man who seemed the simplest, the least aware.

It was the stockbroker, oddly enough. He had books on his shelves about flying saucers and Atlantis and Bigfoot, and once he had actually sent a check to a flat earth society. I waited until his turn came around again, then went into the room where he slept alone.

For a while I just worked quietly around him. Then I gathered my courage and ripped one of the legs of his expensive suit.

He slept on. I pretended to trip against his bed and he woke up, his eyes unfocused, beglamoured. "Excuse me, sir," I said, showing him the trousers. "I was wondering if you'd like me to sew this up."

"Mmmm," he said.

I glanced behind me. That Person had appeared, just like I'd thought he would. He watched me intently, that red light deep within his eyes, but so far his cane stayed at his side.

"Would you like this fixed?" I asked. My heart tripped so loudly I thought That Person must surely hear it. "I can tailor it for you."

"Sure," the man said. "Sure, I'd like that."

"Like what?"

"If you will tailor it for me."

The man behind me screamed. I turned and laughed wildly. "He said my name!" I said. "I'm free!"

"Shut up," That Person said. "Yes, you're free, but don't think we're done with you. Shut your mouth!"

I couldn't stop laughing, though. "I'm Rumpelstiltskin!" I said. "He guessed my name!"

The room around me disappeared, and I was in darkness again. I was falling; I reached out and grabbed for something, anything. No, I was standing still, but I couldn't see, couldn't hear.

Tiny flames of light sparked around me. Or was I imagining them? I heard faint music, the music that Livvy and the others had danced to.

Two gibbous circles shone in the darkness like moons. They came closer, and I saw they were spectacles. The gloom lessened, and the witch appeared in front of me.

What did That Person mean, they weren't done with me? What would happen now? I couldn't focus, couldn't think what to do next. My heart pounded.

"You've caused us a great deal of trouble, haven't you?" the witch said.

"I hope so," I said.

"My, you're a stubborn lad. There's never been such a one as you before, not in all the long years of our bargain. Very well, then—we'll have to make a new bargain, just for you. What would you take to leave us alone?"

"Nothing. No, wait—Livvy. Give me Livvy and I'll go away."

"Ah, you nearly misspoke there, didn't you? What if I'd been about to offer you Livvy just then? You think you're so clever, my pretty little manling, but you're no match for us."

The music grew louder, more complex. The notes spiraled out and then twisted inward, turning in on themselves. I followed the melody for a while, then realized to my horror that I'd missed what the witch had said.

She laughed. Her laughter would have sent shivers up a steel rod. "I'm offering you a new bargain, my little lambkin. We give you one of our treasures, and you go away. Leave us alone for seven years, until your love returns to you."

All my instincts told me to agree, to take whatever she gave me and then run like hell. It took everything I had to stand my ground, to try to think.

"Why should I?" I asked. "You don't have anything I want, except for Livvy."

"Ah, but we do. We have many things, wonderful things. Treasures your people have coveted for centuries."

"Give me Livvy, and I'll go."

"Goodness me, but you're impatient. Here—come and look." She waved her hand and a long table appeared. "Choose any of these, any one of our lovely treasures."

The music changed subtly, became more intricate. I moved closer, curious now. The witch picked up a black cloak and swung it out toward me. "Wear this cloak, and you will become invisible," she said. She set it down and moved along the table, then lifted a sword. Light from the candles shot up along the blade. "Fight with this sword, and you will defeat all your enemies." She put the sword back on the table. "And finally, the third thing." She picked up a sack. "Ask for anything, and it will appear in this sack." She set the sack down and waved her hand across the table. "Infinite wealth. Power. Whichever you choose, my pretty little fellow, along with the good fortune you'll have when you marry Livvy."

The pattern of the music changed, changed again. "Choose wisely," the witch said, and laughed.

I tried to think but the pattern overwhelmed me, trapped me within the music. Where was all my knowledge of fairy tales now? I'd known the right answer once, though, I was pretty sure.

I stared hard at the three objects, forcing myself to concentrate. The next moment I found myself following a climbing run of notes like an elaborate staircase. The candles pulsed in rhythm with the music, and I looked away. "I'd like—I want the sack," I said.

The witch laughed again. Instantly I was sure I'd made the wrong choice. I felt defeated, lost.

Before I could take it back the witch spoke. "Very good, my little cock," she said, handing me the sack.

The lights went out. This time, though, I could make out a soft blur to my left. I was inside the hill again, I realized, and the blur was the entrance.

I hurried through it. It closed behind me. I looked down at what I held in my hand, an ordinary burlap bag. "Livvy," I said. "I want Livvy to appear in this sack."

The sack sagged toward the ground, suddenly heavy. Something moved inside it. I struggled with it, got it open.

I heard a shriek behind me, within the hill. Livvy stepped out of the sack, awake, alive. She looked at me, her eyes unfocused. "Where—where am I?" she whispered. "Who are you?"

She fell against me. I held her up, and together we went back to the house.

9

I BET YOU THOUGHT the story would end there. That it would end like a fairy tale: "And then they all lived happily ever after." And I thought so too, even though by this point I knew quite a lot about fairy tales. I knew, for example, that there was one tale, "The Death of the Hen," that ended "And then everyone was dead."

But I should tell it in order. The first thing that happened, the most important thing, was that Livvy was all right. Not great, not ready to face the world, but I saw her start to recognize me, to remember what we had been to each other.

I led her past the old garage, the other outbuildings, and into the house. Sylvie and Maddie and Rose were sitting around the dinner table, and for a moment I thought I'd returned the same night as I'd left. But Ben wasn't with them, and there was only one knife at each place setting. All of them started exclaiming loudly when they saw us.

"What—what day is it?" I asked, cutting them off.

"What do you mean?" Maddie said. "It's Thursday. January twenty-seventh."

It didn't seem like it could be, not after everything I'd gone through. "What year?"

"What happened, Will?" Sylvie asked, looking worried—worried and afraid. I would see that fear many times over the years on the faces of the family, even Maddie, even Livvy.

"Lots of things," I said.

I started to tell them what had happened, what I'd done. Then I noticed that Livvy looked exhausted, and I cut short my story and took her to bed. I wasn't tired at all, still on a high from outwitting the witch and That Person, but I was determined to stay with Livvy, worried that the other realm might somehow try to take her back.

Her sleep was different in some subtle way, though. Before it had been heavy and troubled; now she slept lightly, her movements natural. I lay next to her, up on my elbow and looking down into her face, as happy as I had ever been in my life. I noticed, pleased, that her bracelet or shackle had disappeared.

The second thing I discovered was that the sack no longer worked. I tried it out while Livvy slept; I got up and asked it for a bouquet of roses for Livvy, just testing. Nothing happened. I hadn't thought that it would, not really. I had not kept my part of the bargain; I had not simply taken what I was offered, tricking them instead into giving me Livvy. I wondered if they were done with us now, if they would make their bargains with someone else.

I woke up before Livvy the next day. My back and head were sore, my hands roughened from the work I'd done, but I felt surprisingly good, eager to start my life again, to put everything about the other realm behind me. Then Livvy moved, and opened her eyes, and I saw how fragile she still looked, how lost and uncertain.

I got up and called Ben, and found out that classes had already started. I spent a couple days with Livvy and then returned to Berkeley. My energy carried me through my classes, and I quickly made up the time I'd lost.

Livvy stayed on at the farmhouse, though, resting and getting used to being back in the world. I called her every night and we talked for a few minutes, about inconsequential things, until she felt tired.

For the first time I heard that someone in the family had called the university and gotten Livvy excused from all her classes due to illness. I have to say I felt surprised; I'd never known them to be so practical.

She wasn't able to register for the new semester either, but she spent only a month at the farmhouse before she decided to come back to Berkeley, to her apartment. It felt like a victory; obviously she would rather be with me than her family. I spent all the time I could with her, and meanwhile she read the textbooks for the classes she'd missed, trying to catch up.

She was still hesitant, though, nervous around Berkeley's freaks and crazy people, wary of all the students who seemed to know exactly where they were going. And she seemed to lean on me more. I thought I'd enjoy that, but as it turned out I didn't; she was so different from the strong woman I'd known. We took it slowly, eating dinner at her place, going outside only once or twice a week.

There was a psychological reason for the differences between us, I knew. I had done something, had worked to free us, while she had been passive, unable to change anything around her. Knowing this didn't help, though. Her progress seemed terribly slow, sometimes even nonexistent; there were too many times where I felt like giving up in frustration.

Finally, when I thought she was ready, I asked her if she wanted to talk about the other realm. "Sure, all right," she said, and then, as if to deny her words, she said nothing else for a long time.

"We were fighting," she said after a while. "A great troop of us, men with swords and silver armor, and swarms of these—these tiny creatures, with wings and their own swords, or riding on what looked like hummingbirds... We rode out during storms, or maybe we were the storm—anyway we made this hideous noise, all of us together, the men screaming and clashing their weapons and—and laughing, horses neighing and dogs barking. It was chaos, thunder and lightning all around us—I was never really sure what was happening. And then after the battle we celebrated, we danced, although I didn't want to... I was tired, always so tired."

"I saw you," I said.

"You did? When?"

I described my first visit to the other realm, but she said she hadn't seen me. "How did you—how did you get me out?" she asked.

I looked at her, startled. How could she not know? I told her the story, how I had chosen the sack and then asked for her. She laughed—the first time I'd heard her laugh since she came back—and kissed me.

"It wasn't my idea," I said. "I read about it in a fairy tale."

"We aren't supposed to read fairy tales. The crows told us not to. We read some of them anyway, of course, when we were kids."

"That's all over. You don't have to worry about them ever again—you can read or do anything you want."

The skin between her eyebrows creased, a frown line that had appeared sometime in the past months. "Are you sure?"

"Yeah. I'm sure."

"Maddie said so too. But she said that you broke the bargain, that we don't have our good luck anymore. She's mad at you—she said you didn't have any right to speak for our family. Though of course she says she's glad I'm back."

"What do you think?"

"Well, I'm happy to be back too. Of course I am."

She sounded uncertain, though, and my heart felt heavy as lead.

Around that time I got a letter from someone at the *Oxford English Dictionary*. So much had happened I'd completely forgotten about the letter I'd sent them, asking about the entry for the word "bondmaid." To my surprise, they actually answered my question.

"Thank you for your interest in the *Oxford English Dictionary*," the letter said. "You are correct in pointing out that the word 'bondmaid' was left out of the main volume of the *OED*, and the story behind that is quite an interesting one. In compiling the dictionary the editors used volunteer readers from all over the world, who sent in slips of paper with quotations illustrating how a specific word should be used. After the dictionary was finished, in 1928, the slips for 'bondmaid' were found to have fallen behind a pile of books. The word was later added to the Supplement."

I was sure that the person who wrote me thought that this story was true. I was equally sure that what had really happened was a lot more interesting than that. By this time I understood enough about the Feierabend family to work out the true story: someone had discovered that a quotation from a book revealing the bargain was about to be published and had stolen the slip of paper—and dropped all the other slips behind some books for good measure. I wondered what else the family had intercepted over the years, besides fairy tales and old quotations.

The next important thing happened about a week later. I was walking to campus along Telegraph Avenue when I heard someone say "Hey—can I talk to you?" I didn't stop; Telegraph was filled with crazies who would engage you in long pointless conversation if you let them.

"Hey," the voice said again. "Hey, Will. I want to make a bargain with you."

I spun around. One of those short furry men stood there, dressed like a denizen of Telegraph: a green Army-surplus jacket, torn green T-shirt and trousers, everything so filthy he looked like he'd slept in an oil spill.

"What do you want?" I asked.

"We'd like the sack back," he said.

"You would, would you?"

"That's right. And if you give us the sack, we promise never to take a bondmaid from Livvy's family ever again."

I nearly agreed right then. But I remembered the witch's scream and I knew that she had to be furious with me, that she would want to get back at me any way she could. And I knew from reading fairy tales how clever the people of the other realm could be, how tricky. I stood and thought, going over each of his words as if biting them for authenticity.

He misinterpreted my silence and said, "We know the sack doesn't work for you."

"Why do you want it, then?"

"That's our business."

"Can you make it work again?"

"Not for you."

"Okay," I said. "Let me see if I got this straight. You will never take a bondmaid from the Feierabends—" I stopped. What if they changed their name? "From Livvy's family, from any of her descendants or anyone descended from anyone who's related to her."

"That's right."

"What about their good fortune? Do they get to keep that, or get it back again?"

"You broke the bargain, didn't you? Why should we keep our side of it?"

"Maybe because I won't give you the sack if you don't."

He shrugged. "It's not worth that much to us."

He seemed to mean it. Well, it had been a long shot anyway, and I saw his point. "All right," I said. "Never mind that. But everything else goes."

"Agreed," he said, and we arranged to meet on Telegraph the next day.

I called Livvy and told her all of this. A day later my phone rang. "Why on earth did you give him that sack?" the person on the other end said.

It was Maddie, of course. "Didn't Livvy tell you the rest of it?" I asked.

"They're never going to take a bondmaid from your family again."

"And what about our good fortune? You're just going to give it up without a fight? Why didn't you ask for that instead?"

"I did. But they're not giving that back, not without the bondmaids."

"So? Let them have the bondmaids, let everything be the same as it was, in exchange for their stupid sack."

Suddenly I felt as if I had no air at all in my chest. I took a deep breath. "Let them—after what happened to Livvy?"

"Sure. They aren't going to take her again, are they? Not with all the problems she caused them. They might even take me the next time. You don't hear me complaining."

"Look," I said. I'd done some thinking about this, going over and over what the little man had said. "He never said your good fortune was gone. It might still be there—you never know."

"I do know. I know because I grew up in this family, because our family's lived with this for hundreds of years. It doesn't work like that."

"Really? And who brought Livvy back?"

"That's what I mean. You took Livvy, so they took back our luck. They never give up something for nothing."

"Sure they do. That crow told you not to read fairy tales, but I did, I read all of them. They make bargains like that all the time."

Maddie laughed scornfully. "That's what you think," she said.

But weeks passed, and then months, and nothing terrible happened. Livvy went back to school in the spring quarter. Maddie got cast in another play, and then in a few small parts in movies and on television. Her disgust toward me and my foolishness never mellowed, though, even as her career started to take off. Once I made the mistake of congratulating her on her success, and she told me angrily how much better she would be doing if I hadn't meddled.

At the end of the school year Livvy agreed to move in with me. We found a place together, and Ben got another roommate.

You can never recapture old happiness, though; that was something I learned then. Livvy and I got together with Ben, or with Maddie when she was in town, but our foursome, our charmed circle, was broken. It didn't feel the same; we had none of our old wild energy, the laughter and excitement.

Still, if I wasn't ecstatically happy I was at least content—which, I realized, was the next best thing. I found myself humming my old song, "Everyone Says I Love You," but this time it was Harpo's version on the harp I thought of, wordless but full of feeling.

And all this time I looked for omens, trying to discover whether or not our luck had run out. Maybe there was some loophole I didn't know about, maybe the family would be allowed to keep their good fortune after their long and faithful service. I juggled signs and portents constantly, trying to decide what it meant when I found a dollar bill on the sidewalk or a bus left just as I reached the bus stop. I didn't know it then, but I was going to make these calculations for the next fourteen years.

I looked for crows, too, and furry men dressed in green, and I felt Livvy shiver on stormy nights when thunder and lightning crashed all around us. But in my two remaining years as an undergraduate I saw only one thing out of the ordinary, one time I knew for certain that the other realm had reached again into our lives.

10

IN THE SUMMER OF 1972 Maddie came up from Los Angeles to visit, and Livvy and I drove up to the farmhouse to see her. "How nice you're all here," Sylvie said, greeting us at the door. "Lem's restaurant is finally open, the Moon Bridge Café."

My ears swiveled toward her, satellite dishes finding evidence of alien life at last. Lem, that was the cousin's name, the one I couldn't remember. "Why don't we go there for dinner?" I asked.

Livvy and Maddie decided to come, though Sylvie and Rose stayed behind. I had my own car by then, a necessity if I wanted to visit the farmhouse without Ben, and we headed down into the valley. Fog came up as soon as we left, huge billowing sheets of it; I felt like I was driving through someone's white hanging laundry.

Livvy and Maddie were busy catching up, paying no attention to my struggles with the road. "What are you in town for?" Livvy asked.

"The demonstration, of course," Maddie said.

"What demonstration?"

"You're kidding me. You have noticed that the Vietnam War is still going on, that workers are still oppressed all over the world? Or are you too busy staring into each other's eyes to care?"

That seemed unfair. I'd marched in my share of anti-war demonstrations, been sprayed with my share of teargas. "I didn't hear about any demonstration," I said.

"Of course not. Like I said, you don't even care. The YSA—"

"Great. Now we get to hear what the Trotskyites say."

"Trotskyists."

"Yeah, you said that before. And what's wrong with being called a Trotskyite? Is it like Trekkers and Trekkies?"

"You have no idea what a Trotskyist is, do you?"

I didn't, not really. I was starting to feel sorry, just a bit, for making fun of her. She wasn't finished, though. "You don't care because you never had to worry about going to Vietnam. And do you know why?"

"Well, because my birthday was number 336 in the draft lottery. What's your point?"

"Is that what you think? After all this time? You got a high number because they thought you were going to marry Livvy. They didn't want you going off to Vietnam, you or Ben."

"What?" I knew immediately who she meant by "they." I tried to remember back to that time, watching the lottery on television, the blessed relief when it looked like my birthday would be in the last third of the numbers called. "I didn't know Livvy then. Ben hadn't even met you yet."

"That doesn't matter. They knew you were going to date Livvy, and Ben was going to date me. It's ironic, isn't it? You benefited from the bargain more than anyone in this family, and you're the one who destroyed it."

Was that the way it worked? Could they look into the future like that? And what about all those other people who'd been born on my birthday—did they owe their good fortune to a coincidence they didn't even know about? Did the other realm really have that kind of power?

"Watch out!" Livvy said.

I looked up to see my front bumper about a foot from the mountainside. I swerved back.

"Stop arguing, children," Livvy said.

Somehow, with Livvy and Maddie helping out, we made it to the Valley floor and into downtown Napa. Downtown was small but very solid, with those huge blocky buildings they used to construct for banks and department stores. Now they mostly housed small shops for furniture and clothing.

"Turn right here," said Livvy, who'd gotten directions from her mother. She indicated a small street away from the main one.

"I never thought—what if we need a reservation?" I said. "Shouldn't we have called?"

"Nah—it's Uncle Lem."

I'd noticed that the family still acted as if everything would arrange itself for their benefit. They had always been more spontaneous than other people, trusting that whatever they had in mind would work out. If they'd decided to travel somewhere, for example, there would be a plane leaving half an hour after they got to the airport—and the tickets would be on sale as well.

And I'd never known them to make a reservation at a restaurant. Probably they didn't know any other way; they'd grown up lucky, after all. As for me, as I said, I had started to measure good omens against bad, a complex algebra of fortune and misfortune.

"Left here," Livvy said.

I turned left onto a tiny unlit street. Ahead of me I saw a neon sign, with the words MOON BRIDGE CAFÉ running like paint in the fog. We got out of the car and went inside.

The fog reached into the restaurant too, or maybe it was just full of smoke; I could barely see across the room. A figure came toward us, moving out of the haze like someone parting a curtain: a small man, with white hair. He had a lantern jaw edged with a white beard, and half-moon glasses perched on the tip of his nose. The tail of his frock coat streamed out behind him.

"Livvy!" he said, beaming at them. "Maddie!"

"Hi, Lem," Livvy said. "Will, this is my uncle Lemuel. My cousin, really, or my father's cousin, or something—anyway, this is Will."

"Hi," I said.

A group of people were just leaving a table, and Lemuel led us toward it. Faint music played somewhere. I looked around for a band but couldn't see one.

The fog seemed to have faded from this part of the room, as if it had its own microclimate. Now I could see flowers everywhere, in pots hanging from macramé holders and in giant urns standing on the floor, even painted on the walls. Beads and sequins hung across the doorways, candles shone on tables, and behind the bar a stuffed wombat with wire-rim glasses sat on one of the shelves. On the wall ahead of us was a poster of Groucho Marx and John Lennon with a banner that said, "All hail Marx and Lennon." The place smelled like spilled wine and baking chocolate.

We sat down. I turned to Maddie, about to show her the poster and tell her that those were my politics, when a woman came toward us.

"This is my wife Nell," Lem said. "She'll be your waitress tonight."

Maddie gasped. Livvy actually jerked back away from her, scraping her chair along the floor. "Lem, how could you?" she said.

"What?" I asked. There was nothing very odd about Nell, or nothing I could see. She was shorter than Lem and much younger, a little plump, with long reddish-brown hair that hung in waves down her back.

"It's not what you think," Lem said. "Listen, she's told me some things—"

"I don't care what she told you—you know how stupid this is," Maddie said.

"*What?*" I said again. I felt a familiar emotion, a frustration and bafflement that seemed to happen only around the Feierabends.

"She's from the other realm," Livvy said, taking pity on me finally. "Isn't she, Uncle Lem?"

Lem nodded.

"And your sister Violet was a bondmaid, too," Maddie said. "I have to agree with Livvy on this—how could you?"

"Listen," Lem said. "We can be revenged on them—she's told me how. We can revenge my sister. She has some ideas, a way we can get our good fortune back."

Livvy shook her head, and even Maddie, who had said she'd sacrifice herself to remake the bargain, looked horrified.

"No way," Livvy said. "They trick you. You can't trust them, not ever."

Nell was watching us, smiling slightly. She brushed her hair back and I saw her ears for a quick moment. They looked pointed.

"Wait a minute," I said, finally catching up. "You, Lem—you *married* her?" I'd had no idea that the denizens of the other realm could live in our world, let alone get married here.

"I did," Lem said. "Best thing that ever happened to me."

"Someone does it every few generations," Livvy said. "That's what Rose says, anyway."

"So you could—you might be related to her? To people from the other realm?"

"I guess."

She played with the salt and pepper shakers, pottery figures of a fiddler and a goose, obviously not wanting to talk about it. I remembered something Hilbert had said, that they'd had some extraordinary people in their family. At the time I'd thought he'd meant that the other realm had given them gifts, like all those godmothers in all those fairy tales, but now I realized they might be closer to that realm than I'd thought. That Livvy...

But Lem was speaking. "Listen," he said again. "Just hear what she has to say."

"Maybe we should," I said. I had some idea of making another clever bargain, winning the admiration of a grateful family, Maddie admitting that I'd been right all along. "How can it hurt?"

"You have no idea," Maddie said. "I told you—you didn't grow up in this family."

"Oh, let her talk," Livvy said. "He'll see."

"Livvy—"

"Don't worry. We'll stop it if it gets too dangerous." She made a grand gesture, more like Maddie than Livvy, telling Nell to go ahead.

It was Lem who spoke first, though. "You were doing battle there, right?" he said to Livvy. "In the other realm. That's what everyone who comes back says, the bondmaids. Did you ever wonder who you were fighting? What the sides are?"

Livvy said nothing.

"The queen has enemies in that land," Nell said. There was something odd about her voice, though pleasantly so, as if she were purring, or speaking through fur. "That queen who imprisoned you, who put you through such horrors. Those enemies are your allies, Livvy. They're fighting to win free of the queen, of her dominion."

"The queen?" I asked. "That witch I saw?"

"Witch, that's right. That's what she is. You can fight her, join with her foes. Win out against her tyranny."

Livvy laughed scornfully. "Right. If I could have gotten away, which I couldn't, and if I hadn't been so tired all the time..."

"Not you," Nell said. "But there are others who can."

"Who?" I asked.

Nell shrugged. "I don't know. Someone from your family, though, someone already marked out by the other realm."

"I still don't understand. Why would we want to fight her? Why should we go back, now that I have Livvy?"

"Why? For the rewards, of course. Anything you'd like—riches, power, a queen's ransom, literally. Good fortune for you and your descendants until the end of time, happily ever after. And no bondmaids this time, not ever."

I must have looked doubtful, because she went on. "I'm one of them, one of the people fighting the queen. I'd be there now, if I hadn't escaped into this world." She smiled at Lem, then looked back at me, her expression grave. "That's why I'm giving away their secrets like this, even though they'd kill me if they knew. I'm asking you for your help against her."

I shook my head. "Me? I don't even know how to get there."

"There are no maps to that realm—it's not anchored, like your lands. But there are places where our realm and theirs overlap. The boundaries aren't fixed, you know. They're more like tides, one flowing into the other."

"Well, that's a big help," Livvy said, cutting in sharply. I realized I'd been lulled by Nell's soft voice, dreaming of fierce battles and stunning victories. "Thank you very much. There's a way in, only you don't know it, and you can't tell us how to find it, and what's more there aren't even any maps."

Nell bowed her head, as if chastened. "I've told you all I can," she said. "As for the doorways leading in—"

Something was happening to the restaurant while she was talking; it had grown even dimmer, the fog swirling and eddying through the chairs and tables. The couches and shelves faded into white. A candle behind the bar guttered out, then another, then several all at once. The band—which I hadn't seen anywhere, though the music sounded live—grew louder.

The fog thickened. The music became louder still. It changed, coiling and twisting like the fog, until it resolved into the song I had heard when I'd rescued Livvy.

Livvy stood, her eyes wide with fear. "They're here," she said. "The other realm. She called them, Nell did. I told you—"

"No," Nell said. She looked frightened as well, and that more than anything made me realize the danger we were in. "They've come for me. I should never have told you so much."

Livvy ran for the door, and I followed her. Something crashed behind us; it sounded like a chair falling over. Other people were standing, even running, though they couldn't possibly have known what was happening.

The fog hid everything now. I pushed my way through the crowd, calling out for Livvy. I bumped into a man standing still and listening, his face transfixed by the music, and I hurried past him.

Something the size of a dog ran in front of me. A fox, I realized with a start. It stopped and looked back at me, grinning, showing its sharp teeth. It dragged its tail across the floor, and fire bloomed in its wake.

I forced myself to keep moving. I shouted Livvy's name again, but it was drowned out by screams and music, by the smashing of glass behind me.

A short while later I hit a wall made out of something cold. Ice? I felt my way along it, realized it was a window. Air blew against my face, and I could see through an open door to the vague light of the street. I groped my way toward it.

"Here," someone said in my ear, a soft, low voice.

I turned quickly. Nell stood behind me. Something had happened to the restaurant beyond her: it was dissolving, turning into a winding road. On either side of the road stood squat, fat houses, with thatched roofs and wide chimneys.

As I watched, a cloud of smoke blew up, covering everything. "Take this," Nell said. "It will help you."

She pushed something into my palm. I glanced down, and when I looked up again I could see flame glowing within the smoke. Nell's hair looked red now, outlining her face in fire.

I closed my hand around what she had given me, and then a crush of people pressed me against the window and carried me along with them. We reached the door and squeezed through.

People stood outside, talking and pointing at the restaurant. Maddie came out of the door, and then Livvy. I ran to them and hugged Livvy, realizing at that moment what I'd been afraid of—that the other realm had come to take her back.

Finally we broke apart. Livvy looked at the crowd. "Did you see Lem anywhere?" she asked.

"No," I said. "I saw Nell for a bit." And something else, I thought, but I decided not to mention that just now.

A siren sounded, then another. I smelled smoke and turned quickly to look at the restaurant. Flames ate along the front wall, black edged with gold. Livvy looked at Maddie. Something seemed to pass between them and they went toward the restaurant.

"What are you doing?" I asked.

"Lem's still inside," Maddie said. "We have to go back."

"Are you kidding?" I said. "It's burning up in there. Wait for the fire trucks."

The sirens seemed no closer, though. The fire flared outward, burning along the restaurant's façade. The crowd backed away from the heat and stood watching, their faces intent, an orange light reflected in their eyes.

Livvy rocked back and forth impatiently. We waited for what seemed like hours, though it was probably only five or ten minutes. Finally two fire trucks pulled up in front of the restaurant. Men dragged out the hoses and shot streams of water into the flames.

The light of the blaze grew stronger. I realized I was clenching my hand, that something was pressing into my palm. I opened my hand and saw an ancient key, with long pins and a round head.

Without thinking I dropped it in my pocket. I looked around for Livvy and saw that she had moved closer to the fire. "Get back, lady," one of the firemen called out. "It isn't safe here."

"I'm looking for my uncle," she yelled back.

"We'll find him. Right now I need you to stand away from the fire."

She headed back toward me. There was a huge roar as the roof of the restaurant caved in. "Ahhh," the crowd said together, a soft sigh, almost of satisfaction.

Slowly, very slowly, the firemen got control of the blaze, then broke down the walls and went inside. We heard the sound of axes cracking against walls, furniture dragged across the floor, people shouting back and forth.

Finally the man Livvy had talked to came back outside. "There's no one in there, ma'am," he said.

"No one?" Livvy said. "But my uncle—he never came out, him and his wife—"

"He isn't there. We'd have found him if he was."

"Are you sure? Can I look?"

"Not a chance—it's still much too dangerous. He probably went out the back door."

"The back door," I said, feeling stupid. "That must be it."

"Sure," the man said. "All restaurants have to have a back door—it's the law."

Livvy looked at me for reassurance. "You think so?" she said.

"Definitely," I said.

"But where is he?"

I shrugged. "Maybe he went home?"

"He wouldn't have done that, not without talking to us first. Oh, God, what if the other realm, if they—"

"Look," I said. "Let's go back to the house and try to call him from there."

We went to the car and started up the hill. Did I really think Lem had escaped out the back? I did if it made Livvy happy. But then what had happened to Nell? She had been right next to me, at the front of the restaurant.

When we got to the farmhouse Livvy and Maddie took turns calling Lem, but there was no answer.

11

WE NEVER DID FIND LEM, or Nell. We drove to their house the next day and knocked on their door, but we heard nothing from inside. Maddie pulled up a window—with typical Feierabend disdain for the fates, Lem had left them unlocked—and we went inside, but the house was empty. We went back to the restaurant too; it was boarded over where the fire had eaten at it, with vivid black stains reaching to the roof.

I carried the key with me for a while, trying it in doors at the farmhouse and even in my apartment, but it didn't fit anywhere. In the light of day I noticed an engraving on the head I hadn't seen before, a spider, and I remembered the motto over the fireplace: *spider in the evening.*

Nothing much happened for a while after that. Ben and I graduated two years later, in 1974. To my surprise he'd stuck with his English major, and after graduation he got a job in a bookstore and told us he was going to write a novel.

I went on to graduate school and started working with actual patients, poor, desperate people who couldn't afford therapy and came to the campus to be treated free. It was so frustrating that many days I would come home determined to go into something easier, government bureaucracy maybe.

Livvy graduated, two quarters behind me because of all the time she'd missed. As we got ready for her graduation ceremony she seemed anxious, worried about something. "What's wrong?" I asked.

"I—" she said. "Well, I'm pregnant."

My first impulse was to take her and spin her around the room. Fortunately something, my training in psychology maybe, came to my aid and I asked her how she felt about it.

She hesitated. "Good, I think," she said. The frown line appeared between her eyebrows, deeper now, and she said, "I'm pretty sure."

Every so often, ever since her return from the other realm, she would seem a little cold to me, not quite of this world, and this was one of those times. How could she not be overjoyed? Didn't she want us to have a family together?

She seemed to sense my thoughts, because she laughed nervously. "Well, you know. What if it's a girl?"

There was no technology back then to tell you what the sex of your child would be; you had to wait all the long months until the birth itself. Still, this was a problem I could deal with. "They said they wouldn't take a bondmaid from your family ever again," I said.

"That's right," she said. She sounded uncertain, though. Maddie had said, often, that the other realm could not be trusted. That they would keep their bargains, but never in the way you expected.

"Do you—" I said. My heart tripped and stopped and started again, and I forced myself to go on. But she was saying something, and just as I said, "Will you marry me?" she said, "Maybe we should get married, what do you think?"

She smiled, wider and more brilliant than her usual mysterious smile. "Well, yeah," she said, and I said, "Yes, of course."

We had a quick wedding on the lawn behind the farmhouse. None of us knew how to plan a wedding, but we left it for as long as possible, the Feierabends trusting to luck, and me out of general ignorance. Livvy and I had no idea how to find a minister, for example, and we kept putting it off or trying to delegate another member of the family to work on it. Finally, at the last minute, I ran into a friend who had become a Universal Life Church minister by answering an ad at the back of a magazine, and he agreed to marry us.

We asked Sylvie for her permission before we invited Hilbert. "Well, of course you can," she said. "He's your father, after all." He had come by the farmhouse a few times since Livvy had woken up, awkward visits where he lectured about political scandals (Nixon had resigned the year before, because of Watergate) and left after half an hour. Still, I felt I had gotten to know him better.

On one of these visits he gave me a list of his relatives, telling me that he had gotten it from his father Henry the last time they'd talked. I was certain that that wasn't true, that he had always known where every last Feierabend was and hadn't wanted to tell me earlier. I didn't accuse him, though; I wanted to stay on his good side.

Livvy and I took a day to address invitations, with Livvy providing commentary on the relatives I'd never met. There was her grandfather Henry and his brother Peter, whose son Lem had disappeared, and Lem's sons from an earlier marriage, and his sister Violet and her son.

"Wait a minute," I said, stopped by one of the stranger names. "You have a relative named Lettuce?"

She laughed. "*Lettice*," she said. "It's pronounced Le-ti-che. Like Leticia." She looked solemn for a moment, and then said, "She was a bondmaid too."

Livvy spent the day before the wedding filling the kitchen with food, including a duck that needed to be cooked for five hours. I asked if I could help, and was sternly told to get out of the kitchen and not come back until she was done.

The actual ceremony passed in a blur. Partly this was because I felt so happy, but partly because I went through the whole thing in a haze of champagne and a hit of the killer weed Ben had given me beforehand.

Afterward we set out Livvy's buffet, then mingled with the guests. I felt serenely goofy by this time, tolerant and enlightened and wise beyond my years—also sure I was making a fool of myself many times over, but in my newfound wisdom I told myself I didn't have to care. I was part of the family now, included within the circle of enchantment that surrounded them, the magic that had held and protected them for three hundred years or longer. Nothing could ever go wrong now.

I met Lettuce, and then kept trying to catch glimpses of her, to see how sleeping for seven years had changed her. And Livvy introduced me to some other relatives too, Lem's sons, his sister Violet, also a bondmaid, and her son. Henry and Peter had been too fragile to make the ceremony, but they had sent their best wishes.

I'd seen Ben only briefly before the ceremony, when he'd passed me the joint he'd been smoking. There had been a woman hovering near him, and I'd wondered if he'd brought a date. If so I definitely approved—he still sometimes mentioned Maddie, and I worried that he'd never gotten over her.

Finally I found him at the buffet table, the woman I'd seen standing next to him. To my horror she was someone I knew, a patient of mine named Marya.

"Hey, Ben," I said.

"Will!" he said. "Congratulations, man."

I walked with him a few paces away from the table. To my relief the woman didn't follow us. "Did you bring her?" I asked.

"Yeah," he said. "She came into the bookstore and said she needed a ride. Why, is something wrong?"

I couldn't believe that Ben, of all people, could be this naïve. What happened to the guy who'd given me the yellow strawberry, who used to point and say "Hey, look—it's Halley's comet!" when he wanted to steal something off my plate? "Yeah, there's something wrong, man. I didn't invite her. She's one of my patients."

"Really? Wow—sorry, man. She told me she's a friend of yours."

I glanced back at the woman. In therapy sessions she'd told me about four conflicting stories about her family and her living situation, but I was coming to think she lived on the street, at least part of the time, and that her name wasn't really Marya. Sometimes we seemed to be making progress, but at other times her behavior was wildly inappropriate; she'd kissed me on the mouth once after a session, for example. And now this, coming uninvited to my wedding—I guess you'd have to say that was inappropriate too.

"It's probably my fault too," I said. "I told her I was getting married."

"Yeah, but how'd she know I was your friend? That's disturbing, man."

It was. Had she been following me around, seen me with Ben? I was going to have to have a serious conversation with her, maybe even stop treating her. It could keep until later, though; this was my day.

I looked over at her again. She put some stuffed vine leaves on her plate and stood there eating while people struggled to move around her—eating quickly, as if she thought the food would be taken away from her at any moment. She turned to the man next to her and said something, then laughed wildly. The man scowled and walked away.

"Didn't you notice anything odd about her?" I asked.

Ben shrugged. "Who am I to make judgments about your friends?" he asked.

"She's not—"

"Just kidding. But, you know, I really didn't. I think she was on her best behavior in the car."

I nodded. She could do that, for a while. I couldn't tell him so, though, couldn't break patient confidentiality. "Oh, well," I said. "I should probably go talk to the guests. But it's good to see you."

I was feeling pretty strange by this time. Too many of my worlds were crashing into each other like bumper cars—friends from high school and college were here, and my parents and older brothers, and Ben's parents, who were divorced by this time and pointedly not speaking to each other. And then there were the Feierabends—Hilbert and his lectures, vague Sylvie, Maddie and her drama and fiery politics. What would they all make of each other?

And every so often I would see people out of the corner of my eye, then turn and find that no one was there. I caught glimpses of the little furry men, for example, dressed in green tuxedos with green bowties, and once I saw, or thought I saw, a woman with a lion's head. Another time I stared idly at an old bald man before I realized he had wings. I tried to look for more of these creatures but they seemed to hide themselves, to slip away as I focused on them. Faces appeared in the trees, then resolved into twigs and leaves.

They weren't really there, I told myself. We were done with them, all those denizens of the other realm. I had conjured them up out of excitement and marijuana fumes.

A man headed toward me, juggling plates and bottles and pie tins. For a moment I thought he was from the other realm too, but as he came closer I saw he was with Maddie.

"Will!" she said. "I'd like you to meet my boyfriend, Andre. Andre, this is Will."

Andre caught the objects as they dropped. "Pleased to meet you," he said.

I was so disoriented by then that I blurted out something I would never have said if I'd been thinking. "Hey, Ben knows how to juggle too," I said.

"Well, of course," Maddie said. "I like men with balls."

We all laughed, and Andre, luckily, didn't ask me who Ben was.

Hilbert came over, dressed in a black jacket and tie and a white shirt that had come loose from his trousers. "Reminds me of my own wedding, really," he said, looking up at me from his chest. "It's a terrible feeling, nostalgia. It used to be an actual medical diagnosis—'nostos' means returning home, and 'algos' means pain, like neuralgia. Well, anyway. Congratulations."

A tiny shape flitted behind him, a woman on a hummingbird. I watched it until it grew too small to see, and then forced myself back to Hilbert.

12

SEVEN MONTHS AFTER the wedding, in October 1975, our child was born, a boy. We were so delighted, so relieved, that the nurse, obviously a feminist, made no secret of her disapproval. In those years it seemed that every boy was named either Jason or Dylan, and at first the only thing we could agree on was that we would call him something else. Finally we decided on Nicholas.

Livvy stayed home with him for a while, then started grad school in the fall of 1976. A year later I graduated and set up as a therapist. I still saw some patients without charge, though, including Marya. I had never stopped treating her, despite my resolution at the wedding. For one thing, it would have been too disruptive for her to start with another therapist. There was another reason, though, one that didn't reflect well on me—if I'd transferred her to someone else, I would have had to tell my adviser that I'd screwed up, that I'd told Marya I was getting married. We were supposed to be able to judge how much personal information a patient could handle.

Livvy graduated in 1978. She had a brief flirtation with med school but then decided to go into research—and I couldn't help but wonder how much of that had to do with her fears, the fact that she still felt nervous around other people. I never said anything, though, and she found a job she liked almost immediately.

A year later we were doing so well we bought a house. At the housewarming party Maddie told us she had gotten the starring role in an independent movie. She had long since broken up with Andre.

Nick turned out to be a shy boy, uncertain in groups and in new situations, but also very brave, determined to overcome his fear. Sometimes when I watched him I could tell how hard he was working, and I felt my heart being wrung like a dishcloth. When he knew he was safe and among friends, though, he was the happiest kid I'd ever seen.

I added and subtracted these signs obsessively and decided that, on the whole, the other realm was still disposed to wish us well. Either that, or they had forgotten all about us.

One day in 1980 I got a call at work. I was with a patient, so I knew the receptionist must have thought it was important. Even so, I wasn't prepared for the news at the other end. Livvy had been in a car accident.

I managed to make out that she had been taken to a hospital nearby. Then everything contracted down to the size of a sheet of paper, and high wind roared in my ears.

"Is she—is she sick?" I asked, because, after all, why else would you go to a hospital? In my panic I couldn't think of the word "hurt"—couldn't, or didn't want to.

"She broke her arm," the person at the hospital said. "And she—well, you'd better come in, sir."

The patient with me right then was, unfortunately, Marya. "I have to go," I told her.

"What? We were just getting started."

"I'm afraid it's an emergency."

"But we were just getting to the important part. I have to tell you what my mother said after that." In this version of her history Marya's mother was an Italian countess. I was sure that none of it was true, and I felt impatient with all of it, wishing, unprofessionally, that she would just get to the point.

"It's a family emergency," I said.

"Really? What happened?" She looked at me avidly. I noticed, not for the first time, what a strange color her eyes were, as flat and metallic as ball bearings.

"I don't know yet. I have to get to the hospital."

"Who's sick?"

I didn't answer, just bustled her out and put on my coat. I had enough presence of mind to tell the receptionist to cancel my patients for the day, and then I got into my car and headed out.

Livvy worked in San Francisco, and they had taken her to a hospital nearby. I crossed the Bay Bridge and got off at what I thought was the right freeway exit, and found myself in an unfamiliar part of town.

I drove around frantically for a while. All the streets seemed to go one way and it was impossible to make a left turn, and somehow I ended up getting farther and farther away from where I thought I should be. Finally I rolled down the passenger window and asked people on the sidewalk for directions.

Most of them shrugged and walked on a little faster. One or two said they didn't know. Then I heard a voice saying, "Turn right at the light, and then right again five blocks down, and pull into the parking garage."

"What?" I asked, looking around for the voice.

"Here." A woman stepped out from behind a crowd of people. She was very short, and she wore a green dress that fell down to her feet, with a darker green shawl over it. Her long tangled hair blew into her face.

"Could you give me those directions again?" I asked.

Cars honked behind me, and someone shouted at me to get a move on, but I ignored them. The woman repeated her directions and I drove away.

It was only when I was pulling into the parking garage that I realized who she had to have been. It had never occurred to me that there were women helpers, as well as men.

I found Livvy in a cubicle off the emergency room. She had a cast on her arm, and a nurse was putting it in a sling when I walked in.

I hugged Livvy, and she put her good arm around me. "What happened?" I asked.

"Well, I blacked out," she said.

"What!"

"I was driving, and suddenly I felt this horrible pain, right here"—she put her hand on her chest—"and then I guess I passed out and hit a parked car."

She was speaking slowly, drugged, probably. "What was it?" I asked the nurse. She shrugged, as if she couldn't possibly be expected to know anything about medicine.

"They don't know," Livvy said. "They're going to keep me here a while, try and figure it out. Luckily they gave me something for the pain."

It all seemed to be getting worse and worse. First the phone call and the horrible few seconds imagining what had happened to her, then the relief that she had only broken her arm, and now this, some unknown, possibly terrifying illness.

I thought about calling her family, Maddie and Sylvie. Then another thought occurred to me, this one so bad I had to sit down. Had the family's luck run out? Did this happen because I'd broken the bargain? Was it all my fault?

I had been so young then, back when I'd rescued Livvy. I'd thought, like everyone my age, that we'd live forever, that nothing terrible would ever happen to us. Now I felt completely alone, cut adrift, unprotected from death, disaster, illness. I felt like a man in a haunted house, waiting for midnight; like a man who had suddenly lost his faith in God. What had I done?

I noticed that Livvy was looking worried too, and that scared me as much as anything. She and her family had always been so certain they would be safe, no matter what happened.

"Don't look so worried," Livvy said. She tried to smile; it moved so slowly across her face it looked more like a grimace. "I'm sure it's nothing."

"Sure," I said.

"They're going to transfer me to another room," she said. "Run some more tests."

We sat and waited for a bed to become available. I would learn a lot of things about hospitals in the next few days, and one of them was that you spent most of your time waiting. Hospitals were a lot like what I had heard about war—hours of boredom followed by brief moments of terror.

Finally they moved Livvy to her new room, a sterile place that smelled like some kind of astringent cleaning liquid. She went to sleep almost immediately, and I sat by her bed, watching her. A male nurse came in and started talking to me, a list of instructions on how to take care of Livvy's cast. I forgot all of them as soon as he had finished.

I picked up Nick from school and took him back to the hospital, telling him only that his mother had broken her arm. Someone had to take care of him while I was with Livvy, I realized, and I hesitated between Sylvie and my mother. Finally I called my mother, putting off telling Sylvie about Livvy's accident for a few more hours.

Then I moved into the hospital, eating bad cafeteria food and sleeping on hard hospital chairs. Every so often Livvy would be wheeled away for tests, or someone would come into her room and take more blood.

A day passed, and still no one seemed to know anything. Well, they knew what it wasn't—she hadn't had a heart attack or a stroke. This didn't reassure me; instead it made me even more anxious. Did she have some kind of strange disease no one understood? I felt cold all the time, shivering as though the hospital had turned their air conditioners up as far as they could go.

Finally I prayed. Not to God—instead I prayed to something I knew for sure existed, the other realm. I asked them to take a bondmaid, anyone, even Livvy—I would far rather she went to sleep for seven years than—well, than the alternative, which even then I couldn't name to myself. I told them I accepted the bargain, all of it. I begged their forgiveness for my youthful arrogance, when I thought I'd known better than they did.

Maddie came the next morning during visitors' hours. We had a whispered conversation out in the corridor about what I knew, which wasn't much. By this time I was desperate to talk to someone about what I feared, and although I knew Maddie was exactly the wrong person I couldn't seem to help myself.

"I—well, I asked the other realm to help her," I said.

To her credit she didn't smirk or look superior. "Yeah," she said. "So did I."

"They still might be protecting us," I said, trying to put the best face on it. "I saw one of those helpers when I got lost, this short woman dressed in green, and she told me how to get to the hospital. She even showed me the cheapest parking lot in the neighborhood."

"I don't think so. I just got turned down for another part. They said I was too old."

"But you're, what—twenty-nine?"

"Yeah. That's too old for Hollywood."

"Oh," I said, stupidly. She would never have the career she wanted, and it was all because of me. For the first time I understood the full extent of what I'd done. And what about Sylvie? A few bad harvests, and she could lose the farmhouse. What would she do then? As far as I knew, she had no job skills whatsoever.

"Well, we're on the same side now," Maddie said. She smiled, and we went inside to see Livvy.

Livvy was feeling better; the pain had gone away, which seemed to baffle the doctors even more. She and Maddie were soon talking in that shorthand the sisters had, a conversation of shared jokes and stories and made-up words that managed to cut out everyone not related to them.

The doctor came into the room and they fell silent. He looked down at a chart in his hand and said brusquely, "So, you have pancreatitis?"

"What?" Livvy said. "I don't know. Is that what it is?"

"What's pancreatitis?" I asked. I think my heart had stopped. I'd known someone with pancreatic cancer, and he'd lived two weeks after his diagnosis.

"Yeah." The doctor turned a few pages on the chart, flipped them back. "Usually people feel the pain in their back, not their chest—that's why it took us so long to figure it out. Do you have gallstones?"

"Not that I know of," Livvy said.

"What *is* it?" I asked. What was wrong with this guy? He had the worst bedside manner of anyone I'd ever heard of.

"It's an inflammation of the pancreas. Sometimes a gallstone leaves the gallbladder and winds up in the pancreas, that's why I asked. Do you eat a lot of fatty foods?"

"Yeah," Livvy said.

Maddie laughed. "Yeah, I guess you could say that."

"What about alcohol? Drink a lot of wine, or beer?"

Now Livvy was the one to laugh. "Well, my family owns a vineyard," she said.

"Well, you should moderate your diet," the doctor said. "Okay, I guess that's it. The nurse will be coming in to help you get dressed."

"That's it?" I asked. "What about—what if it happens again?"

"Then she comes back and we examine her again." The doctor glanced at his watch and left.

We stared at each other, each of us looking stunned, the survivors of some disaster. Then Maddie started to laugh again, and Livvy and I joined in. "I'm sorry—you've already had the six seconds of your allotted time," Maddie said, in a perfect imitation of the doctor. "The nurse will be coming in to help us throw you out."

I know, it wasn't that funny—but we laughed until we howled. Someone came in the door, and at first I thought it was a nurse telling us to quiet down, there were people here trying to sleep.

It was Ben. I was glowing now; you could have put me in a lighthouse and used me to signal to ships. I hugged him quickly, slapping him on the back, and said, "It's pancreatitis!"

"Must be a funny disease," he said, catching the mood in the room. "What—she's going to grow a clown nose and big feet?"

"Something like that," I said.

"She'll need new shoes, though," Maddie said.

"I'll borrow yours," Livvy said. "They're probably big enough."

Just for a moment we were back again, the four of us. Then Ben said, "I knew she'd be okay."

"What do you mean?" Maddie asked.

"Well, you know. Your family's always okay."

"Not anymore."

"Sure you are. Look at Will and Livvy, buying that fancy house. What do you call that except good luck?"

The house, not really all that fancy, had inspired a lot of jokes on Ben's part over the past year: we were the bourgeoisie now, the enemy. Usually he was good-natured about it, but sometimes he slipped over into envy. He was still working at the bookstore, still living in the old apartment with the roommate he'd found after I'd left, a deadly dull man Livvy and I called the Television Zombie.

I remembered what he'd told me about the meetings at Professor Rothapfel's house, the way he'd gone looking for luck. Sometimes it seemed to me that he thought he was owed good fortune. I'd told him, several times, that I had probably broken the bargain, but I don't think he believed me.

"I mean, look at you," he said now. "You have the perfect life, both of you. Happily married, a terrific kid, enough money for anything you want—and on top of everything else you're going to inherit part of a vineyard. What else do you need?"

"Health," I said, and at the same time Maddie said, "And what about me? No one could say my life is perfect."

"Sure it is. You starred in a movie, for God's sake."

"Yeah, and it disappeared the day after it opened."

I hadn't heard that. I remembered what she'd said to me out in the hallway, that she was already too old to be an actress.

"You're having fun, though, right?" Ben said.

"Yeah, right," Maddie said sarcastically. "It's lots of fun."

I already knew what Ben would say next: If it wasn't fun, why was she doing it? And I knew what he would really mean by it: Why had she left him?

"Come on, Ben," I said. "This is a stupid thing to argue about. You know they took back the bargain. And there's nothing mysterious about the house. We have good-paying jobs, both of us, and we work hard, and we were able to afford it."

"You come on," he said. "If I had your luck my novel would have been published years ago."

"How's the novel going, by the way?" I asked. I wasn't just trying to change the subject; I really wanted to know. He hadn't said anything about it for at least a year; I had never even seen it.

"Never mind that. That's not what I'm talking about. You know, it's funny—I was the one who introduced you to the family, Maddie and—"

"Hello, everyone," someone at the door said.

I turned in relief. My relief slammed headlong into impatience when I saw who it was. Marya.

"What are you doing here?" I asked.

"What do you mean?" she said. "I wanted to see how your wife was doing. That's not very friendly, Will."

"How'd you know she was here?"

"I heard you on the phone. You said 'she,' so I knew you had to be talking about Livvy, and then I just called around to all the hospitals in the Bay Area. I know you were about to tell me where she was, but you rushed out so fast you forgot. That's all right—it's obvious you were worried about her."

Impatience turned into annoyance, annoyance into anger, a screeching four-car pile-up of emotions. "Could you come out into the hall with me, Marya?" I asked.

"Why? I want to see Livvy."

"Just for a second." To my relief she followed me outside. "Remember when you started seeing me, and we talked about what therapy would be like? That we would have to have a strictly professional relationship, one where you talk to me and I use my skills to help you understand what's going on in your life. There have to be boundaries between us, otherwise it isn't going to work."

"Well, but I thought we were friends."

I understood, of course, that something like this was supposed to happen between a therapist and patient. It's called transference—the patient transfers all her irresolvable emotions onto the therapist, who stands in for parents, lovers, friends, enemies. What I didn't get was why it had been going on for five years, why we hadn't progressed beyond it. A few years ago she had spent a month calling me at all hours, so often I had to have our number changed.

"Look, this isn't a good place to talk about this," I said. "Why don't we work on it at our next session?"

"I'm thinking about quitting, actually. I don't think you're right for me. Not when it's obvious you don't even like me."

"I'm sorry to hear that. Why don't you come back one more time, and we'll talk about why you feel that way?"

Even to myself I sounded awful, answering her with rote shrink-like phrases. To my surprise, though, she smiled and said, "Okay, sure. And give my best to Livvy, would you?"

I watched her walk away, then hurried back to Livvy. "Wasn't she at your wedding five years ago?" Ben asked. "Why does she keep bothering you? What's wrong with her?"

"I wish I could tell you," I said.

"Right. Patient confidentiality, I understand. She's nuts, isn't she?"

I laughed—I couldn't help it. "I do have patients who get better, who go on with their lives," I said. "Really."

"I believe you, man."

The nurse came in then, to help Livvy get into her clothes, and Ben and Maddie left.

When we got home we called my mother in Sacramento to tell her the news, and to make sure Nick was all right. Then Livvy and I sat at the kitchen table, Livvy just looking glad to be back. "You know, I was really mad at you for a while," she said.

"You were?" I asked. "Why?"

"Well, because you brought me back from the other realm, because you changed the bargain. I wondered if—well, I thought I might be dying. And no one was going to protect me. I could just—anything might happen."

"Yeah," I said. "I was scared too. I even asked the other realm for another bargain."

"So did I," she said. "Do you think it worked?"

She reached across the table for my hand. Her arm brushed a vase, and it fell to the floor and shattered. I started to get up, to get a broom, and then saw her expression and stopped. She looked stricken, haunted.

"What's wrong?" I asked, sitting back down.

"Well, what was that?" she said. "That was bad luck, wasn't it?"

"What, you've never broken anything before?"

She laughed, shakily. "You know, I don't think I have."

"Really? You've been *that* lucky?"

"Really."

"I'm sure everything's fine. I mean, look, the doctor said there's nothing wrong with you. Maybe the other realm made a new bargain with us, or they never forgot the old one. Maybe everything's going to be okay."

I wondered how that would work, though. Would the diagnosis have been pancreatitis no matter what? Could it have started as—as something worse, could they have changed it?

"Maybe," Livvy said.

My optimism was for Livvy's benefit; I was nowhere near as hopeful as I sounded. Still, I wanted to believe it. I understood more about life as I'd gotten older; I knew the risks we took just living through every day. And more people depended on me now: I was a husband, a father. I understood Sylvie better, saw how much she had sacrificed to keep her family safe.

And so life went on, years of work, home, raising a child. And then one day, when Nick was ten years old, I went into his room to get him ready for school. But he was deep in sleep, and nothing I could do would wake him.

13

I DID ALL THE THINGS I'd done when Livvy had fallen asleep. I went to the hill, I crossed it and recrossed it, I stood in front and shouted nonsense words. Nothing happened, of course. I'd changed the bargain when I'd returned the sack. I'd been horribly stupid; I had bargained away my son. Maddie was right: I hadn't known what I was doing.

I looked for Feierabend relatives, all those names I had written on wedding invitations eleven years ago. Henry and Peter had died last year, at the ages of eighty and seventy-nine respectively, but now that Nick had fallen asleep even the living relatives seemed to fade away like so many ghosts. I called old phone numbers and wrote to old addresses, but I was unable to find Lem's sons, or his sister Violet and her son.

One day I remembered the key Nell had given me at Lem's restaurant. Sometime over the years I had lost it, and now I turned my house and the farmhouse upside down, looking for it. I finally found it in an old pottery flour canister, though Livvy swore she didn't remember putting it there. Then I went through both houses again, trying every keyhole.

Since I was spending so much time at the farmhouse anyway I started borrowing books from their library. I began to ignore my patients, anxious to get back to my reading, and finally I closed down my practice and referred my clients to other therapists.

After that I was free to drive up to Napa and read all day. There was still the problem of what to do with Nick, though, and I tried to convince Livvy to stay home and watch him, to take a leave of absence from her job.

"We can't afford it," she said. "One of us has to keep working."

"Sure we can," I said.

We were sitting on Nick's bed, watching him. "No," he said. He grimaced, tossing on the bed. "No, please."

I brushed his hair away from his forehead. Where was he now? What was he doing? Was he being made to dance, to stay awake through the night? Or was he fighting, forced to ride a horse, to hold a lance as tall as he was? How was he faring, this son of mine who had always hated uncertainty, the unexpected?

I looked at Livvy, but her expression hadn't changed. "We have to do something," I said.

"What?" she said.

"I told you. Quit your job, look after him. And don't tell me we can't afford it."

"I don't want to."

"What? Why not?"

"Because I don't. What difference does it make?"

"I just want to know. My God, Livvy, you're so cold sometimes. Do you even care about Nick?"

Nick moaned. "Shhh," Livvy said. "Of course I do."

"Then why don't you want to help?"

"How would it help if I stayed home? You could take him up to Napa, let Sylvie look after him."

"But how can you keep working?"

"Because I can't stand to watch him like this! I went through it too, remember?"

I'd nearly forgotten that, had never realized how much worse for her all this must be.

"I have to work, have to do something, or I'll go crazy," she said.

"All right," I said. I reached out for her. She pulled away at first, then moved into my arms.

Livvy was right: Sylvie didn't mind babysitting Nick, and he was certainly easy to take care of. I headed up to the farmhouse every day and went through the shelves one by one, searching for clues. I skipped the books in German, and the dictionaries—even I wasn't stupid enough to read a dictionary from cover to cover—but I took down every book and riffled through it, looking for loose paper, underlines, anything that might help.

The library was typical of the Feierabends, with a hundred years of books about whatever they'd been interested in at the time. I read about mushrooms and solar myths, medical dissections and blacksmithing, heraldry and puppet shows. I read ancient bestsellers like *Forever Amber* and *Trilby*, read a biography of Trotsky—Maddie's, probably—and realized that Maddie had been right; I'd known nothing whatsoever about the man. I paged through train schedules and collections of old maps and a guide to the 1939 San Francisco World's Fair.

Rose was away at college by this time, and Sylvie lived alone at the farmhouse. She'd learned to cook for herself, or at least to buy frozen dinners, and she seemed to be managing all right on her own. I couldn't help but think that that was because she didn't have to worry about her children anymore; now it was my turn.

Livvy came up with me and Nick on the weekends, and we slept over in Livvy's old bedroom. The house was eerily silent even with her there, with none of the laughter or arguments or dogs barking or music playing from years ago. Sometimes I would feel an almost physical pain, thinking about the way we'd been. Hilbert had been right, had perhaps been warning me: nostalgia was a terrible thing.

A month after I started reading I remembered my prayer to the other realm, the time Livvy had fallen sick. It should have been at the forefront of my mind, of course; I might have changed the bargain back then, been responsible for giving them Nick. A part of me hadn't wanted to face that, though. Being a shrink is no guarantee that you're any saner than anyone else.

I remembered as well the terror that had come over me, watching Livvy, pale and drugged, in her hospital bed. I was old enough now to know about the dangers waiting out in the world; horrible things had happened to my friends, my patients, bad luck picking us off one by one like a sniper. And to be protected...

But no, what the hell was I thinking? Of course I wouldn't sacrifice my son just to keep myself safe. But if I could reach the other realm somehow, make some other bargain...

One day I got tired of reading and started wandering through the house. I came to the end of a hallway and reached a door that had been boarded over—to save on heating, Sylvie had said. Suddenly I wondered if that was true, if the answer to all the family's secrets might lurk behind this door. There was an entire house there, after all, the section that looked like a Tudor cottage from the outside. I found a hammer and, without telling Sylvie, I set to work prying off the boards.

The door opened inward, creaking only a little. There was a button near the door, and when I pushed it, surprisingly, a light came on—though why shouldn't it, after all? Sylvie still paid her electricity bill. The first floor turned out to be a warren of dark, tiny rooms, all of them empty: a hallway and a cloakroom, a couple bathrooms, a pantry and a kitchen with a dumbwaiter. I puzzled over this as I climbed up to the second floor; it looked like the infrastructure for a giant party, but where did they hold the party itself?

I got the answer at the top of the stairs, which opened out onto a ballroom with a dark wooden floor. There were dark wood panels on the walls, too, about three feet high, and pink and green wallpaper above that, peeling and water-stained. Two huge chandeliers hung from the ceiling like spiders dangling from a thread, and there was a mural between them, a man sitting on a rock and playing a lyre, with animals standing and listening all around him. It took me a minute but I finally got it—Orpheus, who had tried to bring his wife back from the underworld.

Tried and failed—was this a message to the family from the other realm? Or had the family written this message to remind themselves, had they been the ones to paint the mural?

Or, I wondered, knowing what I did about the other realm, had they painted it as a warning to me? Maddie had said they could see into the future, after all.

No, I was being paranoid. I turned on all the lights, the wall sconces and the chandeliers, then walked through the room, hearing my footsteps echo off the walls. It was even bigger than I'd first thought, stretching the length of the Tudor cottage. Two or three chairs stood near the walls and pages from an ancient newspaper lay on the floor, but otherwise I saw nothing but dust and spiderwebs. Despite the water stains it smelled as dry as the newspapers.

I went back to the library, sat down, and picked up the book I had been reading.

When I got home that evening I was going to tell Livvy about the ballroom, but before I could say anything the phone rang. Livvy answered it and listened for a while, then motioned to me to pick up the other receiver.

"Hi, Will," Rose said on the phone. "I was telling Livvy about some stuff you might be interested in. Turns out there were some other Feierabends who went missing, besides Lem and Nell. A woman named Fiona, for one."

"When was this?" I asked. "And how do you know?"

"Look—summer vacation is coming up. I'll see you in Berkeley and we can talk about it then."

Rose visited the next Sunday. I'm ashamed to say I'd lost track of her, ignoring her in favor of her more vivid sisters. I kept thinking of her as fourteen, her age when we first met, and it was always a shock to see her and realize that she'd grown into an adult. She was twenty-nine now, a lecturer with a Ph.D. in history.

She hadn't changed all that much, though. She still wore her hair long, and she was still plumper than her sisters. To my eye she looked more like Hilbert than ever, though I knew better than to say so.

Livvy had scaled back her meals ever since she'd landed in the hospital, and after Nick had fallen asleep she had more or less stopped cooking altogether. The day Rose came, though, she spent all day in the kitchen, making us cucumber soup and lamb in mint butter. After dinner we sat around the table to talk, all of us heavily aware that Nick lay sleeping upstairs.

"So when did Fiona disappear?" I asked.

"In the twenties," Rose said. "The Feierabends were bootleggers then, you know."

"What!" Livvy said.

"Well, sure. How do you think they survived during Prohibition? Some of the people in Napa made religious wine, sacramental wine, but our family didn't have those kinds of connections to the church. But they had a boat, and they'd sail from Sausalito to San Francisco with barrels of wine in the hold. The Golden Gate Bridge hadn't been built yet."

She was starting to remind me of Hilbert in another way, his nerdy obsession with facts, pieces of history. "How do you know all this?" I asked.

"I talked to Henry and Peter a few years ago. They died last year, you know, within a few weeks of each other."

I nodded. Sylvie was finally starting to trust me with the family news.

"So I wondered if they'd ever been arrested," Rose went on. "I went through a bunch of old records—the Coast Guard, and the Bureau of Prohibition—but I didn't find anything. It was the Feierabend luck, I guess—other people got caught all the time, but they never did. I gave up for a while, and then a few weeks ago I wondered if there might be something in the local Napa County police records. And I found this."

She took out a stack of Xeroxed pages, and we began to read.

Officers' note: Here's our interview with Leeanne Summers, just the way we took it down and transcribed it. It's a pretty unbelievable tale, though, and we don't think Miss Summers was on the level. We went on to ask her plenty of questions, but we couldn't shake her from her story.

—Officer Fred Alonzo and Officer Frank Alter, July 23, 1927, Napa County

Okay, I'll tell you what happened. Yes, all of it—everything I understand, anyway. I'll do anything I can to help Fiona. Just promise me again that you aren't Prohibition agents. The last thing I want is to get her family in trouble.

And I hope you're interviewing that Walter, too. Walter Arbuthnot—he's the reason we lost her. No, he didn't throw her overboard. I'll get to it—just let me tell it in order.

Oh, and can I have another cup of coffee? I'm still shivering, I can't seem to get warm even with all these blankets. Thank you.

It started at a party at Fiona's house. Fiona and I used to go to school together, in San Francisco, but now that we've graduated she mostly stays with her family in the Napa Valley. They have this very strange house, half of it like an old Victorian and half like a Tudor cottage, and now they're building a whole new section, something Fiona called a Craftsman bungalow. The cottage part is mostly a huge ballroom, and that's where the parties start, the gramophone playing "Sweet Georgia Brown" and "Don't Bring Lulu," people out on the floor dancing the Charleston and the foxtrot. They have a bandstand, and sometimes they even bring in real bands. Fiona's family is rich, I think, though they don't act like it.

That's not all of it, though—their parties last for days. You can go swimming or boating out on the river, or play charades or croquet or mah-jongg, or if you want some quiet you can just sit in their library and close the door and read—they have all the latest books, and some pretty strange old books too.

And they have interesting guests, chess champions and water dowsers, Mexican grape pickers and defrocked priests, Communist Party members and vaudeville actors. Once they had that woman who swam the English Channel—what's her name? Gertrude Ederle, that's right. But my favorite is Fiona's great-aunt Alva, this ancient woman who tells fortunes with a German accent, and who wears a snake draped around her shoulders like a necklace.

Fiona's cousins were at this party I'm talking about, Henry and Peter. Fiona has a sister too, Lettice, but there's something wrong with her—she's sick in some way that no one ever really explained. I never saw her at any of the parties, anyway, and I thought they'd sent her to a sanitarium, when all the time—well, I'll get to that later.

Yeah, they serve booze there. Of course they do. They own a vineyard, after all. You promised me you wouldn't arrest them if I told you about their bootlegging, right? That you just want to know what happened to Fiona?

Okay, then. The family has this barn that they keep padlocked, and every so often you can hear a loud noise coming from it, like someone's running a generator. And people visit the house at all hours, and whisper something to Fiona's mother or father, and then one of the parents takes them outside, to the barn. So I knew the family bootlegged, without anyone ever coming right out and saying it. Everyone knew it.

No, of course I don't just go for the booze. I told you, Fiona and I were—are—friends. Anyway, you can always find the stuff in San Francisco if you really want it—there's a bar right across the street from the Hall of Justice, for goodness sake—so Napa Valley is a hell of a long way to go for it. They keep talking about putting a bridge across the bay but it never seems to happen, so when I go I have to get a ride with some of the other guests—we take the ferry to Sausalito and then drive for hours up a winding road to Napa.

No, I go because I really like Fiona and her family. There's something—I don't know—magical about her, about all of them. Yes, I know that sounds precious, like I've seen too many performances of *Peter Pan*. I can't think how else to explain it, though.

Anyway, I was standing on the side of the dance floor, looking up at the ceiling and trying to figure out who the fellow with the harp was, when there was a commotion at the door and this large woman came in. Sailed in, really, like a barge—she wore a long pale-blue dress with lace foaming at her neck and arms and hemline, and she had rows of necklaces and a pair of eyeglasses on her breast. Someone said she was an actress on Broadway, but I didn't catch her name.

Then this smaller guy walked in after her, like a tugboat to her barge. Fiona came back with a drink for me, and when I took it the new fellow walked up to us and said, "Ah, I'd heard there was hooch at this party. Heard the family makes it themselves, though, so it's probably panther piss. Where can I get some?"

Right then Henry came by with a tray, and the man took a glass. "It is pretty awful," I said, with a sidelong look at Fiona and Henry to keep quiet.

The man steeled himself, closed his eyes, and took a sip. Then he opened his eyes in surprise, and we all laughed.

"It's my family that makes the wine," Fiona said.

"Ah," he said, only a little embarrassed. "My apologies. So you're the ones with the unpronounceable German name."

"Feierabend," Henry said, as if to show him how easy it was to pronounce.

"I'm Walter Arbuthnot," he said.

We introduced ourselves. He took another sip of wine, and this time I noticed that the index finger on his right hand was missing. He saw me looking and said, "Old war injury."

"Applesauce," I said. "You're not old enough." He looked just a little older than we were, twenty-two or twenty-three.

"I'm twenty-seven, in fact," he said. "And there are other wars besides the Great War."

I was getting pretty tired of Walter by this time, with his insults and enigmatic remarks, and I was glad when Fiona turned to me and asked, "How was the drive up, Leelee?"

"Fine, mostly," I said. "There was some fog at the end, though."

Fiona looked at Henry. "Fog, you hear that?" she said. "And there isn't any moon."

"We could, I guess," he said.

"We could what?" I said.

"Henry's ready to make a run," Fiona said. "Want to come?"

"Sounds like fun," I said. I had this idea we'd drive down to the valley and drop off some bottles, maybe get invited inside for drinks. And, all right, I didn't know a lot of the people at the party. Mostly I stuck around Fiona and her cousins, and if they left I wouldn't have anyone to talk to.

Fiona grinned. Henry went to talk to Peter, but it turned out he didn't want to leave the party. "He says someone has to look after the guests," Henry said.

"Ah, Peter's all wet," Fiona said.

"Those barrels are heavy, though. You girls been exercising those muscles?"

"Sure," I said.

Henry laughed. "No, I was just kidding. But we do need someone else—I can't do it by myself."

"I'll go," Walter said.

We looked at him. "Not a chance," Fiona said. "How do we know you're not a Prohi agent?"

"Wouldn't I have arrested you already, if I were?"

"Oooh—if I *were*," Fiona said. "Listen to him."

Walter smiled ruefully. "It's my Harvard education—I can't help it."

"Do you have any identification?" Henry asked. "A driver's license or something?"

He gave that smile again, his hands out, palms up, as if to show us he was harmless. "I don't drive."

"Oh, the hell with it," Fiona said. "Come along, then. And if you turn out to be a Prohi we'll throw you overboard."

"Shouldn't you change your clothes?" Henry asked.

"What does the well-dressed girl wear to a bootlegging?" Fiona said, laughing.

Fiona and I started back to our room. Great-aunt Alva shouted out something as we left, but we were in a hurry and didn't stay to find out what she wanted. Maybe we should have—she might have warned us, told us something. Yeah, probably we should have.

Anyway, I was wearing a chemise and high heels, not exactly working clothes, so I was very glad to change into a tweed skirt and sweater and more comfortable shoes. Fiona picked up an old polo coat she'd borrowed from one of the cousins and we were ready to go.

We walked over to the stables, where the family kept their cars, and Henry headed us toward the touring car, the big five-passenger Moon. He opened the rear door and ushered Fiona and me in, and when we sat down I heard something rolling around beneath us.

"We took the bottom of the seats out," Fiona said. "There are barrels of booze under here."

"Is there actual booze inside here, that's the question," Walter called out from the front seat.

"Hush," Henry said. "No. We have to be careful."

"Yes, sir," Fiona said, mock serious.

Despite what Henry said Walter took out a silver pocket flask and drank from it. Henry looked at him but didn't say anything. Walter wiped the mouth of the flask with a handkerchief and passed it back to us, but we shook our heads.

Meanwhile Henry had started the car and we set off. The fog seemed to have gone, but Fiona was right—there wasn't any moon. We drove over the bridge, and I laughed.

"What?" Fiona asked.

"I just got why you call it the Moon Bridge," I said. "It's because you drive the Moon car over it."

She and Henry laughed too. At that moment I felt like part of the family, someone who knew all their jokes and secrets.

The road to the valley was unlit, not to mention winding and badly paved, so Henry took his time driving. We talked about Prohibition—Walter thought it would be over soon, but Henry, who was supposed to take over the vineyards when Fiona's father retired, said the family expected it to go on for another five years at least.

"What are you going to do if it does end?" I asked.

"It doesn't matter," Henry said. "We'll make wine, just like we always did."

"Yeah, but you'll have more competition then," I said.

"Oh, we'll be all right," Fiona said.

I wondered how she could be so sure, but just then I noticed that we'd left the valley. “Hey,” I said. “Where are we going? To the ferry?”

“We don’t need a ferry,” Fiona said. “We have a boat.”

See what I mean about them being rich? I mean, who do you know that has his own boat?

“Where do you put the barrels?” I asked. “Downstairs?”

Walter laughed. “Downstairs!” he said.

Fiona took pity on me. “It’s called ‘below’ on a ship,” she said. She leaned forward to Walter in the front seat. “How was she supposed to know?”

“Thank you,” I said to her.

“Everything is called something else on a ship,” she said. “I don’t know why—I imagine these sailors talking to landlubbers like us and just making it up as they went along. ‘The front? No, that’s the, um, the bow. And the back? Yeah, we call that, let’s see, the stern.’ And then they go away and have a terrific laugh about how they put one over on everybody.”

The car hit a pothole then, and one of the barrels underneath us banged against something and rolled around. I had a picture of the barrel breaking open and pouring out wine as we drove, leaving a trail for the Prohi agents to follow, like Hansel and Gretel with their breadcrumbs.

Henry stopped the car in Sausalito, near the army base where the fishing fleet is, and we got out. He looked around him, checking for agents, I guess. Then he opened the trunk and pulled up a false bottom, and he and Walter lifted out the barrels and rolled them down to a boat at the dock.

They took the barrels below, and Fiona and I got on the boat. Henry went to the pilot-house and started the engine. It was dark now—night had come, and Henry kept most of the lights off so the Coast Guard couldn’t see us. All we could hear was the engine, and water slapping against the sides of the boat.

Then we saw fog coming toward us across the water, and suddenly everything turned cold, cold and white. And the sounds changed too, became muffled, like we’d stuffed our ears with cotton.

I shivered and pulled my coat tighter around me. “How is he going to find his way in all of this?” I asked.

“Fellow seems pretty competent,” Walter said.

“He is,” Fiona said. “Don’t worry.”

I shivered again, but not from the cold this time. For some reason I’d never thought that the trip might be dangerous. I'd lived a pretty sheltered life until then, I guess.

We went on. Every so often I thought I heard a creaking noise or the rattle of machinery, like another ship coming toward us, but it was only my ears deceiving me.

Suddenly Henry swore and hit one of his instruments, something that looked like a small wooden chimney. "What is it?" Fiona asked, sticking her head through the open window of the pilot-house.

"The compass," Henry said. "It swung around just now. I thought we were going south, toward San Francisco, but somewhere or other we turned west. We've been sailing out into the ocean."

He turned the wheel and went on for a while, muttering every so often under his breath. Then he swore again and looked up through the windshield of the pilot-house, I guess trying to find stars to guide him. But of course there were no stars, only the fog all around us.

I don't know how long we went on like that. It felt like hours, though it might have been only ten or fifteen minutes. Then suddenly we heard bells, like someone was riding a sleigh over the water. I was sure that this was an illusion too, but the sound got louder, heading toward us. I looked at Henry, but he seemed as surprised as I was.

The prow of another ship broke through the fog, and then a ship like nothing I'd ever seen before came up on our left side. There was a house on its deck, for one thing, made out of stone and nearly covered in wisteria. And there was a garden there, too, laid out in front of it, with paving stones and hedges and trellises.

We all looked at each other. "What—" Henry said.

Then men came out of the house, ran up to the ship's railing, and threw out ropes with grappling hooks at the ends. The hooks caught on our rails and the men started to pull.

The ropes looked thin, not really all that strong. Henry gunned the motor a couple of times, and the ropes pulled tight but didn't break. He swore.

"Who are these people?" I asked.

"I don't know, but we're about to be boarded," Henry said.

There was only about six feet between us now. The men jumped the distance like it was nothing and dropped down on our deck. One of them held a sword in his mouth, and the others were pulling out swords too, out of their—what's the word? Scabbards, that's it.

I know, I didn't believe it either. You'll just have to take my word for it. And it just gets stranger, so if you don't believe this part you're going to have a real hard time with the rest.

I moved back, closer to the pilot-house. Fiona's a lot braver than I am, though, and she stayed right where she was. "All right," Henry said. "The stuff's in the hold. Take what you want, but don't hurt the passengers."

"Your hold, yes," one of them said. You could hear laughter in his voice, a little like the bells we heard earlier, but he looked as serious as anything. "Your hold holds nothing that interests us."

I could see them better now. They were tall and thin, with long brown hair and eyes that looked silver, like their swords. Their boots and clothes were made out of soft brown leather.

"What do you want, then?" Henry asked.

"Nothing very much," the leader said. "Only what you stole from us. Give us the pipe and we'll go."

"Pipe? What pipe?"

"The whistle. We know that one of you has it."

"I don't know what you're talking about. No one here has any—"

"What will you give me for it?" Walter asked, interrupting.

The leader looked at him quickly. He started to say something, but Fiona got there first. "We'll trade it for Lettice," she said. "For my sister."

The men laughed. "Ah, but is it yours to trade?" the leader said.

"Then take me," she said. "Take me instead of her."

"Why should we do that?"

"Because—because we want her back. Because we miss her. Because I'm begging you. Please—you can't be as hard-hearted as all that, you have to have some feeling."

They laughed again, and started walking toward Walter. Walter took something out of his coat pocket. Henry dropped to the floor—now I realize he thought Walter had a gun, but at the time I had no idea what he was doing. Walter put the thing up to his lips and blew on it.

It was a pipe, the pipe they wanted. It sounded deep, nothing like the shrill whistle you'd expect from something so small. The men stepped back and looked at each other.

"What the hell are you doing?" Henry asked, standing up. "Are you nuts?"

Walter didn't say anything, just kept playing his pipe. Another ship came toward us out of the fog, and drew up on our right. And then it happened all over again—the men on board threw out grappling hooks, and the ships came closer together, and the men jumped over the railings and hit our deck.

Then they ran toward the first crew, drawing their swords. The swords hit against each other, and they started fighting up and down the deck.

"Get out of here!" Henry yelled at us. "Go below!"

But Fiona didn't move, and so I didn't either, though we did try to stay out of their way. And I have to say that some of it was beautiful, like a dance, even though I knew that they were out to kill each other. A step up, a step back, swords hitting overhead. Retreat, advance, their swords lower this time, then up again, attack, defend, back, forward. And all that time their boots made no sound on the deck; and their breath was silent; the only noise was their swords, like loud bells.

Two men fought their way close to us. One of them swung his sword and the other man ducked underneath it, his long hair flying out behind him. They wore the same clothes and they looked the same, and I wondered how they told each other apart, how they knew which ones to attack. Then one of them spun away and the other leapt after him, and I lost them in the crowd.

When I looked back the fight was still going on, the swords flashing up and back. One man jumped to the top of the pilot-house and another one followed him, and they cut and thrust for a while. Then the first man dropped down and landed on the railing, the thin rail that was only five or six inches wide. He danced back and forth with his arms flung out, like he was daring the other man to follow him.

The other man jumped down to the deck and looked around for his crew. One group looked like they were winning now, pushing back against their opponents, their swords rising and falling. The other group dropped back, then back again, until they hit the ship's railing and had to stop. The deck started tilting under their weight.

Some of the men turned and fought, and some of the others reached out for the ropes and pulled. The ship with the house on its deck came toward us out of the fog, and when it got close enough the men jumped back over the rail. Then they were gone, casting off the ropes and sailing into the fog.

The group that had won stood against the rail, facing us. Fiona looked at them, trying to figure out what to do. Finally she curtseyed. "Thanks for your help," she said.

The men raised their swords. The swords seemed to leave a trail of fire behind them, and I rubbed my eyes, not believing what I saw. The swords made patterns, waves and circles and stars, and wherever they went the fire followed them. Then the men started to dance with each other, two, three, four at a time, going back and forth, touching their swords together, making these—these designs, like giant webs only more complicated.

We stared at them—we couldn't look away. I thought about a novel I had read in Fiona's library, about a man named Svengali who had hypnotized a woman, Trilby. Somewhere far away I was horribly frightened, but the fear didn't seem to matter very much.

I made a terrific effort and looked away. The shapes were too much for me, though, and I had to turn back. The web was tightening around us, coming closer.

"Get away!" Fiona shouted. She pushed me but I didn't move—I couldn't. My mouth was open, and I could feel the cold air freezing my tongue and teeth. I tried to say something, but my words seemed frozen too.

Fiona turned to Walter. "Can you...play your pipe?" she asked.

"The pipe...was what...summoned them," he said.

The net closed in on us. Then it—well—it sliced through me, and I felt colder than I'd ever been in my life.

The swords still danced around Fiona, though, back and forth, up and down, trapping her inside the pattern. "No!" I said. I broke away and pushed my way toward her. Then I stopped, remembering the cold.

"Go away!" Fiona said, her voice muffled. "Run!"

The strands around her were as thick as ropes now. I grabbed for one of them but it slipped through my hand, just sliced thought it. I felt a freezing shock, and then my hand went numb all over.

The web covered Fiona completely. Bits of fire still sparked along the lines. The men put their swords back into their scabbards—and the spell broke, and I started screaming.

The men didn't seem to notice. They lifted Fiona on their shoulders and carried her to where their ship waited, then tossed her over the railing like a rag doll. Someone caught her on the other side and the men jumped after her, and then the ship cast off and disappeared in the fog.

I was still screaming—I had to make an effort to stop. "We have to get her back!" I shouted at Henry. "Hurry—go after them!"

Henry and Walter were staring off into the fog, looking dazed. "How?" Henry asked. "How do we follow them?"

"Just go," I said. I pointed to where I saw the ship last. "That way. Or are you going to let them take her?"

Henry seemed to break out of his trance. He turned the ship and we sailed for a long time, but there was nothing but fog ahead of us. "Who were those people?" I asked finally.

No one said anything.

"Come on," I said. "You know something about this, both of you. What did Fiona mean when she asked them to take her instead?" I turned to Walter. "And you—what was that pipe you blew into? Why did they want it?"

Walter put his hand into his pocket. Then suddenly he started patting all his pockets, taking out his keys and his flask and a piece of paper with, I saw, Fiona's address on it. "It isn't here," he said. "Goddammit, what happened to it?"

"Never mind that," I said. "Where did you get it?"

"Can you turn on the lights?" he asked Henry.

"Sure, and have the Coast Guard come after us," Henry said.

"Just the deck lights, just for a little while. I have to find that pipe."

The lights came on. Walter looked all over the deck, even in the pilothouse, where he had never been. Finally he came back and stood near me, cursing softly.

"Where did you get the pipe?" I asked again, as Henry turned the lights off.

"Just a junk shop somewhere. They said to play it whenever I needed help."

"Who said? How did it summon those—those—"

"I don't know. Honestly."

I didn't trust him, not at all. He had something to do with Fiona's disappearance, I was sure of it. I remembered how he had come into the house, following that actress. "How do you know the Feierabends?"

"I don't, not really. Someone told me they had these fantastic parties, so I waited by the house until one of the guests went inside and I just followed her."

He had a glib answer for everything—I didn't think I'd get anything more from him. I looked into the pilot-house, at Henry. "So what did Fiona mean when she said to take her instead of Lettice? Take her where? And don't tell me you don't know."

Henry stood with his hands on the wheel for a long time, not saying anything. "All right, I guess you deserve to know," he said. "There are these two factions, two armies. They're fighting a war, and they—well, our family's involved. Lettice, Fiona's sister—she's been asleep for four years."

I gasped, but he didn't seem to hear me. "She's in—in their realm somehow," he went on. "I mean really she's in one of the bedrooms upstairs, sleeping, but in their realm she's helping them fight. After seven years, three more years now, she'll wake up. And in exchange for that our family—well, everything we do prospers. Our winery never gets raided, and the Coast Guard never stops us when we make a run."

I didn't know what to make of this, but I did register one thing. "Turn on your damn lights, then," I said. "If they're not going to stop you."

"We try not to tempt fate," he said.

I looked at Walter. He seemed to be taking all this talk of other realms very calmly, and once again I got the idea that he must know more than he let on.

"What I think happened—I think that first group knew the pipe was here," Henry said. "And when they came, Fiona saw a chance to get Lettice back." He paused again. "And then when Walter summoned that other faction he gave them permission to enter our world. They could do anything they wanted then, including take Fiona away. Maybe they need her, need one of us, the way the other group needs Lettice."

"Why *does* the other group need Lettice?"

Henry shook his head. "We don't really know. We give one side an advantage somehow. So I guess the other side wants that advantage too."

I didn't understand any of this. And I see by your faces that you don't either—or you don't believe me. What? No, of course I didn't concoct this story with Henry and Walter. Why would we do that?

All right, that's enough. I'm leaving. I don't have to talk to you—Peter said so, and he's studying law at Berkeley. Of course we didn't kill Fiona. And she didn't accidentally fall over the side, either. If she had I would have said so.

No, I'm not in love with Henry, or Peter either, not that it's any of your business. Yes, they're handsome men—it's a good-looking family. But they didn't make up some story and then convince me to lie to the police. I'm not some foolish young thing, easily swayed by a pretty face.

Okay, I'm glad we got that settled. Yes, I did believe Henry, as much as I understood of what he said, anyway. You would have too, if you'd seen what those men did with their swords, and if you'd felt that net go through you like that. I'm still cold, even with all these blankets, and I still can't move my hand.

Could you get me some more coffee, please? And there's some brandy in that cupboard over there. See, I'm giving away all their secrets.

After that? Well, we knew it was hopeless by then, but we didn't want to turn around. The last thing Henry and I wanted was to face Fiona's mother and father, Peter and Great-aunt Alva, and tell them we hadn't been able to get her back.

I argued with Walter a lot, on and off, while we went. It was his fault that those people had come and taken Fiona away, after all. He never added anything to what he said, though. Maybe you can get more out of him, arrest him or something.

At one point I looked around the deck and realized something strange—there were no dead bodies, none of them had died. I looked down and thought I could see some blood, a dark stain on the wood, but there was nothing else.

"Well, of course," Henry said when I mentioned this to him. "They're immortal, after all."

"Immortal?" I said.

"Practically immortal, anyway. I think they can die, but it's harder to kill them."

Just then I saw something a few feet away from me, next to the pilothouse. I bent down and picked it up. It was Walter's whistle.

I didn't give it back to him, though. I just put it in my pocket without saying anything.

Finally Henry decided to head back. He turned, and the compass swung around—he thought it might have started working again, now that we weren't following the other ship. But it took us a long time to find our way back to Sausalito, and another long while to drive back up to the family's house.

It was morning by then, and everyone was sleeping in, tired out from the party last night. We woke up Fiona's father and he called the police, and here you are.

That sound? That's Fiona's mother, crying. She's lost both her children now. She hasn't stopped since we told her about Fiona. No, I wouldn't try to interview her. The doctor's coming with something to help her sleep—you're going to have to wait until she wakes up to talk to her.

What? Yeah, I still have the whistle. Just a minute, all these blankets are in the way. Here it is. Now do you believe me? No, for God's sake don't blow into it. Can I have it back, please?

14

"WOW," I SAID, when we'd finished reading. "Fairy pirates. Whenever I think I understand your family it always turns out I don't know the half of it."

"I never heard this story either," Rose said. "I don't think even Hilbert knows what happened to Fiona. They try not to talk about it."

"Oh, I know that, believe me." I was still trying to absorb what I'd read. Bootleggers, wild parties, a magic whistle. "I still don't see how it helps us, though."

"I thought we'd go visit this woman, Leeanne Summers," Rose said. "And Walter Arbuthnot, too. I don't think Ms. Summers told the cops everything, and I never found an interview with Walter, though she asked them to talk to him."

"Okay, but how are we going to find them? Ms. Summers probably changed her name when she got married."

"I bet she didn't," Rose said, smiling slightly.

"All right, I'll bet. How could you possibly know that?"

"There are clues," Rose said.

Livvy laughed. She took the stack of pages and flipped to the beginning. "Oh, I get it," she said.

"What?" I said. I felt that frustration I got around the sisters sometimes, when they seemed to be reading each other's minds.

Livvy took pity on me. "Here," she said. "When Leeanne says, 'Fiona and I started back to our room.' Why would they share a bedroom, with all the rooms at the farmhouse? And what about this—'Yes, they're handsome men—it's a good-looking family'?"

"I still don't—Oh. You think Leeanne and Fiona were a couple?"

Livvy nodded. "She seems pretty broken up about Fiona—more than if they were just friends. She's ready to give up all the family secrets just to get her back."

"She still might have gotten married, though," I said. "Everyone did back then, even if they were gay."

"Five dollars says she didn't," Rose said.

"You're on," I said.

It was one bet I was glad to lose. Rose came back a few days later to say she'd found Leeanne Summers: she was living just across the bay, in San Francisco.

The day after that was Saturday. I dropped Nick off at the farmhouse, and then drove Livvy and Rose to Leeanne Summers's house. "Did you call to tell her we're coming?" I asked Rose as we went over the Bay Bridge.

"No," she said. "It's usually better to just show up—that way they can't come up with some excuse for not seeing you."

"But what if her mind's gone? If she has no idea what we're talking about?"

"Then we haven't lost anything, have we?"

"I'll have lost a day of reading."

"Do you really think those books will help? I went through a lot of them when I was a kid, and I never saw anything about the family, or the bargain."

"Yeah, but you didn't read them all, did you?"

"No, but—"

"You read those books?" Livvy said to Rose. "I didn't know that. I never went in there as a kid—it always seemed so dark and spooky to me."

"You never noticed anything I did," Rose said. "You and Maddie were always off playing some game, and if I asked to join you you told me I was too young."

"Oh, come on. When did we do that?"

"All the time. Remember when you both went around the house and tried to find a flying carpet? You sat on every Persian rug we had and you crossed your arms and asked them to fly—"

"Really?" I asked. Even in the midst of all my worries I couldn't help but think what a brilliant story this was, how typical of Livvy and Maddie.

"Yeah," Rose said. "And when I asked if I could help you you told me you'd done them all, you were finished."

"Well, maybe we were. I don't even remember this."

"Well, it sure wasn't the only time you wouldn't let me play with you. And you can guess what Sylvie said when I told her—she couldn't be bothered."

"Okay, I'm sorry. I'm sorry, all right? I didn't realize. What's the big deal, anyway? All that was twenty years ago."

Rose said nothing. Livvy looked at the map on her lap and told me to take the next exit. Almost immediately the road split in two directions, one marked east and the other west.

"Which way?" I asked.

"Hell, I don't know," Livvy said. "It doesn't look east or west on the map—"

The choice was nearly upon us. "Well, I have to take one of them."

"West!"

I swung out onto the west road. "Yeah, this is right," Livvy said after a while. "Turn left here."

Livvy's directions were usually right. Was this the other realm protecting her, making sure she got to her destination? It was ironic, if so—they were leading us to a woman who might help us get free of them.

"It *is* a big deal," Rose said, picking up where she'd left off. "No one paid attention to me when I was growing up, and you know why? Because Sylvie and Hilbert thought I'd be the bondmaid. They'd already fallen in love with you and Maddie, so they tried to keep their distance from me—that way it wouldn't matter so much if I fell asleep. Maddie was the talented one, and you were the smart one, and I—I was the afterthought."

We were driving up a hill now, through a part of San Francisco I'd never heard of, Bernal Heights. It looked like a small town, with tiny bright gardens and stairways climbing up from one level to the next. At one point we passed a slide that ran the length of a city block, and I thought about how much Nick would like it. Then I remembered, and I felt the dread that went everywhere with me these days like an unwelcome companion.

"I'm sure that isn't true," Livvy said.

"Yeah?" Rose said. "They even gave you and Maddie longer names. Rose—how long does it take to say that?"

"Oh, come on. Rose is a beautiful name."

"You're not listening. I'm saying—"

"I know what you're saying. Turn right here. And I'm saying that it isn't true. Sylvie and Hilbert paid just as much attention to you as they did to us. Which wasn't a lot, I admit."

In my professional opinion, though, it did sound like Rose was speaking from real experience. Usually I would have suggested that she go see a therapist, but how on earth could she explain her family's problems to anyone else? Maybe I could talk with her later, after all this was over. Not as a therapist—I was too close to her for that—but to try to find a way to help her.

"I barely even remember Hilbert," Rose said. "He left when I was nine."

"Sylvie says Hilbert's been hanging around the house a lot," Livvy said. "She thinks he might want to come back."

"You're kidding me. Does she want him back?"

"She didn't say. She thinks he got shaken up when his father died, that he wants to change his life somehow. Anyway, you might get to know him better than you'd like, sooner or later. Turn left at the light, up ahead."

"Yeah, he wants to come back now," I said. "Now that he doesn't have to worry about his daughters anymore."

"Here, this is it," Livvy said. "No, you passed it. Can you back up? Okay, over there."

I pulled up in front of a small wooden house, and we got out. Rose opened the gate and we walked through a garden filled with flowers, an explosion of color.

Rose knocked. For a long time nothing happened, and I was just about to suggest we come back, when I heard footsteps approaching. The door opened.

"Hello," the woman standing there said. Then, "Oh, my," she said, and fell to the floor in a dead faint.

We all knelt to help her. "No, wait," Rose said. "She needs some air. Here, Will, Livvy, back up." She fanned the woman lightly.

The woman on the floor opened her eyes. "I'm all right," she said. She looked at Rose. "I think I'm all right. It was a shock, that's all. You look just like her, you know."

"Who?" Rose said. "Fiona?"

"Fiona, that's right. I thought she'd come back, only a little older. And why not? They don't age in that place she went to, or at least I don't think they do."

"Ms. Summers?" Rose said.

"Oh, call me Leeanne. Could you help me up, please?" We helped her sit and then stand, and she wobbled over to a couch, leaning on Rose. "Please, sit down," she said. "Tell me what the family's been doing. I saw your—was it your sister?—in a movie, and I knew who she was right away, but I don't know anything more that that."

Rose sat next to Leeanne on the couch. There was only one chair, opposite the couch, so I let Livvy have it and I sat on the floor.

"I'd bring you tea, but I'm still a little shaky," Leeanne said. "Tell me who all of you are. You're Henry's grandchildren, isn't that right? Or Peter's?"

"Henry's," Rose said. We introduced ourselves, and then she said, "Look, Ms. Summers—Leeanne—we need your help."

"Of course, dear." She seemed unable to look away from Rose; she had barely noticed Livvy, and she didn't even seem to realize that I wasn't related to the family. It was funny, almost, after all of Rose's complaints that no one ever paid attention to her.

Rose told her everything that had happened, starting from when Livvy had fallen asleep. Leeanne listened intently, and I noticed something I hadn't seen before, that she had been not just good-looking when she was young but beautiful, extraordinary. She had deep blue eyes, high cheekbones, a nose that curved outward like a bow, a full mouth. Her face was a mass of wrinkles now, but you could still see what she'd looked like once.

"And then we read that interview you gave to the police," Rose finished. "And we wondered, well—"

"I'd forgotten all about that interview," Leeanne said. "How strange to think a record of it still exists, in some file cabinet somewhere."

"Is there anything else you could tell us about that day? What they did afterward, Henry and the others?"

"Well, I only visited a few times after that," Leeanne said. "I asked if I could help, of course, but they said there was nothing I could do. And the parties stopped, not that I came for the parties. Really, I was more at home in their library, or wandering around outdoors with Fiona."

She paused. "That whole time, it was so different from everything that came before it, and after—it was like an enchantment. I don't think I could have stayed around that family for very long, you know. It would have taken too much out of me, like an addiction. You can't live in that place, or even visit for a while—it's not meant for people like me."

I stirred. I knew what she meant, certainly, but was she right? Or was she just trying to convince herself? Still, look at what had happened to Sylvie.

"What was I saying?" Leeanne said. "Oh, yes—that they never stopped looking for Fiona. They put ads in all the papers, and they even hired a private detective, but they never found her. But it was strange—it almost seemed as if they knew they wouldn't get her back, as if they were just going through the motions. Well, you read that interview, you know what they thought. That those people, the ones who took her, that they needed her for something."

"Did you ever see Walter again?" Rose asked.

"I did, as a matter of fact. He visited me a short time later and he said—well, it was a funny thing, he said he'd tried to find the Feierabends again but he never could. He knew the address, but whenever he tried to go back he'd get lost among all those winding roads. As if the house was hiding itself from him, he said.

"That wasn't what he wanted, though. He wanted his whistle back. I told him I didn't have it and he—well, he nearly strangled me, just put his hands around my throat and shook me back and forth. He kept saying that he saw me take it, and that it was rightfully his. Luckily my friend Sally came home just then, and he went away and never came back."

"But you did have the whistle, didn't you? That's what you told the police."

"Here," Leeanne said, looking at me. "Bill, was it? Could you open that drawer there, please, the one at the top?"

I went to a bureau behind me and opened the drawer. "The whistle is in there," she said. "Be careful with it, though."

I saw it as soon as she finished speaking. It was shaped like a fish; the mouth was open and it was flattened at the tail, with a row of holes down the body.

"I didn't want Walter to have it," she said. "Well, especially after he attacked me like that."

"Did you ever try it?" Rose asked.

She nodded. "I did want to see Fiona again, that badly. But nothing happened. I wonder if it's—well—if it's somehow used up."

A key sounded in the door. "Oh, dear, it's Sally," Leeanne said. "I never told her about the Feierabends, about Fiona going missing... I wasn't hiding anything, I just couldn't think how to explain it."

Sally came inside, carrying bags of groceries. "Hello, dear," Leeanne said. "These are relatives of someone I knew a very long time ago, Rose and—I'm sorry, I've forgotten your names. And this is my friend, Sally Day."

"Didn't you give them tea, dear?" Sally asked. "And what about those cookies I baked yesterday?"

"Well, I felt a little woozy."

"Woozy?" Sally said, looking worried. "What do you mean?"

"I'm fine now—I can—"

"No, you sit down. I have to put the groceries away anyway."

Sally left the room, and a short while later we heard her moving around in the kitchen. Leeanne turned to Rose and said in a low voice, "You can keep the whistle if you like. Maybe it'll help you, maybe you can figure out how to use it."

"Are you sure?" Rose asked.

"Oh, yes. I'm too old for all of that, anyway."

I passed the whistle to Rose. We talked a bit about the Feierabends, the sisters' careers, Henry's and Peter's deaths, all of us aware that Sally could hear us just as we could hear her. Then Sally came back into the room, carrying a tray with a teapot and cups and a plate of cookies.

"So who was this person you knew?" she asked, pouring the tea and handing out cups.

"A woman named Fiona," Leeanne said. She reached for her cup, holding it with her right hand and then steadying it with her left.

"Your hand—does it—" I asked.

"It's just a little numb," she said, then, "Oh, I see. Yes—it's never really felt right since that day."

"What day?" Sally said. "What happened?"

"Well, I went bootlegging."

"What? What an interesting life you had, before I met you."

"Much more interesting since I met you, dear. Anyway, I knew this family up in Napa, people who had a vineyard and made a little wine, and I went sailing with them from Sausalito to San Francisco with a hold full of booze. And then we were boarded by...by pirates—"

"What!"

"And they abducted Fiona, and she—well, we never saw her again, poor woman."

"Oh. How sad."

"It was, very sad. And here's their grandchildren, come to find out about their history. I think I've told them all I can, though."

She raised her eyebrows at us over the rim of her cup, as if warning us not to ask any more questions. I thought we were about finished, though—I couldn't think of anything else. We drank our tea and said our goodbyes, with Leeanne calling after us to come back and tell her everything we'd learned.

As we left I noticed a small wooden sign on the mailbox, saying "Summers-Day." I smiled and showed it to Livvy and Rose.

Leeanne must have lived with Sally for a long time—she'd said that Sally had come home while Walter was there, and Walter had visited only a short time after Fiona had disappeared. She seemed to have turned away from the Feierabends' magic completely, to have embraced domesticity with a nice but perfectly ordinary woman.

Or had she? What did I know about the two of them, about the summers' days behind that door? Was I just feeling superior because I had stayed and fought for Livvy, for Nick?

15

I WENT TO THE FARMHOUSE the next day and tried to read, but I couldn't pay attention to any of the books in the library. I kept thinking about Walter's pipe, and wishing I hadn't handed it over so quickly to Rose. Had he really found it in a junk store? What would happen if we used it, if we summoned people from the other realm? Could we bargain with them, like I'd bargained with the witch?

Rose came back that night looking discouraged; she'd been unable to find Walter in the local phone books. "Did you ever try that pipe?" I asked her, before we'd even sat down for dinner.

"Not yet," she said.

"Well, what about now? Do you have it on you?"

"Yeah, but—"

"But what? Are you afraid?"

"Maybe. Or maybe I'm afraid nothing will happen, and then we'd be right back at the beginning."

"Afraid of what?" Livvy asked, coming out of the kitchen and wiping her hands on a towel.

"Of using the whistle," Rose said.

"Then don't do it," Livvy said.

"But what if it—if it could help Nick?" I asked.

"If she doesn't want to—" Livvy said.

"Oh, all right," Rose said, interrupting her. She opened her briefcase and started rummaging through it.

"Wait," Livvy said. "We should get ready, prepare ourselves..."

"How do you prepare yourself for this?" I asked.

Rose found the whistle and raised it to her mouth.

"Get a—a weapon, maybe—" Livvy said.

Rose closed her eyes and blew. Nothing happened.

"Well, there you are," I said, feeling foolish. "It's used up, just like Leeanne said."

"I guess so," Rose said.

She spent a few more days doing research, then returned late on Thursday looking triumphant. "He had to go to bankruptcy court," she told us over a dinner of pepper steak. "Walter. He'd apparently borrowed a lot of money and never paid it back." She took a bite of her steak. "I can't get a handle on this guy. He's a Harvard graduate in Leeanne's story, a little sleazy but with enough charm for them to invite him along when they go bootlegging, and then he turns up later and tries to strangle Leeanne. And now he's bankrupt—and I got the feeling from the court documents that he was running some kind of scam, that he never intended to pay the money back."

"Maybe he just got worse and worse as he got older," I said. "Either that or he managed to hide what a jerk he was from Fiona and Henry."

"It sounded almost like he was flirting with them," Livvy said. "With Leeanne and Fiona. At least at first."

Rose laughed. "Yeah, good luck with that," she said.

"And what about that whistle?" I asked. "I don't believe he found it in a junk store, like he said. And I don't think he came to the farmhouse just for the drinks, not with the way he snuck in. He knew something about the family."

"Well, I know where he lives now, so we can go ask him. Or where he lived, anyway—the bankruptcy was three years ago, in 1983, so he might not still be there. It's about a mile from Leeanne and Sally's house—luckily they never seem to have run into him."

"Do you want to go tomorrow?" I asked. I turned to Livvy. "Or wait—you have to work tomorrow, don't you?"

I wanted to leave that evening, no matter how late it was, to confront Walter and make him give up all his secrets. To be honest, I wanted to take him by the throat and shake him, just like he'd done to Leeanne. But Livvy had a right to be there, as least as much as I did.

Livvy seemed to understand what I was feeling, though. "Why don't you and Rose go?" she said. "I'll be fine."

Walter may have lived only a mile from Leeanne and Sally, but his neighborhood, the Mission District, looked like an entirely different city. It was in the flatlands, down from the hill we'd driven through, and seemed to be home to immigrants from any number of countries: when we got out of the car we heard soft ripples of Spanish, mostly, but also other languages I couldn't identify, though Rose thought one of them might be Arabic. Cars were parked two deep in the streets, and the paint on the houses was old and peeling, though the houses themselves seemed neat enough.

Despite all the cars we found a parking space right away—the Feierabend luck, once again. Walter lived in an old building that had been subdivided into apartments. The front door wasn't locked, and Rose and I let ourselves in and climbed up the stairs. Different styles of music played on every floor, Mexican, then punk, and finally as we got to the third floor we heard minor chords that sounded Middle Eastern. Someone was cooking something; a strong smell of nutmeg filled the hallway.

Rose knocked at Walter's apartment. The door opened a fraction, still locked with a flimsy chain, and a middle-aged woman peered out at us. "Hello," she said.

"Does Walter Arbuthnot live here?" Rose asked.

"I don't owe you anything," the woman said happily. "The court said so."

"We don't want money. We just want to talk to him. Is he here?"

"He's dead, actually," the woman said, still sounding cheerful. "I'm his daughter."

I hope to God Nick never announces my death in that tone. "Do you—do you know anything about him?" I asked. "We're interested in a family called Feierabend, people he knew once. Did he ever tell you about them?"

"Feierabend," she said. "You know, he wrote a story with that name in it, or something like it. I thought he made it up."

"Do you still have it? We can pay you for it."

The slice of her face that I could see turned angry, and she stood up taller. At the same time Rose gave me a warning look. "I don't want your money," the woman said.

"I'm sorry. I didn't mean to imply—I didn't mean to give you the wrong impression. This is Rose Feierabend—Walter knew her grandfather. I'm Will, her brother-in-law. We're doing some family research."

She thought a minute, then said, "Okay, come on in. I'll see if I can find the story. My name's Valerie, by the way. Valerie McCrae."

She unlocked the chain and motioned us inside. She was plump and had unruly brown hair, with gray hairs springing out from it like wires. She wore a T-shirt and beads, and a long skirt patched together with different colors. Her feet were bare, and, I couldn't help but notice, pretty dirty.

The living room was about as I'd expected, an old carpet with stains and discolorations, a sagging couch covered with an Indian bedspread, a few puffy beanbag cushions. An ancient stereo stood against the wall, along with records in milk crates, their covers coming apart at the edges. I was starting to hear people like Valerie called "aging hippies"—said with scornful laughter, as though they should have had sense enough to jump onto the next fashion bandwagon. As an aging hippie myself, I wasn't sure what to make of it.

"Sit down," she said. "Do you want anything to drink? I have some wine, and I think some orange juice. Or water, I guess." We shook our heads and sat gingerly on the couch. "Okay, I'll just be a minute."

She went over to a closet and started pulling down cardboard boxes. "Do you need any help?" I asked.

"No. No, I'm fine." She took down another box and opened it. "Walter," she said, shaking her head in admiration. "He was a piece of work, that man, a real skunk. Look at this—it's a deed for some land he owned once. He sold that land three times, at least. And here—here's some stock certificates for a company that never existed."

She sat back, brushing her hair out of her eyes. "I was dumb enough to sign something for him one time. I ended up going to court for years after he died, all those people wanting their money back. All settled now, though. Maybe I can finally start getting my life back."

"He went to Harvard, didn't he?" I asked.

"Is that what he told you? Well, it's not as much of a stretch as some of the other things. He did go there for a year, I think. Then his father lost his business—and this was before the Depression, too, it's just our family's luck that we can't even make money in the boom times. Anyway, he had to leave school to support the family. That's what he said, anyway. Who knows if it's true?"

"And he'd lost one of his fingers? Do you know how that happened?"

She laughed again. "Which story do you want to hear? It got shot off in World War I—though I think he managed to avoid the draft somehow—or World War II, or he was attacked in the Himalayas—"

"The Himalayas?"

"Yeah. He'd been initiated into this secret cult—ah, forget it, it's ridiculous. And there's another explanation in that story he wrote, this one even more unbelievable. He always had to dramatize his life, make it more exciting. He said—wait a minute, here it is."

She pulled out a folder and came over and handed it to us. I noticed then that she limped when she walked, and I wondered if that was why she wore that long skirt, to cover up whatever was wrong with her legs.

"Can we borrow this?" Rose asked.

Valerie thought for a while. "Better not," she said finally. "I don't want to let any of this stuff go, just in case I get sued again. You can read it here, if you want."

Rose opened her briefcase and took out a pen and a legal pad, and we started reading.

My father having lost all our fortune in 1923, I set out in the world to win it back. I traveled to many exotic places and saw a great many unbelievable things—things I would not credit myself, were I to hear them from another man. I sat at the feet of a hidden master in the Himalayas, flew antiques out of Persia, owned a mining company in Peru. The mining company went bust due to the negligence of my partner, and I scuffled around and somehow found myself in Berlin.

I was despondent over the loss of my business, and it was during that time I took up the teachings of Emile Coué. Each morning when I got up I would recite the phrase he had given the world—"Every day in every way I am getting better and better"—and then, refreshed, I would set out from my lodgings to look for work.

And I discovered another way to bear my misfortunes: it helped to think of myself as a character in a fairy tale. I was the third son of a feckless father, after all, a man who had sent me out to seek my fortune with nothing but bad advice, no better than if he had abandoned me in a forest. My brothers, each of whom had amassed a great deal of wealth, refused to help me; I was alone in all the world.

So I was pleased to find myself in Germany, the country that had given fairy tales to the world. I had a great deal of time on my hands, in between looking for work, and I spent hours searching out bookstores, re-reading those tales that had once given me such innocent happiness.

One day I found an ancient volume in English called *Spiderweb and Candlelight*, by John Woodhouse. I paged through it absently and came upon the following sentence: "The Elf made him this Bargain, that his Daughter would be a Bondmaid to the Fair Folk, in exchange for which he and his Family would live for ay in pleasure and comfort."

Naturally, I was intrigued. Who would not want to live in pleasure and comfort? I read on and discovered that in exchange for this boon a daughter would have to fall asleep for seven years. The family in this story repudiated the bargain, though, and "the Elf sought to make this same Bargain with another Family."

The author went on to state that "there were many who put themselves forth as Candidates, wishing good Fortune for themselves and their Families," but to my great frustration the story ended there. Did the elf find another candidate? How did one go about putting oneself forward?

I bought the book immediately, of course, and over the next few days I read it from cover to cover. I felt as if I had finally found my purpose in life. I was the third son, and this was the fairy tale that would be my destiny.

I was quickly disappointed, though; none of the other anecdotes in the book dealt with this bargain, being mostly boring accounts of famous men Woodhouse had known. Still, I was in Germany, the place where, according to the story, the bargain had first been made. I had a small sum of money I had salvaged from the ruin of the mining company, and on a whim I took a train to Kassel, the home of the Brothers Grimm.

I found lodgings at a small inn and set out to explore the town. The citizens were eager to point out the house where the brothers had lived—houses, I should say, since they seemed to have moved a great deal. I made cautious inquiries about a bargain, though not to everyone; I did not want to get a reputation as a lunatic.

But no one knew anything, and I began to grow discouraged. I even considered returning to Berlin, a city with more diversions than the dull rustic place in which I found myself. Still, every morning I would recite Coué's phrase, and thus fortified I would set out into the town in a more hopeful frame of mind.

One day as I was walking past the earliest of the Grimms' houses I saw a beggar loitering in the street, a short, thin man dressed in rags. He came over to me and asked for money, but I had almost nothing in those days and I told him so.

"Ah," he said. "Not even to learn about the bargain?"

I should perhaps mention here that I had picked up some German in my travels, and had learned a good deal more since I had come to Germany. I have always been quick with languages, something that has served me in good stead all over the world. Still, this fellow's rough Hessian accent was almost incomprehensible, and it took me a moment to understand what he had said.

When I did, though, I stopped in my tracks. "What do you know about it?" I asked.

"Nothing. Not if you don't have any money."

"I may have a little. How do I know you're telling the truth?"

"You'll know when I tell you my story."

"I'm not paying you anything until I hear it."

A tedious negotiation followed, one in which I agreed to pay him some money at once and some after he finished. Then he wanted me to buy him a meal, but with his dirty clothes and knotted hair I doubted any restaurant would serve him. Instead I led him to a bench in a nearby park. We sat down and I smelled his sour odor, as if he had gone several months without a bath.

His name was Hans, he told me. "My family lived next door to the Grimms," he said. "That first house, the one you were looking at. The family had moved to Kassel so Jacob and Wilhelm could start going to school. Very studious they were—their father had died young, and they had to support their family, their mother and the four younger children."

I stirred impatiently, wishing he would get to the meat of the matter.

My father had lost his fortune and had asked his children to support him, a request I'd found intolerable. Surely fathers should support their sons, not the other way around. I could only assume that children in those days were more under the thumb of their parents.

"Jacob was studying law, you know," Hans went on. "Funny, to think about it—he could have been a lawyer, and we would have never had those stories. Anyway, he had a professor who was going to France, to Paris, to look at law books in the libraries there, and this professor asked Jacob to come along. And then—well, the histories say that Jacob got interested in legends then, in the folk stories that he found in old books, but my great-grandfather said that something different happened. That Jacob read a book in a library in Paris that mentioned a wealthy family, people who were enchanted in some way, who prospered in good times and bad. The book said nothing more than that, but it made reference to other stories about this family, stories that had been lost.

"Life was very hard back then, in the early 1800s. Napoleon had just invaded Germany—well, there wasn't a united Germany then, but Napoleon took over the various states and provinces, and he set his younger brother Jérôme up as king here in Kassel. So maybe Jacob thought that he should try anything, whatever would help his family. He got a job when he came back from Paris, working in Jérôme's library, but it didn't pay very much. Really, though, he was looking for stories about this family, in the library and elsewhere.

"So that was when he and Wilhelm started to collect fairy tales. But at first Jacob didn't tell Wilhelm what he was looking for. Maybe he felt guilty—he and his brother believed in hard work above everything, not in supernatural tricks. Maybe he thought he was taking a path Wilhelm would disapprove of.

"Anyway, they'd been collecting stories for a few months when this old woman came to visit Wilhelm. Jacob was out then, working at the library. You know the story about the bargain, and the bondmaid who has to sleep for seven years?"

"Not all of it. How did the bargain come about? Where did the family meet—well, meet that elf they made the bargain with?"

"I don't know. Jacob—"

"You don't *know*? Isn't that what I paid you for, to tell me—"

"Ah, but I know something better. Patience, and I'll get to it. So here was Wilhelm, with the story Jacob had spent all this time looking for, and he thought of it as just another fairy tale, didn't even think to mention it to his brother when he came home from work. And that night—well, according to what Wilhelm told my great-grandfather, some tiny people, people about six inches high, broke a window and slid down the curtains. Then they ran all over the house, screaming and laughing and breaking dishes, tearing the curtains and bed sheets, calling everyone names—Wilhelm said he'd never heard such profanity, but then he was pretty innocent, my great-grandfather said. And of course they tore up the papers the brothers had been working on, and scattered them all over the house. Jacob and Wilhelm tried to sort them out the next day, and that was when Wilhelm noticed that the story was missing."

"So what?" I asked. "He could still remember it, couldn't he?"

"Not really. He hadn't paid all that much attention—remember, he didn't know the story was all that important. He only told Jacob about it when he realized it was missing. Poor man—Jacob kept asking him about it for the rest of their lives. He was still doing it when the brothers moved back here, thirty years later. By then Wilhelm had forgotten all of it, of course, had made himself forget—"

"Wait. He'd forgotten it? So you don't know the story either? What the hell do you know, then?"

"What do I know? I know what Wilhelm did next."

I forced myself to be patient. "And what was that?" I asked.

"Well, Wilhelm liked going for long walks. They both did, but they liked to take different paths and think about different things, about what they were working on. One day Wilhelm went into the woods and saw those little people again. One of them was playing a great golden trumpet as tall as he was, and some of the others were working to the music, carrying blackberries as big as their heads.

"As soon as they saw him they dropped the berries and went swarming all over him, screeching in these loud high voices. They shot arrows at him, Wilhelm said, and they climbed him and stabbed him with their swords—tiny arrows, and tiny swords, but they hurt all the same, and there were a lot of them. He screamed and tried to brush them off, he tried to run away but he only ended up getting lost. And this was a place he walked through every day, a place he knew as well as his own study.

"Finally he found a way out of the woods, and he shook the last of the little people out of his hair. But he was never the same after. His heart would start to race for no reason, and he couldn't catch his breath, and he'd feel terror overwhelm him, even when he was standing outside in his own garden, in bright sunlight. Finally he had to go away, to a sanitarium, they said, but really to someone who claimed he could cure him of his fears. Elf-shot, they called it back then, or elf-struck, someone who had been cursed by the elves.

"A lot of what they did at that sanitarium was nonsense, of course. He had to rub his neck with mercury, and rub his heart with spirits, and wear a magnet over his heart. But they must have known something there, because they gave him some advice that seemed to help, at least a little. They told him to forget the story he'd been told, to put it out of his mind.

"So he came back, and he spent a lot of his time rewriting the fairy tales that he and Jacob had collected. The tales went into seven editions, and each time he changed them just a little. Jacob was traveling a lot by then, and was busy with his own work, and he never seemed to notice how different the tales had become."

"But why? Why did he change them?"

"Ah, now we're coming to it. It happened in the woods again, of course. He saw a small bird there, a beautiful bird with bright wings and long tail-feathers of gold and purple. He followed it, enchanted, not noticing where he was going. And after a while he came to a hill deep within the woods.

"The bird lit on the hill and stayed there, singing and preening its wings. He realized that the place was important somehow, and he remembered a tale he'd collected, about a man who'd stuck his finger in a hill and seen a door open in front of him. He reached out his hand cautiously and put a finger in a hole—and suddenly the side of the mountain slid inward, and he saw a table covered with food, and a soft bed piled high with blankets.

"He was hungry by that time, so he sat down at the table and ate the food. It was delicious, he said, but he could never remember afterward what it was. Then he felt tired, and he lay down on the bed and went to sleep. And in his dreams he saw and heard the things the elves wanted him to change. The stories gave too much away, you see, told too much about the places the elves lived—not just the story they'd torn up, though that was the worst of them, but some of the others as well.

"He did this all his life—wherever he was he would manage to get back to Kassel, to the hill. He would say he wanted to visit old friends, and he did that, but he would also spend a night under the hill. The elves tormented him, you see. They'd marked him in the woods, and they followed him for the rest of his life. His health was always poor, from then on, especially when he'd stayed away from the hill for too long."

"So where is this hill? Do you know?"

"I do, yes. My great-grandfather told my grandfather, and my grandfather told my father, and my father told me. I'm hungry, though, as hungry as Wilhelm was. If I could just have a bite of food before we go—"

"Not so fast. How do I know you didn't make this whole story up? Show me the hill first, and we'll see."

He nodded, clearly disappointed, and stood and headed toward the woods outside of town. With his short legs he moved very slowly, and he seemed ill in some way as well, perhaps from having lived so long outdoors. I was frantic to urge him on, but I made myself keep to his pace.

Finally we reached the woods and went in under the trees. He followed a path I could barely see, and I took note of various landmarks in case I decided to come back. "Why did Wilhelm tell your great-grandfather all this?" I asked.

"I don't know," Hans said. "It was on his last visit to Kassel—Wilhelm was an old man by then, and I think he wanted to tell someone, to get it off his chest. He couldn't talk to Jacob about it—Jacob would only nag him about the missing tale—and I think that bothered him. They were very close, they usually told each other everything."

I tried not to sound eager when I asked my next question, not wanting Hans to hear how important it was to me. "Did your father ever tell you the name of that old woman? The one who told Wilhelm the story about the bargain?"

"He did," Hans said. He paused for a long time, working his way around some tangled roots in the path, and I nearly screamed out loud. "Feierabend."

We continued into the woods. "Wilhelm had a theory," he said. The path began to slope upward, and he spoke with difficulty now, taking deep breaths between his phrases. "He thought that the elves, or whatever they were...he thought that they only showed themselves in what he called the uncertain places. Where the sea meets the land, for example...or inside meets outside... or at dawn or twilight..."

Just then we saw a hill in front of us. "Or where a forest ends and a hill begins," he said.

He stood there awhile, catching his breath. I brushed him aside and put my finger into a hole in the side of the hill.

I felt a sudden excruciating pain, and I jerked my hand back. My finger had been cut off. I stared at the stump where it had been, at the blood flowing down my arm. "You idiot!" I said. "You stupid, stupid fool! Why the hell didn't you warn me? Look at this, it's cut off my finger! My finger's been cut off!"

"I—I didn't know," he said. "I didn't know that would happen."

"Look at this," I said. I think I was going into shock, at the pain and loss of blood—I kept saying the same thing over and over again. "Look, my finger's been cut off."

At that moment a part of the hill slid inward. Hans stared at the opening, witlessly, and I hurried inside, my pain nearly forgotten.

A light came from somewhere, from the walls, maybe. I didn't see the food Hans had mentioned, or the bed. There was just a table in front of me, and a whistle on top of it, a small pipe made out of clay. And there was a note next to it, written in those Gothic German letters, that said, "Play this when you need our help."

The door to the hill began to close. I grabbed the pipe, instinctively using my left hand, my unharmed hand, and ran outside.

"What's that?" Hans asked.

"Nothing," I said, closing my fingers around it.

"You took something—I saw you."

"Never mind that—it doesn't concern you. Obviously they wanted me to have it."

I headed back along the path. He followed after me, and I walked faster to lose him.

"Where's that money you promised me?" he called out. "And what about my dinner?"

"You can't be serious," I said, not turning around. "After you made me lose my finger? I should sue you—and I would, too, if you had any money."

"I didn't make you do anything. I told you—I didn't know that would happen. I've never even been able to get inside."

He dropped further and further behind, until I could barely hear him. "Do you know why it cut your finger off?" he said, shouting now.

I stopped and looked at him. "No, why?"

"Because you wouldn't give me dinner, that's why. You've read fairy tales—you know how they work. When someone asks for something you have to be generous, otherwise you don't get what you want. You're like the bad sons in the stories, the ones who refuse to help."

"You're crazy. I did get what I want—they gave me something, something they never gave you. And I'm not the bad son at all—I'm the third son, my father's third son. You didn't know that, did you?"

I started to run, trying to put him behind me. A short time later I reached the edge of the woods and hurried on to my lodgings.

I stayed for some time in Kassel, convalescing. Then I began searching for the Feierabends, and I learned that before Prohibition a family with that name had owned one of the largest vineyards in the United States. I sailed for the States and found the family easily enough; in fact, they were making wine from their grapes, though illegally.

My experience with the Feierabends was inconclusive, though. Even worse, I lost the pipe. But I came to believe that the pipe wasn't what they had said it was, something that would help me. Quite the opposite—they had tricked me somehow, worked events to their advantage.

Only one thing remains to tell. It happened exactly a year ago, on March 19, 1950. I was in Wyoming, with an eye to buying a mine there. I had spent the day down in the mine with the owner, and I returned to my hotel dirty and exhausted. I fell asleep immediately after dinner.

Sometime in the middle of the night I felt someone shaking my arm. "Walter," a voice said. "Walter, wake up."

I opened my eyes. Hans stood there, of all people. I wanted to sit up, to stand and defend myself. What was he doing here? Did he plan to rob me?

A lassitude had come over me, though, and I could barely keep my eyes open. And somehow Hans's appearance in my room, half a world away from where I had last seen him, seemed completely natural, as if we had made plans to meet there.

"What are you doing here?" I asked.

"I'm cleaning your room," he said.

Even this didn't seem terribly strange. "What? Why?"

"Say my name," he said. "Please."

"Why?"

"Just say it. Or give me something, one of your shirts, maybe."

"I'm not going to do anything until you tell me why you're here."

He glanced behind him as if looking for someone, and then spoke softly, quickly. "Do you remember when I took you to the woods, and that hill?"

I nodded.

"Well, it turned out that they didn't like that, they didn't want me showing you all those things. And this is my punishment, to clean houses for fifty years."

"Your—your punishment? What do you mean?"

He looked behind him again. "What I said. I was crazy then, a madman—well, you saw what I was like. I'd wanted to get under that hill for so long, I'd heard stories about the food, and the wonderful dreams... And then you went in so easily, and that made me even crazier. I followed you back to your inn that day, remember, and then I ran into the center of town and started screaming, and, and—well, I don't really remember exactly what I did."

He slowed. He seemed to have been waiting a long time to tell someone his story. "They put me away, of course. The good burghers of Kassel, I mean, not...well, you know. Not the folks under the hill. They put me in an asylum, where I could go mad in peace. I was there a long time, fifteen years. And then the world around me went mad too, even madder than I was, and suddenly Germany was at war, and they took me out of the asylum to make me a soldier. I ran away, though, and I went to the hill, I put my finger into the side, and it opened. Finally, after all this time, it opened. I went under the hill, and that's when they caught me. It turned out they were ready for me, they'd been waiting years to punish me. And I've been working for them, for Those People, ever since."

I forced myself to overcome my tiredness and study him. He looked better, surprisingly; he was cleaner, and he had filled out some, even grown stout. He wore a black coat with a long tail, and a black hat and gloves. A duster made out of peacock feathers stuck out of his belt.

"Say my name," he said again.

"Why?"

"Because then I'll go free."

"How long have you been doing this?"

"Ten years now," he said. "That's what the calendars say, anyway, in the houses I clean. Forty years to go. Say my name, or give me something. Please."

I tried to think. Did I want to free him, to go against that other realm, against the ones he had called Those People? I knew what they could do to me; my finger reminded me of that every day.

"I'm not sure—" I started.

Someone appeared behind him, and a cane whipped down on his back. He cried out. "Have you washed the dishes?" the man behind him said.

Hans left quickly, and the other man followed him out. I had caught only a glimpse of him, tall, with black clothes and what had looked like red eyes in the dark. I had been right not to meddle with him.

I am still waiting for him, have been waiting for a year now. Surely he knows how I helped him, how I stayed silent, resisting all of Hans's entreaties. Will he come and reward me for my forbearance? Will my luck finally change? I believe so. After all, every day in every way I am getting better and better.

—Walter Arbuthnot

—Los Angeles, California

—March 19, 1951

16

"WOW," I SAID. There was a lot here to think about, a lot I wanted to discuss with Rose. But Valerie stopped rearranging the boxes in her closet and looked at me, waiting for me to go on, and I had to say something that would make sense to her. "You were right—he wasn't a nice guy. Or at least he wasn't very nice to Hans."

"You don't think all that's true, do you?" Valerie said. She sat on one of her beanbag chairs. "That stuff about the door in the hill, and those men coming to clean at night? I think he was trying to write a story for kids, a fairy tale, but he didn't know how. Just another thing he wasn't very good at."

I looked at Rose, wondering how much I could tell Valerie. She shook her head. For the first time I understood some of the reasons for the family's secrecy. They kept silent in part because no one would ever believe them.

"It's funny, because he did tell me some cool stories," Valerie said. "All about him, of course, and how he was smarter or better than other people, how he tricked someone into something. He left my mother and me when I was four, but he would show up every so often, and I was always thrilled to see him. He would bring me these far-out presents, things from Japan or Mexico or someplace, and I always begged my mother to let me go away with him. I must have driven her crazy—here she'd been trying to raise me, make some kind of home for me, and all I wanted was to leave her. To leave and go off with a man who hadn't been all that nice to her, really."

I had a very dark thought then—that Walter had married Valerie's mother to have a child, someone he could offer up in exchange for good fortune. I don't think he'd ever stopped looking for those elves he'd read about.

She saw my expression, I think, because she went on. "What I mean is, he wasn't all bad. He was sure exciting to be around, even fun sometimes. I was in a car with him once when someone started chasing us, and we drove across the Bay Bridge at like a hundred miles an hour. He hit another car, of course, and then someone hit him—that's how my legs got screwed up."

The story didn't seem to prove her point—just the opposite, in fact—but she hurried on. "He managed to get my name on the lease to this apartment," she said. "It's rent controlled—I don't pay hardly anything for it. I think he felt guilty for some things, toward the end of his life."

I could think of a few things he might have felt guilty for. "Well, thanks for letting us read this," I said.

"Did it help you any?"

"Yeah, I think it did."

"Hey, groovy. Let me know if you find out anything else about Walter."

I hadn't heard anyone say "groovy" for years. "Sure," I said.

She stood up to walk us to the door. We went downstairs and waited until we got in the car before saying anything. "Wow," Rose said.

"Yeah, I know what you mean," I said, pulling out into traffic.

"How can she be so cheerful, so—so forgiving? Her father messed up her life, really. She can't even walk right because of him. I just don't get it."

I remembered something I'd read in the family's library. "Some are born to sweet delight," I said. "Some are born to endless night."

"What?"

"It's a poem. Blake, I think. I wonder... Your family has all that luck, you're the ones born to sweet delight. And I wonder if that means that other people have to suffer, the ones born to endless night. If you somehow take away all the luck they would have had. Remember, she said her family couldn't even make money in the boom times."

"Of course not. That's ridiculous. And we suffer too. I mean, you know that as well as anyone."

"Sure," I said, not wanting to argue.

"Did you ever have a patient like that? Someone whose life is all screwed up but who manages to go on, even to be happy?"

"Those aren't the kind of people who go see a shrink. I get the just opposite, people who are hurting for some reason or another. Some of them would probably fall apart if they had the kind of life she did." I shook my head. "Man, her father was even worse than we thought."

"He wouldn't even let that guy go free, the one who was cleaning the hotel. I mean, what harm could it have done?" She hesitated. "Do you think he's the same one who cleans our house?"

"Yeah, I do." I realized, amazed, that I'd never even thought of him over the years. I'd been under a glamour, of course, but that didn't seem enough to excuse me.

"Well, at least we know where he comes from," Rose said. "Now I'm going to feel guilty every time I wake up and see all the work he's done. If he started in 1940, he has—let's see, just four years left."

"Maybe I'll stay up and talk to him."

"Why?"

"I don't know, maybe he knows something. At the very least I can say his name, or give him a shirt or something. You remember when they trapped me, when I had to do all that work? I can't imagine doing it for fifty years."

I'd told the family all about working for Those People. She nodded but didn't say anything.

"What?" I said. "Don't tell me you want him to keep working. What, you think Sylvie won't be able to manage without him?"

"No. No, I just thought it might be dangerous, that's all. What if they get you again?"

I'd been trying not to think about that. I wasn't looking forward to having to face them again, especially the man with the cane. I didn't have a choice, though, not if I wanted to save Nick. "I think—I think the way it works is that they can't trap me again. They'll have to find some other way to stop me."

"I hope so."

I laughed. "Yeah, me too."

I called Sylvie that evening and asked her when Those People were coming. At first she pretended she didn't know, but I kept at her, even browbeat her a little, I'm ashamed to say. "Come on, Sylvie, you put out food for him on the nights he cleans your house. You have to know."

"All right," she said finally. "They come every other Friday."

The next Friday I stayed over at the farmhouse, taking a book from the library and sitting out in the hall to wait. I couldn't concentrate, though. I thought about the time I worked for Those People, about what Rose had said about them capturing me again, about the man with cane. The house was so quiet I could hear the blood pounding in my ears.

He showed up at a little past three in the morning. One minute he wasn't there, the next I saw a flash of movement and looked up as he went into one of the bedrooms down the hall. I hurried after him.

"Hello, Hans," I said.

He turned quickly. "How—how do you know my name?"

"I read something your friend Walter wrote. Tell me your last name and I'll free you."

He looked behind him. "Hurry up," I said. "We don't have a lot of time."

"I don't—I don't know if I want to be free," he said.

I realized I'd never heard him speak before. He had a thick German accent. "What do you mean?" I said. "Look—I did what you're doing now, cleaning, working for that guy with the cane. I know how horrible it is. Just tell me your name. Or here—" I started taking my shirt off.

"No, wait. I—what did you read? What did Walter say about me?"

I put the shirt back on. I was still shivering, though, and the skin on my back crawled with the memory of the cane. I wanted to hurry, but I couldn't seem to organize my thoughts. "He said—God, I don't know. That you asked him for money, that you showed him the hill, the one that opened, that you cleaned his room. That you asked him to free you. So if you'd just tell me your damn name—"

"Did he say that I had become a crazy man? That I wanted to go into the hill and have dreams, and the people of the town had to lock me away?"

"Yeah. All of that."

"It was true, you know. I very much wanted those dreams. And it was a long time before I was again sane. Years and years. Not in the asylum, they couldn't help, but here, this work helps me. It is like—I don't know how you say it. Like a monk, working in a monastery. I have four years only to go now, and I think that by the time I am finished I will be again sane, I can go out into the world. I don't become older, you know, while I work here. I was forty years old when I started, and I am forty now, but with the wisdom of a man of eighty-five."

He stopped suddenly, looking past me. A terrified expression appeared on his face. I turned around. The man with the cane stood there, smiling.

"So now you know," the man said to me. "He doesn't want you to help him. Get out of here."

"Wait," I said. I turned back to Hans, trying to ignore the other man. "I need your help. My son fell asleep, he's going to sleep for seven years. Do you know how to free him?"

There was a strange look of longing on his face. I don't know how to describe it except to say that I had seen that exact expression on one of my patients, a man who used to be a heroin addict—he looked like that whenever he talked about heroin. "Ah, he has those dreams now," Hans said. "The beautiful dreams. I don't know why they want some people and not others, why they didn't want me. I think maybe they are bound to the bargain, just like you are, they can take only someone from your family."

"Do you know anything? Anything that can help?"

"No. No, I am sorry. I would take his place if I could. I would take his dreams. But I can't help you."

The other man moved so I could see him, and raised his cane. "All right, all right," I said, holding my hands up in what I hoped was a peaceful gesture. "I'm leaving."

For years Ben had been stopping by to eat dinner with us every couple of weeks, and luckily Livvy didn't mind having someone else to feed. But the next time he visited, coming in without knocking as usual, we were just leaving for the farmhouse.

"Hi, everybody," he said. "Hey, Rose—when did you get into town?"

"About a week ago," she said.

"Listen," I said to him. "Livvy didn't make dinner today. Maddie's in town, and we're going up to visit her."

I could see he was disappointed, though he tried to hide it. I couldn't help it—I said, "Hey, why don't you come along with us?"

Livvy gave me a complex look, one that somehow encapsulated fifteen years of history and at the same time managed to tell me what an idiot I'd been.

Maddie didn't like Ben, Ben might not have gotten over Maddie, Maddie was still not all that happy with me...I shrugged back, trying to convey that I'd felt sorry for Ben, that it had been the polite thing to do. Apparently I wasn't as fluent in gestures as she was; she frowned, not understanding, and turned away.

We had to put Nick in the back seat of our car, which meant there was no room for Ben and Rose; they ended up taking Rose's car. I spent most of the trip with my attention on Nick, listening as he tossed and mumbled.

At the farmhouse we put Nick in Livvy's old bed, then went downstairs for dinner. Rose and Ben had arrived while we'd been upstairs. Maddie came in and glanced at Ben, but to my relief she didn't say anything. I saw now that she'd cut her hair short and dyed it green.

"It's for a part," she said when she saw me looking at it. "I like it, though—maybe I'll keep it."

The three sisters sat together on the bench across from me, and in some odd way Maddie's hair seemed to emphasize their similarities. They could have been a frontispiece in a book of fairy tales: "Once there were three princesses, one with black hair, one with brown, and one with green..."

I realized with a start that here we all were again, eating dinner, just like when I had first met them. It had been fifteen years, at least, since we'd first gotten together, that charmed circle at the beginning. And so much had happened since then, I'd learned so many things...

Sylvie brought out dinner—made from packages, but I was still impressed. "So, you here on vacation?" Ben asked Rose.

"I'm doing some research for Will and Livvy," she said.

"Yeah? How's it going?"

"Not too good."

We started telling Ben and Sylvie what Rose had found out, Leeanne's police transcript and Walter's story. Recounting everything took a long time, and we'd finished dinner by the time we were done with it.

"So Hilbert's father was a bootlegger," Sylvie said. "I never knew that—I'll have to ask him about it, the next time I see him."

"Sounds like you've done a lot of work so far," Ben said to Rose. "How did you know where to look?"

"Well, I talk to people," Rose said. She flushed, not used to so much attention from her family, I thought. "And I look at old documents, like court cases and newspapers and telephone books. It's what I do, after all."

"Yeah, but we still haven't gotten anywhere," I said. "We don't know how to get Nick back, or even how to find the other realm."

"Well, we know they like," Rose said. "They like—what did Wilhelm call it, in Walter's story? The uncertain places."

"Sure," I said. "And Nell said something similar, at the restaurant. That there are places where our realm and theirs overlap. But how does that help us? Where are those places?"

"Telegraph Avenue," Livvy said.

"Lem's restaurant," Rose said.

"I looked for the restaurant," I said. "I went out there one day, but I couldn't find it. I wasn't even sure I had the right street, and no one I talked to remembered it."

"Wilhelm's hill," Ben said.

I laughed briefly. "I thought about that too, believe it or not. I had the idea of going to Kassel and looking for it, but that's too crazy even for me. Walter never even said where it was."

"You're forgetting the most obvious place," Sylvie said. "What about right here—the farmhouse?"

We all looked at her. I'd gone back to the hill near the house, of course, but I'd never really thought about the farmhouse itself. "Yeah, but where?" I asked. "How?"

"I don't know," she said. "Never mind—it was just an idea."

"No, it was a good one," I said.

None of us said anything for a while. "You know what I'd like?" Livvy said finally. "To see that ballroom Leeanne mentioned. We were never allowed in there as kids."

"There isn't really anything to see," I said.

"What?" she said. "When did you go there?"

"One day when I got tired of reading. It's easy enough to get into—I just pried the boards off."

"Okay, let's do it," Maddie said.

"What, now?" Sylvie said. "What about—well, isn't it too dark?"

"The lights there still work," I said.

We got up, and I found the hammer in the kitchen drawer where I'd left it. Everyone followed me into the hallway, then through the dogleg where the bungalow joined up with the Victorian house. We reached the boarded-up doorway and I set to work.

The boards came off, easier this time, and I opened the door and turned on the lights. I showed them past the cloakroom to the kitchen and pantry, and then we climbed the stairs to the ballroom.

They looked around, taking in the chandeliers and the mural, the water-stained wallpaper and the dark wooden floor. "Orpheus," I said to Livvy, indicating the mural.

"What?" she said. "Oh."

"It must have been something once," Maddie said. "Couples on the dance floor, servants in dinner jackets standing by with drinks and hors d'oeuvres. Look, there was a bandstand, up front. I wish I'd been there."

She'd have started a union for the servants, I thought, but I didn't say so; I'd stopped making fun of her politics by then. "Look!" she said.

At first I didn't see anything. Then, as I followed her finger, I saw a man and a woman dance by, the woman's scarves flowing as she passed. More couples joined them, and I heard thin music playing and someone singing: "You can bring Pearl, she's a darn nice girl, but don't bring Lulu. You can bring Rose, with the turned up nose, but don't bring Lulu."

Why hadn't I seen this before, the first time I was here? Did it only happen when a member of the family was present, someone who'd been born into it, who truly believed that their rugs might be flying carpets? We stood, unable to move, as the dancers swept across the floor. A man and a woman sailed toward Ben and then passed through him; he watched them go with his mouth open, astonished.

Was Fiona here, or Leeanne? I glanced around but didn't see anyone who looked like them. Someone headed toward me, though, a stout woman with a cane, wearing a heavy green necklace.

No, not a necklace—a snake. It was Great-aunt Alva.

"You know vhat to do," she said. She had a thick German accent. "You know vhat vords to say."

At first I didn't realize she was talking to me. Even after I figured it out I didn't understand. What words?

Then, suddenly, I remembered. *"Rick rack ruck!"* I shouted.

The gauzy scarves and dresses of the women billowed outward. The air took on their pastel colors, became translucent. An animal ran past, a fox, I thought.

"What—" Livvy said. She reached out and took my hand.

The colors parted in front of us.

17

AT FIRST I DIDN'T UNDERSTAND what I was seeing, it was all so strange. A market, maybe, or a play, a game or a celebration...

Instead of the ballroom I saw a wide green meadow, with all sorts of people (and other things, but I put them aside for later) coming and going. There were booths and tables and makeshift counters, with men and women standing or sitting behind them, selling their wares. There were people walking through the crowd singing or performing, and athletes playing a complicated game with a ball, and a procession of people dressed in streamers of bright colors, scattering ribbons and flowers. The sound of a drum came from far away, and I smelled spices and animal dung, meat stew and wine, and something else, sharp and unfamiliar.

And there were others here, too, the same sorts of creatures that had come to Livvy's and my wedding. People with animal heads, people with wings, a small brown shape that darted behind a tree and never reappeared...

I glanced around for the others, and saw them staring around in amazement. "Where are we?" Ben asked.

"It's where—it's where I was, that time," Livvy said softly. She put her hand to her mouth, her eyes wide. I hadn't seen her so afraid for a long time, and I felt distressed to see it; I'd hoped her fear had gone forever. I put my arm around her, but she didn't seem to notice. "Are they going to keep me here? And make me dance, and—and fight in their wars?"

"No," I said firmly, or at least trying to sound firm. "We're all here this time—we won't let anything happen to you."

"And this time they didn't come for you," Rose said. "We found them—they might not even know we're here."

We started walking along a path. A counter stood in front of us, with carved and painted wooden boxes on top. I opened one up and a golden light streamed out.

The woman behind the counter smacked my hand, hard, with a ladle. "Stop that!" she said. "Don't let it escape!"

People turned to stare at me. Something small and bright buzzed near my face—a small bird or an insect maybe, but I thought I'd seen a human face.

I closed the box quickly and we continued down the path. "Shouldn't we get out of the open?" Ben said.

I wanted to be bold, to walk up to that witch, wherever she was, and demand Nick back. At the same time, though, I felt alarm at the very idea of seeing her again. I scanned the crowd for the man in the top hat.

"Let's see where we are first," I said.

The next stall displayed cages made out of what looked like bone. At the one after that we saw fish, swimming in the air on top of a counter, their colors glinting like metal: cobalt, copper, bronze. "Fish, fine fish!" the man behind the counter said. "Buy some fine fresh fish here!"

Suddenly we heard the sound of hooves, and a troop of men in uniforms galloped toward us, on shining black horses. People scurried off the path. Terror gripped me, and I ran with them. The troop passed by, shouting and waving.

I started back to the path. Livvy grabbed my arm. "I thought they were coming for us," she said. "Ben's right—we're way too exposed here."

"It's all right," I said. "Look—no one's paying us any attention."

Just then a crow flew overhead, cawing. Conversation faltered, and people looked up into the sky. Even the music seemed to fade.

We started to run. We ran through the stalls and booths and counters, the games and processions. I bumped into a table and overturned it, and I heard the sounds of glass breaking as I hurried on. I dodged what looked like a giant hedgehog, jumped over a narrow stream, then crashed through some low branches. Behind me I heard the others coming on, and I looked back for Livvy.

They had all reached the trees. We stopped at the same time, breathing heavily. I glanced around nervously for the crow, but I didn't see it. Still, I knew that didn't mean anything.

Now I noticed that we were surrounded by tall leafy trees; we'd gone farther than I'd thought into the woods. I couldn't see a path anywhere.

"Guys?" I said. "Do you know where we are?"

"We came in that way, I think," Maddie said.

"No, it was over there," Rose said. "Wasn't it?"

"Livvy?" I asked.

She shook her head. "I never saw this place," she said. "I was always fighting, or—or dancing." She seemed about to say something else, then shook her head again.

It had gotten darker in just the short time we'd been here. I looked up but the leaves seemed to shift, to move like hands, blocking the sun.

The sound of something crashing came from within the forest. I turned around, panicked. A man burst through the trees, brandishing an axe.

We started to run again. It was so dark now that we could barely see our way through the forest, and we had to slow down, to pick our way among the trees. I could hear the man coming after us, shouting something, but it sounded like gibberish.

Suddenly he stood in front of us, his axe slicing left then right through the air. "Look," I said. "Wait—we're not your enemy—"

He stepped closer. "Spinne am morgan," he said.

I looked at the others helplessly. And then, to my surprise, Ben said, "Bringt kummer und sorgen."

"Good!" he said. His voice boomed around us, and some animal scurried away in the distance. "Friends! Come, I'll take you to our meeting-place."

I could see him a little better now, through the gloom of the forest. He was tall and stocky, with long hair and long bushy eyebrows, a lumpy nose, and a beard down to his waist. He shouldered his axe and headed off under the trees.

We followed him. I walked next to Ben. "What the hell was that about?" I whispered.

"Shhh," Ben said. We dropped back, away from the woodsman, and he said, "Remember the writing on the fireplace? At the farmhouse?"

I nodded.

"I asked Professor Rothapfel about it. It's a saying, a proverb. 'A spider in the morning brings sorrow and worry. A spider at midday brings—'"

"But what does it mean? Why did he say it?"

"How should I know?"

"Well, *he* knows what it means. And he seems to think it makes you his best friend. You'd better be careful, not say anything stupid."

"Don't worry, I won't."

We continued on a long way. We went slowly, carefully, straining to see through the gloom. I expected to see an opening through the trees at any minute, to find ourselves back in the meadow, but the woodsman seemed to be taking us in a different direction.

Something rustled within the trees. The fox we'd seen stepped out, walking daintily, and headed toward the woodsman. "Where are you going this night?" the fox asked.

I wasn't even surprised. "To the meeting," the woodsman said.

"Ah," the fox said. "Follow me."

Its golden tail burned as if on fire. It went on ahead of us, lighting the way, and a short time later we came out from under the forest. A winding road stood in front of us, lined with houses.

I'd seen this road before, I realized. I'd gotten a glimpse of it at Lem's restaurant, before it had been blotted out by the smoke. And I'd seen the fox there, too; it had set the floor on fire with its tail. I felt uneasy now, wondering whose side the fox, the woodsman were on.

Small wide houses stood along the road, with thatched roofs and smoke puffing from their chimneys. We passed a couple of them, and then the woodsman knocked on a door.

The door opened. A sharp, skinny man peered out. He had fingers like twigs, I noticed. No, they *were* twigs, long and spindly, and bent in strange places.

"Spinne am morgan," the woodsman said.

"Bringt kummer und sorgen," the man said, waving us into the room. We were in a tavern. People were crowded inside, sitting at every table; a few sat on the bar and one even perched on a rafter. Some huge animal—a cow?—turned on a spit above the fireplace.

The fox went to curl up by the fire. Some people moved over to make room for us, but even so Ben and I and the woodsman had to stand against the back wall. The room smelled like smoke and old wool and garlic.

"Now's the time," a man standing at the front of the room said. "The time to strike against the queen, to destroy her once and for all. To end her wicked rule, and free ourselves from her tyranny."

Everyone around us rumbled "Aye."

"Are we ready, then?" the man said. "Once we set off there'll be no turning back."

"Aye!" everyone said, sounding louder this time.

The man spoke on, something about the road they would have to follow, the battle they'd fight. I had stopped listening, though, and was looking around me with amazement. A man with a stag's head sat at one of the tables, his legs crossed in front of him.

"She's here!" someone said suddenly, interrupting the speaker.

"Who?" he asked.

"Look! The sleeper, the dancer. She's here, in this room!"

A man was staring at Livvy, an expression of shock and astonishment on his face. The people around her pushed away.

"Who are you?" the leader asked. "Are you spies, sent from the queen?"

"Not spies," the woodsman shouted from the back. "They knew the password."

"But she fought with the queen!" someone said.

I tried to force my way through the crowd, to get near Livvy. "I did fight with her, yes, but I escaped," Livvy was saying. "She wanted to keep me for seven years, but I only stayed for a few months."

"You know what she's like, then," the leader said. "She held you captive, as she holds us captive. Are you ready to fight against her?"

Livvy sat silent for a moment. "Yes," she said.

Everyone cheered. A fiddler played a dance tune, and the fox barked from near the fireplace, strange high yips. People grabbed what looked like weapons from underneath the tables—old rusty swords, battered scythes, rakes with teeth missing—and we left the tavern.

It was morning already; faint streaks of light were spreading out across the sky. Ben came up next to me. "How are we going to fight against these people?" he asked. "We don't even have any weapons."

With everything going on around us, I hadn't really thought about what we'd do next. "Well, they know where the queen is," I said. "Let's just follow them, see when we get there."

We started walking. At first I was worried that it might be too much for Sylvie, but we went surprisingly slowly for a group bent on war. Then I saw some of the short fuzzy men among the crowd—including, I think, the one who had fixed Ben's car—and I realized that we were going at their pace.

There were some other strange folk there too—the stag, for one, and a huge man, a giant, and I saw an enormous bird, something like an ostrich, walking along with us, lifting its feet high with every step. A man was riding on its back.

We reached the end of the road and continued on. We walked through fields and meadows, up small hills covered in grass. Someone played a trumpet, and I heard the fiddle music again. People were talking, singing, eating. A man next to me handed me a pie, and I was so hungry I took a bite without wondering what it was. I tasted spicy meat, not bad, and I passed it on to Livvy.

We passed small towns along the way, and more people came out of their houses and joined us. We made a long straggling line, hundreds of people at least, with the small creatures hurrying after us at the rear. Then, around noon, we climbed a rise and came face to face with a line of soldiers spread out across a field.

Everything happened very fast after that. Without thinking about it I ran off to the side, away from the fighting, then looked around for the others. People fought with swords, with rakes and clubs. A soldier ran toward one of the short men, his sword out, and the man danced around him and kicked him in the ass. The stag lunged toward another man, his head down, and the fox dragged his tail along the ground, drawing a line of fire after him.

A woman in front of me lifted a sword far too big for her and waved it around a few times. Then she stumbled forward, sighed, gripped the sword harder and looked up. It was Marya.

I grabbed some rocks and climbed a tree. A man ran toward Marya, his sword raised. Even here, I thought, I couldn't escape her. What was she doing in this place?

"Marya!" I yelled. "Over here!"

She glanced around, saw me, and hurried over. The man with the sword followed her, and I threw a rock that hit him in the head.

"Hey!" he said. I threw another rock; it grazed his shoulder and he looked around.

"Up here!" I said to Marya. "Come on."

She tried climbing the tree while holding the sword, but she could barely lift it. "Leave it!" I said.

"I can't."

"Sure you can. Hurry up."

She dropped the sword and climbed up, then perched on the branch next to me. "How did you get here?" I asked.

"I followed you."

"You—followed me? Into the farmhouse, and up to the ballroom?"

"Well, I was—I was watching the farmhouse. I do that sometimes. And then you drove up, and after a while I saw the lights go on in a part of the house I thought was closed off. So I got into the house and climbed upstairs—"

I sighed. I really thought I'd gotten through to her, back when we'd talked about the doctor-patient relationship.

"I know I'm not supposed to," she said, quickly, before I could say anything. "But I was here before, in this place, and all I ever wanted to do was get back in. That's why I follow you—"

"Shhh," I said. I looked around for Livvy and the others, then dropped a rock on someone who had come too close to the tree. "Did you see Livvy anywhere?"

"No. Yeah, wait—she's over there."

I found Livvy in the midst of a group of people, struggling to get through. "Stay here," I said to Marya. "Don't go anywhere."

I slid down the tree without waiting for an answer. I picked up Marya's sword and ran toward Livvy, shouting her name.

Someone turned toward me and raised a sword. I lifted Marya's sword—God, it was heavy—and then brought it down, wondering what the hell I was doing. More by luck than anything else I managed to connect with the other sword, and the man wielding it ran away.

I worked my way through the crowd, yelling for Livvy. She pushed toward me, and I grabbed her hand and pulled her free.

We headed back, dodging small clashes and skirmishes all around us.

Marya, of course, hadn't listened to me and was standing at the foot of the tree. "Hello, Livvy," she said, as if making conversation at a party somewhere.

"What's she doing here?" Livvy asked.

"I don't know," I said, looking around for the others. "Oh, good—there's Rose."

As I watched, Rose took something out of her pocket and put it to her mouth. The whistle, which she'd carried around ever since Leeanne had given it to her. Suddenly I remembered Leeanne's story, what had happened when Walter had played the pipe, and I realized that she would only call more warriors, make the battle larger, maybe even give them permission to kidnap one of us.

I called out to her, but she didn't seem to hear me over the shouts and screams around us, the horses neighing, the weapons ringing out against each other. No noise came from the whistle, though, or maybe it was drowned out by the din all around us.

And no one came in response, new troops or otherwise. She tried again, but once again nothing happened. Then a group of people moved between us, pushing and shoving and hitting out with rakes and shovels, and when they passed I couldn't see her anymore.

"Hey! Will!" someone called.

It was Ben, running toward us. "Oh, hello, Ben," Marya said.

Ben didn't answer. The fighting headed in our direction. Ben and Livvy hurried up a tree, and Marya and I climbed another one, with me dragging Marya's sword behind us. We settled onto the branches, and I found myself looking into Marya's strange flat eyes once again.

I turned away, only to see the oddest sight yet. Someone beneath us had his sword out and seemed to be fighting with air, with nothing, jumping forward, striking out, jumping back. A thin line sliced through his shirt and he fell back, blood dripping down his sleeve.

The man moved forward cautiously, flailing around with his sword. I dropped a rock on his opponent, or at least where I guessed his opponent might be. I heard someone cry out, and the man with the sword slashed out in front of him. Someone shouted, and blood pattered to the ground. The man moved closer. Suddenly he screamed and clutched his stomach, then turned and ran.

I reached down carefully with Marya's sword. I hit something yielding, felt around a bit more, then caught something up on the point of the sword. A cloak—and just as I had guessed, the cloak's owner now lay exposed beneath us.

"Hey, a cloak of invisibility," Marya said. "Neat."

"Shhh," I said.

The two armies were hurrying off the field now, as if they'd made some agreement while we weren't watching. Marya and Ben and Livvy climbed down from the trees, but I stayed up for a while and looked around for the others.

"Did you see anyone else?" Livvy asked when I'd joined them.

"No," I said.

"Where are they?" she said, turning around, distracted. "Oh, God—you don't think they were captured, do you? Taken away, and—and—"

"No," I said, trying to sound certain. "Look, they know we're going to the castle—they'll find us there."

"Is that where we're going?" Marya asked. "The castle?"

The familiar feeling of exasperation rose within me. "You knew about this place—is that what you said?" I asked. "How did you know?"

"I came here before," she said. "I was just walking down Telegraph, and then suddenly I was here. And I walked around for hours, and I saw the talking horses, and the flowers that turned into people, and the dances... And then I spent the rest of my life, all my life, trying to get back."

Like Hans, I thought, though she'd been luckier than Hans, she'd actually made it into the other realm. Or maybe she hadn't been all that lucky, because the other realm had driven her crazy too. "But how did you know to follow me?"

"We can recognize each other, you know, recognize the glamour. I knew you'd been here the moment I saw you."

Was that true? Had I seen something in her, was that why I had treated her for so long, against my better judgment?

"So what do we do now?" she asked. "Are we going to the castle?"

The sun was setting, the land in front of us growing dark. We needed to eat something, and sleep, and catch up with the others. And God—there was Nick to worry about. How had I forgotten him?

"What about Nick?" Livvy said—she'd obviously had the same thought.

"How long can we leave him alone in the farmhouse?"

"I don't know," I said. I shook my head. "He'll be okay—we just have to find him here, in this realm, and wake him up. We have to get to the castle. Not now, though. Let's eat dinner first, and find a place to sleep."

The rocks and hillocks on the field cast long shadows in front of us, and for a moment they looked like soldiers, still lying where they'd fallen. But there was no one on the field, everyone had gone. Even the man I'd uncovered, the one who had worn the invisibility cloak, was no longer at the base of the tree. Had someone come and carried him away?

Like in Leeanne's story, I thought. They don't die, or not very often. How would their wars work, then? I had a vague idea about them; I tried to grasp it but it slipped away as quickly as it had come.

18

I PICKED UP MARYA'S SWORD and shouldered it gingerly, trying to keep the sharp edge away from my neck. It was heavy as hell. "Where did you get this?" I asked her.

"I bought it," she said. "From someone on Telegraph. I knew I'd need it when I got here. Can I have it back now?"

It figured, I thought. She was like one of those people who pack four suitcases for a simple overnight stay. And apparently no one in Berkeley had stopped her from carrying such a dangerous-looking weapon; no doubt they had seen stranger sights.

I handed her the sword. She took it, staggering a little, then shouldered it the way I had done.

We decided to head back to the last town we'd seen. Nobody said anything as we went, each of us thinking our own thoughts. I was worrying about Rose and Maddie and Sylvie, and of course wondering about Nick, and where the castle might be, and what we would do when we got there. I had a cloak of invisibility, though, one of the treasures the queen had offered me—that had to count for something.

After a while we saw the lights of the town up ahead. We walked faster now, more cheerful, and found a tavern along the main road. It was dark inside, candles in sconces dripping greasy wax along the walls, but from what I could see it was less crowded than the last one.

"Wait a minute," Livvy said. "How are we going to pay for anything?"

Marya walked straight up to the bar. Behind it stood a large woman with a bird's head—and I'd seen so many strange sights by then I only gave her a single extra look, to make sure I'd seen what I thought I'd seen. She wore a voluminous white apron, and had what looked like a nightcap on her head.

"Here," Marya said, taking money from her pocket and scattering it on the counter. "We're from a long way away, and this is all the money we have. Can we buy some dinner?"

The coins gleamed in the candlelight from behind the bar. The woman brushed aside the dollar bills, then took one of the quarters and bit down on it with her beak. "Ah, very good," she said, sweeping all of Marya's change into her hand and dropping it into her apron pocket. "What would you like to eat?"

We grinned. "Whatever it is that smells so good," Livvy said. "Some kind of stew?"

The food was terrific. Marya talked nonstop during dinner: "Did you see that woman, with the bird's head? And those people on the battlefield, the giant, and there was this guy with a bird's nest in his hair, with birds inside it... It's so great, just being here, isn't it?" None of the rest of us said anything, but she didn't seem to mind.

After dinner we asked for rooms for the night. The woman led us upstairs and showed us into a room with two narrow beds. Livvy and Marya took one and Ben and I the other—not the sleeping partner I would have chosen, unfortunately, but there was no other way to do it.

I awoke rested and well fed, and feeling more optimistic than I had the day before. We came downstairs, and I asked the tavern-keeper how to get to the castle.

"The castle?" she said. Her eyes changed quickly, like a chemical reaction, from cheerful to suspicious. "Why would you want to go to there?"

"We—we have business with the queen," I said, stammering.

"And what business would that be?"

"Spinne am morgan," Ben said, tentatively, as if he wasn't sure it would work.

"Ah. Of course. But I'm afraid I couldn't tell you where the castle is. I've lived my life in this town, never wanted to leave it."

Ben thanked her and we left, then started along the main road out of town. I looked around for someone who could give us directions, but it was strangely deserted.

"Man, that queen's really unpopular," Ben said. "No one likes her."

"Someone has to," I said. "You saw all those soldiers yesterday." And there it was again, the thought that had come to me the night before—but it slipped away before I could catch it.

"Maybe that's why she needs Livvy, and, and Nick," he said. "They prop up her kingdom somehow."

"How, though?"

He shrugged. "I don't know."

We reached the outskirts of the town and came to a crossroad, with paths leading off to the left and right; we hadn't seen it last night in the dark. "Okay, now what?" I asked.

"We could wait here until someone comes along," Ben said.

"Yeah, but how long would that take? And how would we know we could trust them?"

"The password—"

"Maybe." I looked around. "Did you and Rothapfel read fairy tales in that group of his?"

"Yeah, sure. Why?"

I picked up a feather from the ground, lifted it to my mouth, and blew. It fluttered down and came to rest on the left-hand path.

"That way," I said.

"Are you sure?" Livvy said.

"That's the way they do it in fairy tales."

"Yeah, but—but what if you're wrong? We'd have to backtrack, and we've already been here over a day, and—and what about Nick?"

"Can you think of anything else?"

She shook her head. It had been an unfair question, I knew. She'd stayed away from those stories even after she'd woken up, had never even read any to Nick.

"I've read fairy tales," Marya said. "I think Will's right."

It was amazing, I thought, how well Marya fit into this place. Of course she had been here before; she might even know more about this realm than I did.

We turned left and continued walking. We came to another crossroad, and then a fork in the road, and each time I picked up a feather and blew on it to show me which way to go. After a while we found ourselves back in the woods. Or maybe this was a different forest—I couldn't tell.

Hills appeared on either side of us, small humps at first and then larger. Then we passed a bizarre sight—a brass keyhole in the side of the hill, flat against the rock.

I stopped. "Hey," I said to Ben and Livvy. "Look at this," I said.

"So?" Ben said.

He didn't know, I realized. I reached into my pocket and took out the key Nell had given me. It was attached to my keychain; after I'd found it again I hadn't wanted to let it out of my sight. "Livvy's cousin's wife gave me this," I said. "She was from here, from this realm."

"Hey," Ben said. "Cool."

I raised it toward the hole in the rock. "Wait," Livvy said. "Don't open it."

"Why not?" I asked. "Nell said the key would help us."

"Well, but how do you know she was telling the truth?"

"Because she looked afraid, remember? Like she was giving away the queen's secrets. And you saw that battle, back there—that's what she was talking about. The two sides fighting."

"Yeah, and the last time we saw Nell we nearly got cooked in a fire. And she and Lem are still missing—we don't know what happened to them."

"Maybe they're in here," I said, looking at the hillside. "Maybe we can rescue them."

Livvy shook her head. "I don't trust her," she said. "I don't trust any of them."

I wasn't listening, though. I was caught up in my own story; I felt an almost physical urge to open that lock, like an itch that needed scratching. Bluebeard's wives had probably felt something similar.

I put the key in the lock and turned it.

A part of the hillside swung open, and I stepped inside. Someone called out behind me, but I ignored them and kept going.

I was in a room carved out of the mountainside. A huge man, a giant, sat on a crude wooden stool, smoking a pipe. He took a deep hit off the pipe and blew the smoke toward me.

Everything wobbled and lost definition. I tried to leave the cave, but I had lost my sense of where the entrance was. A glamour, I thought. Glamour, grammar, grimmer.

I staggered outside, but Ben and Livvy were gone.

For a while I just ran around looking for them, frantic with worry, remembering Livvy's fear of this place, of the queen. When I finally came back to myself I was in the middle of the forest. Trees surrounded me, their leaves closing in on me, blocking my view.

I picked up a feather and blew on it, and worked my way back to the path. I went on this way until it got too dark to see, and then I made myself a bed of leaves and lay down.

I couldn't sleep, though. The forest was full of noises: small animals scuttling past, a hoot that might have been an owl, a loud mournful cry. And I was worried about Nick, and about Livvy, how she was getting along and if she was safe, and whether we would find each other at the castle. I woke at dawn, still tired, and continued along the path.

Around noon I came to a river, with a ferryman waiting on the bank. "Hello," I said. "I know you, don't I?"

"I don't know," he said. "I take so many people across this river."

I remembered now, though. I'd tried to put the memory behind me, to forget everything about it. "You used to carry me, when I worked for Those People," I said. "You took me to all those different houses."

"Yes, that's right—I remember you now."

I'd only seen him from the back before, a silent, black-cloaked figure, vaguely menacing. Now I saw how ordinary he looked, his face friendly and open.

I reached into my pocket for some money, but he held up his hand. "I must carry the people who cross here without pay."

"Why?" I asked.

"I don't know. If you find out, please tell me."

I'd blundered into another story, it seemed, like the ones I'd seen working for Those People. "All right," I said, though I was sure I'd never learn the answer. He poled me across the river, and I thanked him and jumped out when we reached the other bank.

A short time later I came to a wide green lawn. A castle loomed up at the end of it, but there was no one else in sight. I walked across the lawn to see the castle better, careful not to get too close.

I'd reached the castle before everyone else, then. Or maybe they weren't coming, maybe something had happened to them.

I turned around, trying not to worry, and saw two women heading toward me. Livvy? I started to run. They were both shorter than Livvy, though, and as I got closer I saw that one of them was Rose.

"Will!" she said.

We hugged each other. "What happened to you?" I asked. "Where is everyone?"

"Oh, you'll never believe it. No, wait, I bet you will—you've been here before, haven't you?" She turned to the other woman, who, I saw now, looked a bit like her. "This is Fiona."

The woman in Leeanne's story. But she looked as young as Rose, or younger, even though she'd lived during Prohibition. Whatever had happened to her in this realm, she hadn't aged.

What did you say to your wife's—what? Great-aunt? I settled on "Hello" and a polite nod.

"Where is everyone else?" Rose asked. "Where's Livvy?"

"I don't know," I said. I told her how I had stupidly used the key, what had happened inside the hill. "What about Maddie and Sylvie?" I asked. "They were with you, last I saw. You were blowing into that pipe."

"The pipe, right. I should just tell it to you straight through, I guess. The pipe didn't work, not then. But after I put it away this dog ran up to me and started barking. And you know who it was? It was Storm, that dog I found the night it was raining so hard, the one with the hurt paw. And she was okay, the paw was fine. I got down and scratched her all over, and I asked her how she was, where she'd been.

"She started skipping around, making these happy whimpering noises. I thought she was trying to tell me something, but I didn't know what it was. And then Sylvie—she came out with one of those things she's always saying, that you don't understand until later. 'She looks like you, doesn't she?' Sylvie said.

"And you know, she sort of did. She was some kind of golden retriever, with hair and eyes the same color as mine. And I had this idea—well, I looked like Fiona, Leeanne had said, and the dog looked like me... And I thought about all the fairy tales I'd read, and I bent over and kissed her, kissed the dog.

"And I was right, she changed. She changed into Fiona."

I looked at the other woman, startled, forced into reassessing her. She wore a tweed skirt and an old polo coat, the clothes Leeanne had said she'd had on when she went bootlegging. "So you were—they'd turned you into a dog?" I asked her.

She nodded. "Walter's pipe—it let them come into our world, and take me away. They changed me into a dog, and I went and fought with them—"

"Fought?"

"In their wars," she said. "Like that battle you saw. Sometimes they can go into your world and fight there, during the great storms. The Wild Hunt, they call that. And I was wounded that one time, and they didn't know what to do—they don't age, you know, or die—and so they left me at the farmhouse. That's a place they know in your world, somewhere they can go when they're far from home. They were hoping someone would take care of me. And then when I was well they came back, and took me away again."

"And you've been a dog, for all this time—"

"What year is it?"

"It's 1986." I thought. "Sixty years."

"It wasn't that terrible, you know. I was happy, most of the time. You know what dogs are like. They fought, and I went with them." She shook herself; she looked like a dog shaking off water. "I am glad to be back, though. What happened to..."

She hesitated, and I realized that she couldn't remember their names. "Henry and Peter died last year," I said. "Henry had a son, Hilbert..."

She shook her head.

"Leeanne," Rose said. "She misses you, but she seems okay. She's with a woman named Sally now."

"Is she happy?"

"I think so," Rose said.

"That's good," Fiona said—but she looked sad, the first time I'd seen that. "How did you get here?"

I told her about Nick, then realized I had to start much further back, when Livvy had fallen asleep. When I got to the part where I rescued Livvy she looked amazed.

"I had no idea," she said. "No idea at all. I could have brought my sister

Lettice back, or tried to. But the family told us over and over not to meddle." She stopped. "Is she still alive? Lettice?"

"Yeah," Rose said.

"So where are Maddie and Sylvie?" I asked Rose. "You still haven't told me."

"Just a minute—I'll get to it." Rose thought a moment and went on. "So then we realized we were still in the middle of the battle, and we all ran off to the side. But we couldn't see you anywhere, or Livvy or Ben."

"We were up hiding in the trees then, I think."

"Anyway, we talked about going to the castle and meeting you there," Rose said, "and Fiona said she could show us the way. So we set off down the road, and then we heard this noise at our feet, something like a rusty spring. And we looked down and saw a frog.

"Maddie picked it up and said, 'Even I know what to do here,' and she put it to her mouth like she was going to kiss it. But Fiona said, right away, 'No—for God's sake, don't kiss him! Do you want to marry him?'

"Maddie looked shocked, like she hadn't even thought of that, and she dropped her hand quickly, though she was still holding the frog. And then the frog said, 'Ah, but I can help you.'

"Maddie didn't even look surprised. None of us were, at that point. All she said was 'How?'

"The frog said, 'I know four secrets, but I tell only three.'

"Maddie said, 'What are they?'

"The frog said, 'Put me back in the well and I'll tell you.'

"We all looked around. 'What well?' Maddie said.

"'Keep going,' the frog said. 'It's at the side of the road.'

"So we kept walking, and we came to a well. Maddie sat down on this stone wall around it, still holding the frog. 'Put me inside,' the frog said. 'I need to get back to the water.'

"But Maddie said, 'How will you tell us your secrets, then?'

"The frog seemed to think about this for a while, and then he said, 'All right. Quickly though. The first is that Ben knew about the family's bargain before he met you. That's why he courted you, because he wanted your luck for himself. But then he found a liking for you as well.'

"Maddie didn't seem to hear that last part, though. 'I knew it!' she said.

'I knew there was something wrong with him, all the time we went out together. How did he know? No, don't tell me—I want to know your secrets instead. What's the second one?"

"'I know how to free Fiona, to take her back to her own world,' the frog said. 'It's very simple. She just stands at the borders of this country and says "Rick rack ruck."'"

"It was that easy," Fiona said, interrupting. "After all these years... I could hardly believe it. Sorry," she said to Rose. "Go on with your story."

"So then Maddie said, 'What about the third secret?'" Rose said.

"'It's about Walter's pipe,' the frog said. 'It only works on the water. That's why he could use it back then, because he was out on a boat.'

"'All right,' Maddie said. 'And the fourth?'

"'I told you,' the frog said. 'I tell only three.'

"'And what if I don't put you back in the well?'

"The frog jerked in Maddie's hand, trying to jump away, but she held onto him tightly. 'That isn't fair,' he said. 'I kept my part of the bargain, I told you everything I said I would. Let me go!'

"'Why should I?' Maddie said 'You and all the people in this place—you've tricked us for generations, for centuries. Well, maybe we can trick you too. And who says it's fair to make someone sleep for seven years?'

"'There's nothing unfair about it. Your family entered into that bargain freely, all those years ago—'

"Well, I'd been standing there, thinking about that third secret, what the frog had said about Walter's pipe. And all I wanted to do was to use it, to see what would happen. I really can't explain it, not now. It was like I was part of this story, part of all those hundreds of fairy tales. Maddie and Livvy never read them, but I did. Once I had the pipe I knew I had to use it."

"I know what you mean," I said. "I felt the same way with the key. It's curiosity, that's how they get us. We want to see how the story ends."

"Yeah, and then we do something really stupid," Rose said. "So I grabbed the frog out of Maddie's hand, and I jumped in the well."

"You—jumped—" I said.

"Yeah. But it was okay—I could breathe in the water. Somehow I knew I'd be able to. I floated down through the water, and then I broke through, and I came to this town lying underneath. It looked like all those other towns we'd seen, with winding roads and thatched cottages.

"I was still holding the frog, and I let him go. He hopped a few steps down the road, and then he came back and puffed up and down a bit. 'Come along,' he said. 'As a reward for letting me go I'll take you to Mother Holle.'

"He jumped away down the road, and I went after him. He stopped on the doorstep of one of the houses and puffed up and down again, impatiently. So I knocked on the door and this woman answered, wiping her hands on her apron.

"She looked at the frog and said, 'Ah, did you bring my helper?' The frog nodded, and she said, 'Very good. Come in, come in.'

"I went inside. And then something weird happened, even weirder, I mean. For a minute, just as I stood there, the room looked huge, as big as the sky. And Mother Holle looked enormous too, like a god or a giant. And then I blinked, and she shrank down to what she'd been before, someone even shorter than me, with white hair and half-moon glasses.

"'Here,' she said, giving me a couple of blankets. 'I need these given a good shaking.'

"I took one and shook it, hard, and feathers flew out. I did this a few times, and somehow I realized that while I was cleaning these blankets I was also, in some way, shaking out snow to fall on the world below—or above, I couldn't work it out. And I saw that Mother Holle was baking these sugar cakes, but at the same time she was making moons, crescent shapes and half-moons and circles, moving trays from the table to the oven and back again.

"I finished the pile of blankets and I tried to look around, but Mother Holle came up to me and handed me a broom. 'Here—this room needs to be swept,' she said. 'It's never done, is it?' She smiled at me, like we were old friends working together.

"I took the broom and started to sweep. I swept out into the middle of the room, and I saw this tree, growing up and out through the roof—I don't know how, but I hadn't noticed it before. I swept around it and reached the other wall, where there was a fire burning in a fireplace.

"'See that the fire doesn't go out, dear,' Mother Holle said.

"I put a log on the fire and then went back to sweeping. And I realized that I was sweeping leaves, that I was making leaves blow out over forests somewhere in the real world.

"I worked all day, and kept on when it started getting dark. Somehow every time I thought about leaving Mother Holle would give me something else to do. I started thinking about all those girls in all those fairy tales I'd read, and I remembered how they'd been rewarded with showers of gold. But I didn't want a shower of gold—I just wanted to get back to my family, to go home.

"But for some reason I kept on working. Once I noticed a loom in one corner, but when I stopped to look at the fabric I felt myself getting dizzy, falling into it, like I was looking at the design of the universe.

"Then finally I saw some light through the windows, and I realized it was morning. I forced myself to go to Mother Holle, to tell her I had to leave, had to find my family.

"'But our work here never ends, my dear,' she said. 'Who will set the stars out every night, and wake the sun from his sleep, and tell the leaves to change color? Who shows the rivers where to go, and shakes the snow out over the world?'

"'Well, who did it before I got here?' I asked.

"'It is hard to find a good apprentice, that's true,' she said.

"I think it was that word apprentice that did it. Did she mean she wanted me to take over from her, to work there forever?

"'But I have to go back,' I said. I was starting to panic. 'I—I have a job, a house, back in the real world. And what about my mother, my sisters?'

"'Oh, we'll find work for them as well, don't you worry,' she said.

"I felt suffocated, frantic. If I didn't get out of that cottage I knew I'd scream. I pushed past her and ran to the door.

"The door was locked, though. I pulled on it, yelling 'Let me out!'

"'Just help me wash these pots and pans,' Mother Holle said.

"I took the whistle out of my pocket and blew on it. 'No, stop!' she said. 'You naughty girl! What are you doing?'

"And then, to my relief, the door opened from the outside. Six or seven men pushed their way into the cottage, and other men jumped through the windows and landed on the floor. They ran toward Mother Holle, backing her into a corner, and drew their swords and pointed them at her neck.

"'Let her go,' one of them said.

"'Please, the winds!' Mother Holle said. 'They have to be set free now—I don't have a moment to waste. Let me get my broom!'

"'Release her, and you can have all the brooms you want,' another man said. They were the warriors in Leeanne's story, I realized, tall and thin, with silver eyes and leather boots and clothing.

"The swords came closer. 'All right,' Mother Holle said. 'She can go.'

"The men dropped back. I grinned at her, feeling smug. I'd won, after all, and she'd lost.

"And then the men raised their swords and moved around me, like they were dancing. Their swords touched and backed away, leaving these lines in the air, lines like fire.

"And of course I knew what was happening. They were doing the same thing they'd done in Leeanne's story, making this pattern around me, building a cage. And I'd brought them here, I'd summoned them with the whistle, just like Walter had. I couldn't believe I'd been so stupid.

"The men came closer and then went back, closer and back, and the patterns grew more complex—and I couldn't look away, it was like I was under a spell. And somewhere, a long way away, I wanted to scream, but I couldn't make a sound.

"Then I heard someone say 'Stop.' I thought it was Mother Holle at first, but it hadn't sounded like her.

"The men stopped, and I looked out through the lines of fire, the bars of my cage. Fiona was standing there.

"'Let her go,' Fiona said.

"The men stared at her. 'It's the Lady Fiona,' one of them said. 'How did you escape the shape we made for you?'

"'I learned how to do a great many things,' Fiona said. 'I know how to leave this place, and return to the world I came from. If you release her, though, I won't go back. I'll stay here with you.'

"She was sacrificing herself," Rose said, looking at Fiona now. "She was going to stay here, exchange herself for me. I wanted to scream at her, to tell her not to do it, but I couldn't move, couldn't speak. A part of it was the spell, holding me, but another part—" She broke off and looked at Fiona again. "Well, it was cowardice. I wanted to go back, to do my work...

"But I couldn't live with myself if I left her trapped down here. 'No,' I said to her, finally managing to speak. 'No, don't do it. You should go back, and—and see the family—'"

"But I knew everyone in the family had to be much older now, older or—or dead," Fiona said now. "I wanted to see Leeanne, of course I did, but I knew I wasn't part of her life any longer, even before you told me about her."

"She kept saying that," Rose said. "She wouldn't listen. She kept telling them to take her and let me go. And meanwhile the men were laughing, and one of them said, 'That family was ever one for bargains. What do you say, my brothers? Should we let this one go, and keep Lady Fiona?'

"Another one shook his head. 'Lady Fiona won't be bound to us, if she stays here,' he said. 'She knows how to free herself from the bonds we placed upon her. She'll be able to go where she wants, visit who she pleases... No, I say let's take this one, the new one, and make her into whatever shape we like.'"

Rose stumbled over this part, thinking about the fate they had planned for her. Fiona took up the story.

"So I said to them, 'You can't do that,'" Fiona said. "'I taught her everything I know.' And I looked at her, warning her not to open her mouth—she's a terrible liar, isn't she?"

Rose laughed. "I really am. But I didn't say anything, didn't let on that I know nothing at all about this place. And finally one of the men said to her, 'Your family has caused us a great deal of trouble, over the years. Very well, we'll take your bargain. We'll toss this one back, and keep you here. And you for your part must agree never to leave.'

"Fiona nodded. The men raised their swords and sliced downward, and the ropes around me fell apart. And Fiona took my hand, and we ran through the door.

"Somehow we found our way back to the road, even though we'd been under water before. We slowed down, and Fiona said, 'We don't have to run, not really. A bargain is binding among them.'

"I asked her again why she'd traded her life for mine, how she could do something like that. And she said—"

"I said that I wouldn't know her world at all," Fiona said. "There were so many new things, back in my time—I can only imagine what life is like for you now. You probably have—I don't know—flying cars, or pills for food."

"But it's not like that," Rose said. "It's different, but you could learn it, learn how to—to be in the world."

"But I really don't want to go back," Fiona said. She must have seen my look of disbelief, mine and Rose's, because she hurried on. "It's—well, it's different here, not like anything I knew back then. Strange, exciting, terrifying... And now that I'm no longer bound to them, I can go anywhere I want." She turned to Rose. "I have you to thank for that, after all."

We stood awhile, thinking about Rose's story. "That frog..." I said finally.

"What about him?" Fiona asked.

"Well, he tricked Rose, didn't he? He said he'd take her to Mother Holle, and all the time he knew she'd put her to work, make her her slave."

"They do trick you, around here. They make bargains, but they'll try to get out of them, if they can. Some of them will help you, though."

"But how do you know the difference?" Rose asked, her voice rising in frustration. "I read a fairy tale—"

"That's right—you said you read them," Fiona said. "We were never allowed to."

"We weren't either," Rose said. "I read them anyway, but I don't get them. There was one about a boy who helped some people, and fought against some others, and in the end he got to marry the king's daughter. So how did he know? What are the rules?"

Fiona laughed. "There are no rules, not really. You just have to trust yourself."

"But I did. I trusted the frog... Oh. I followed him because I wanted to try the pipe, and because I like animals. Not a very good reason, was it?"

"No."

I thought of another question. "How did you find Rose?" I asked.

"I should have come sooner, I know," Fiona said. "We waited for her by the well—her mother and sister thought she had drowned, but I told them that she hadn't, that things work differently here. And then I remembered that she had the whistle, and I realized that if she used it she would call those people, the soldiers, and they would take her just as they'd taken me. So I told them how to get to the castle, and then I jumped in."

"You told them—" Rose said. "Oh, God."

"Why? What's wrong?"

Rose tried to laugh. "Nothing. Nothing, really. It's just that Sylvie has the worst sense of direction in the world. God, I hope they make it."

19

I LOOKED OUT at the road then and saw Maddie and Sylvie heading toward us. I ran to meet them, and we spent a while telling each other our stories—but they had had a pretty uneventful journey, and hadn't seen Livvy. I glanced at the road again, frowning. Where was she? Where was Ben, for that matter?

Just as I was wondering, though, I saw Livvy coming up the road. I hurried toward her, too worried to even say hello. "Where were you?" I asked.

"Oh, God," she said. She looked back down the road, as if afraid someone was following her. "You'll never believe it."

"That's what Rose said. And I'd believe anything at this point."

"Okay, then. Well, that—that giant, or whatever he was, when he blew his smoke I just wandered away, not really thinking about anything. And when I came back to myself I realized I'd lost you, that I was on this much smaller path, winding along a creek. I'd never seen any of it before.

"I looked around, away from the creek, and I saw this cottage underneath the trees. There was some laundry hanging from a rope, and a cow eating grass nearby. And I saw smoke coming from the chimney, so I knew that someone was home, that I could ask directions, but—well, I was afraid to.

"No, not afraid, terrified. I was all by myself, without you or anyone. I thought the queen would come and get me any minute, take me back to the castle, force me to dance, and to fight..."

I wanted to understand her fear, but I couldn't; I hadn't had her experiences. All I felt was a sense of sadness, and an anger that I hadn't been there to help her.

"Anyway," she said. "These people came out from behind the laundry, a short man and an even shorter woman, and I recognized them. It was Uncle Lem, and Nell. This was where they'd ended up, I realized, after the fire at the restaurant.

"I'd just finished telling you I didn't trust them, but I was so glad to see a familiar face that I ran toward them and yelled out their names. And they recognized me too, thank God, and Lem said, 'Livvy! What are you doing here?'

"'We're looking for Nick,' I said.

"Lem seemed confused, and I realized they had no idea who Nick was, that he'd been born after they'd left. 'My son,' I said. 'Mine and Will's. He fell asleep—they started taking boys too, not just girls.'

"'Ah,' Nell said. I'd forgotten what a weird voice she had, that strange velvety sound. 'And now you can help us fight the queen.'

"Now I remembered how much I distrusted her. I told her how you'd used the key she gave you, and what had happened when you opened the door in the hillside. I said she'd tricked us, and why should we listen to anything she said?

"She looked surprised. 'A giant, you say?' she said. 'But I thought—I'd been told there was an army inside that hill. An army that would come to your aid.'

"I didn't say anything. I didn't believe her, but it didn't seem polite to say so in front of Lem. And just then Lem said, 'Come in, come in—tell us about your journey.'

"He put his arm around me and took me inside the cottage. His front room was full of furniture, a long table and a bunch of chairs—wooden and stuffed, and benches and rocking chairs. It looked light and airy, with this wooden floor and long windows high up under the eaves. There was a fire in the fireplace—that was the smoke I'd seen before.

"'Are you hungry?' Lem asked me.

"I realized that I was. We sat down at the table, and Nell headed out into another room. 'How long have you been here?' I asked.

"'Oh, I don't know,' Lem said. 'Since that fire, I think, at the restaurant.'

"There was something wrong with this, but it took me a while to figure it out. 'But didn't Nell say it was dangerous for her here? That they'd kill her, if they found out she was giving away their secrets?'

"'Did she?' Lem said. 'I don't remember.'

"Nell came through the door then, with a platter of food—bread and butter and cheese, apples and beer. She set it on the table, and I started eating. The food was delicious, amazing—the apples were fresh, and the bread was hot and soft, like she'd just made it.

"When I stopped feeling so hungry I asked Lem if he wanted to come back to our world, back to his restaurant.

"'I did once,' he said. 'Not anymore. It's like a circus here, or—or the most exciting fireworks display you ever saw. Something new every day. And of course Nell's been a great help.'

"Nell sat down next to him and took his hand. 'And I can be a help to you as well,' she said to me. 'I know all the queen's weaknesses.'

"I wanted to hear what she said, but just then I realized how tired I was. 'I'm sorry,' I said. 'It's been a long day. Can I stay here for the night?'

"'Of course,' Lem said.

"It had gotten darker while we'd been eating. Lem lit a candle from the fire, and they led me up a staircase and along a corridor. Nell showed me into my room, and I thanked them and fell into the bed.

"It's funny, you know, how much that house looked like the farmhouse in Napa, and Hilbert's house in Oakland. And our house too—it's like everyone in our family ends up re-creating the same place. I tried to think about that some more, but then I fell asleep.

"I woke up in the middle of the night. I think my heart woke me up—it was pounding hard, even before I remembered where I was, it was like my body understood where I was better than my brain. I lay there worrying, wondering what would happen if I never found you, if I had to stay here forever, like Lem and Nell. And I wondered if Lem really liked it here, or if he was under a spell, if Nell had done something...

"Whatever it was, there was something wrong here. I thought about getting up and going through the house, but it was completely dark, and the idea terrified me." Livvy looked at me. "I thought that you'd want to know Nell's secrets."

"Hell, no," I said. "I'd've wanted you to stay safe in bed. Really, I'd've wanted you a hundred miles from that house."

She smiled. "Well, I got up anyway," she said.

That surprised me. I almost said something, that I wouldn't have thought she'd be that brave, but fortunately I stopped myself at the last minute. She was a lot like Nick, I realized, pretending to have courage when she needed to.

"I'd blown out the candle, though, and I had to feel around for it on the nightstand," she said. "I was thinking I'd do this one step at a time, that I could go back whenever I wanted. That's what I told myself, anyway.

"So I picked up the candle and got dressed in the dark, and tried to find my way to the door. Then I ran my hand along the wall until I came to the staircase. From the top of the stairs I could see the fire, still burning in the fireplace, and I went down and lit my candle.

"It was cold in that house, cold and very quiet. I went from room to room, jumping back every time the candle flared and the shadows got bigger. Downstairs was the room with the long table and then a kitchen, a pantry, and another small room that looked like somewhere Nell did her sewing.

"I went back upstairs. The door to the first room I came to was closed, and I pushed it open carefully. And then this loud groan came from inside and I jerked away, nearly dropping my candle.

"I stood there for a long time, but nothing else happened. Finally I looked inside—and saw Lem and Nell, sleeping together in a bed. Lem groaned again and rolled over, and I moved back quickly, hoping I hadn't woken him up. I closed the door as slowly as I could, shivering every time I heard the hinges squeaking.

"Next down the hall was my room, and then another door. This one didn't open, though I tugged on it as hard as I could.

"Finally I saw a keyhole underneath the latch. Don't open the locked door—wasn't that in a fairy tale? I thought it was, that Rose had said something like that once. Maybe it would be better to leave it alone. On the other hand, if they were hiding something it would have to be here.

"Where was the key, though? The idea of going back through the house and searching for it made me shiver all over. I took a deep breath and went back to the stairs.

"I didn't find it in the sewing room, which was my first guess. It wasn't in the kitchen either, and that left only the front room. Or Lem and Nell's bedroom, but there was no way I was going in there.

"I made my way back to the front room and looked around. Now I saw some stuff on the mantelpiece—I think I'd been too hungry to notice it before. A vase and some coins, a pipe and a bag of tobacco, pottery figurines of a fiddler and a goose—and a ring with a key.

"I grabbed it and ran upstairs and along the corridor, then stopped in front of the locked door. I reached out with the key, but my hands were shaking so much I couldn't use it.

"I took another deep breath. This was Lem's house, after all, someone I'd known all my life. I wasn't going to let myself be frightened. I put the key in the keyhole and turned it.

"This loud boom echoed through the house, and the candle flickered and nearly went out. I shrank back, terrified. Then I stood up straight, opened the door, and went through it.

"All I saw were two circles, shining in the darkness. They came closer—and I realized it was the queen's glasses, reflecting the candlelight. I dropped the candle and ran outside, then slammed the door, hard, and locked it.

"And you know what? I didn't feel scared at all. I felt great. It was Bluebeard's wife who wanted to get inside that locked room, right? But the inside wasn't important—that was her mistake. What was important was the outside, everything that wasn't the room. I'd rejected fear, I'd locked it inside where it couldn't get at me.

"I ran back down the stairs and outside the house. I looked up at the stars, I felt the wind on my hair. The stars seemed amazingly bright, and the air smelled delicious.

"Then someone called out behind me. 'Livvy, wait!'

"I didn't want to stop. The voice shouted again—it was Uncle Lem. 'Don't go—I have something to tell you.'

"I ran under the trees. 'What?' I said.

"'You'll need help at the castle,' Lem said. 'Let me come with you.'

"'No way,' I said. 'I saw the queen in your house.'

"'Whatever happened—whatever you saw in our house—that was Nell's doing,' he said. 'I didn't mean to trick you, I promise you. I wanted to help.'

"'But you're married to her,' I said. 'You know what she does.'

"I heard Lem sigh. 'I do, it's true. I can't help it—I love her.'

"'She put a glamour on you.'

"'Maybe. But I still want to come along. I want to help.'

"'I'm sorry—I don't trust you.'

"Lem sighed again. 'All right,' he said. 'Let me tell you something, then, give you a piece of advice.'

"'What?'

"'I know how to free Nick.'

"'What? How?'

"'He wears a shackle around his arm, just like the one you had,' Lem said. 'Take the shackle off, and he'll go free.'

"You know, I'd forgotten about that shackle. For a moment I felt this horrible weight on my arm, just thinking about it.

"I didn't know if he was telling the truth, but I couldn't stop to think about it. I just thanked him and ran away from the cottage. The sun was starting to rise then, and I found the path near the creek and followed it. And when I came to a fork in the road I picked up a feather and blew on it, and after a while I came here."

For a while all of us just stood looking at each other, marveling that we'd made it so far. "Okay," Maddie said. "What do we do now?"

"Well, we have to go in there," Livvy said, indicating the castle.

"Are you sure?" Maddie said. I could hear the concern in her voice, but Livvy nodded.

"Shouldn't we wait for Ben, though?" I asked.

"Ben!" Maddie said. "He was lying to us all this time, the frog said so."

"But what if he's in danger? If he was kidnapped, like Rose?"

"Oh, who cares?"

I hesitated. I was anxious to get into the castle, to confront the queen. But at the same time I was worried about Ben—and now that I thought about it, I didn't see Marya either. She annoyed the hell out of me, but I did have some responsibility for her, as her therapist.

"I can stay here and watch for your friend," Fiona said. "I'll tell him where you are."

I looked at her. I still hadn't adjusted to her presence here. "All right," I said finally, and the five of us headed toward the castle.

20

THE CASTLE HAD double wooden doors, wide and about three stories tall, and a smaller door within one of the larger ones. I pushed on it and we went inside.

The door shut behind us. We were in the place I'd seen before, when I'd come to rescue Livvy. Trees stood around us, holding candles within their branches.

The sisters hesitated, looking around. "Come on," I said.

We went forward. I expected to see the dancers, and the witch sitting and watching them. Above all I expected to see Nick, lying in the witch's lap. I felt fear and hope, both at once.

The space in front of us opened up, but the room was empty. Our feet echoed over the green and gold tiles.

We'd have to go further in. I glanced over at Livvy. "Are you okay?" I asked.

She nodded. And she did seem calm—calmer, anyway. Then something darted out in front of us—a fox? a cat?—and she jumped back. She laughed nervously.

We walked on. We found ourselves in a long hall, with candles on the walls lighting our way. We passed rooms with open doors, and I looked inside as we went by. One held a harp that played itself, a pattern of roses carved in the wood. In another a girl sat on the floor, watching as ants sorted out a pile of grains. More stories we'd stumbled into, tales we would never learn the ends of.

I couldn't stop to wonder about them, though. We continued on. The hall branched out to the left and right, and we stopped.

"Do you want to know the way forward?" someone asked. I looked down and saw a frog.

"You're not going to trust anything he says, are you?" Rose asked. "That's the frog that took me to Mother Holle. And look at all those other things he said—that the pipe would only work on water, for example. He wanted me to try it, to get kidnapped."

"Well, but he also warned us about Ben—" Maddie said.

"Yeah, and how do you know that's true?" Rose said. "I can't believe Ben was lying to us all this time."

"He wasn't lying, not really," I said. I wished Maddie had never met that damn frog. "Yeah, he wanted your family's luck, but he also liked you, he liked going out with you."

"Right," Maddie said. "Where is he, then? What's he doing right now?"

"I don't know. But I'm sure he isn't—"

"Stop fighting, children," Livvy said. "We have to get going."

"Yes, and you need me to lead you to Nick," the frog said. He puffed up and down, up and down. Somehow he looked insufferably smug, and I wanted to smash that expression off his face. "Oh, and I did tell you the truth about Ben," he said to Maddie. "Ben was using you."

"That does it," Maddie said. She picked him up and cocked her arm back.

"Don't!" Rose said, but it was too late—Maddie had thrown the frog against the wall. A man stepped toward her. He wore a white shirt with a great many ruffles, and a velvet hat with a wide brim. He doffed the hat and bowed deeply to Maddie.

"Ah, the woman who broke my enchantment," he said. He looked far too pretty, with waving blond hair and blue eyes, and a mouth that looked ready to kiss somebody. "The woman who is going to marry me."

"I'm not marrying you!" Maddie said, horrified.

"You broke my enchantment. The witch said that whoever did that would be my bride. I was a prince, you know, before she enspelled me."

"I don't care. I'm not marrying you."

"I'm afraid you have to. The witch said—"

"I don't care what your witch said!"

"Quiet!" I said. "Do you want them to find us? You—" I turned to the frog. "Tell me how to get to Nick."

"Good—a man who knows his own mind," the frog said. "Go to the right."

I turned left. "No, wait!" the frog said. "I said right!"

I kept going. "And you also tricked us, like Rose said. I don't believe anything you say."

The man hurried to catch up with me. "Maybe I tricked you, but I never lied to you," he said.

I hesitated. There are no rules, Fiona had said—you just had to trust yourself. So what did I really think? Did I trust the frog or not?

I continued on. And there, in the first room I came to, I saw Nick asleep on a bed. "Nick!" I said. I ran through the door...

...and found myself in an enormous room, music playing, dancers swirling around me. I was back in the ballroom, in the house in Napa.

There were more people this time, it seemed like; the room was crowded with them. And pale colors were unfurling through the air, making it hard to see, the pink and sea-green and violet of the scarves the dancers wore.

"You can bring cake, or Porterhouse steak, but don't bring Lulu," someone sang. "Lulu gets blue, and she goes cuckoo like the clock on the shelf..."

"Will!" someone shouted.

"What?" I shouted back.

"It's me, Ben."

He pushed himself through a crowd of people. Someone else stepped through after him—Marya.

"How did you get here?" I asked him.

"I don't know. I found an inn or tavern or whatever they call it back there, and I walked through the door and ended up here."

Why, though? Had he and Marya failed some kind of test? I thought about what Maddie had said, that Ben had been lying to us all along. And Marya, too—she had always wanted something from me, from the family. Had they joined up, come up with some kind of plan together? And had the other realm pushed them out because of it?

No, that was ridiculous. Ben was my friend; he wouldn't do anything to harm me. And the other realm had sent me here too—though I was pretty sure that was because of the frog, that he had tricked me, had known I would do the opposite of whatever he said.

"Ben told me about the words you had to say," Marya said. She was still carrying that ridiculous sword. "You know—rick rack ruck. So we said them, over and over again, but nothing happened."

"Well, maybe someone from the family has to say them," I said.

I opened my mouth. Ben took hold of my arm, and Marya grabbed his other hand. I didn't know if I wanted them to come with me—I was pretty sure the other realm didn't want them—but I was even more anxious to get back.

"Rick rack ruck!" I said.

I was back in the corridor of the castle, just outside the room where I thought I'd seen Nick. I looked through the door again but of course Nick wasn't there; that had been more of their trickery. Now I saw that Ben and Marya had come along with me and were standing near me in the hallway, glancing around at the castle.

Livvy ran up to me, with Maddie following more slowly. "Where were you?" she asked.

I told her about the frog, the ballroom. "I thought so," Maddie said. "They don't want him here."

"So why did they let me come back?" Ben asked.

"Obviously they made a mistake."

"Quiet!" the frog said. "What's that?"

"What?" I asked.

"Footsteps, it sounds like."

"No one's listening to you," Maddie said. "There aren't any—"

"Quiet," Livvy said. "I do hear something."

A troop of guards turned a corner and came marching toward us, their swords drawn. As soon as I saw them I threw on the cloak of invisibility.

"Stop!" someone shouted, and the guards halted. They formed up two rows, and the witch walked between them.

"It's that family again, isn't it?" she asked. "The ones who have given me so much trouble. All of you here, together in one place. Very good—so much easier to devise your punishment that way."

She turned her glittering spectacles on Livvy. "You first, my little pumpkin," she said.

To my surprise Livvy stared straight back at her. "I wouldn't, if I were you," she said.

The witch laughed. "My but we're brave these days. And where's that meddling husband of yours?"

"Right here," I said. I moved quickly after I spoke, not wanting her to guess where my voice had come from.

She turned and seemed to look directly at me. I felt as if I'd been struck. Could she see through the cloak? Then her gaze moved on, and I went weak with relief.

"A cloak of invisibility," she said. "Very clever. And what if we take your wife prisoner, what then?" She motioned to one of the guards, who stepped behind Livvy and put a sword to her throat. "What if we kill her?"

Livvy's eyes went wide with fear. My mouth was dry, and I couldn't speak.

"Much better," she said. "You'll do as I say for once. All of you will leave this place, all but Nick. Nick will stay here, and sleep out his seven years."

"Are you going to let Livvy go?" I asked.

The witch looked at me, startled. It was only then that I realized what I'd done, that I'd given up on Nick without even thinking, traded him away for Livvy. How could I have done such a thing?

"All of you will leave, I said. All but Nick."

I'd lost, then. The witch had won this time. I'd go back to the world, back to my life, and wait for my son to wake up.

Well, but in exchange Livvy and Nick and I would have good fortune for the rest of our lives. I remembered Livvy in the hospital, the other realm showing us what might become of us if we crossed them, if we broke the bargain. I would never have to worry about illness or poverty or accidents or early death, all the terrifying, unexpected calamities of the world. My family, at least, would be protected.

Nick might even thank me. Livvy had been angry with me after she'd gotten out of the hospital, afraid that I'd put her at risk when I'd rescued her from the other realm. What if Nick felt the same way? He would come into his inheritance when he woke up, he'd be fortune's child. Who wouldn't want that?

I heard sounds from the other direction and turned quickly. Another troop of soldiers was coming toward us, a more motley group than the witch's guard. I saw three or four of the little fuzzy men, the ostrich with the man riding its back, the innkeeper with his long twiggy fingers.

The woodsman strode in front, his ax slung over his shoulder. "Come help us!" he said to us. "We can fight her, win out over her. You can have Nick back."

Marya ran over to them, carrying her unwieldy sword. "What about me?" she said. "Will you let me stay if I help you?"

"Of course we will," the woodsman said.

The guard behind Livvy lowered his sword and went to join the witch's army. Livvy and Maddie and Rose hurried into the nearest room. Sylvie stood in the hall, blinking at the confusion around her, and Livvy ran out again and pulled her back to safety.

I was still at the side of the hallway, covered by the cloak. The woodsman signaled his soldiers forward, and the two armies clashed.

At first all I saw was a blur of movement, people running, swords jumping, the witch urging her men on. And then suddenly, over all the noise, I heard someone sob. I would have recognized that sound anywhere—it was Nick, crying.

I looked around frantically, but couldn't find him. Instead I saw Ben; he had picked up a sword somewhere and was fighting alongside Marya and the woodsman.

Finally I spotted Nick, nearly hidden in the crowd. One of the witch's men was dragging him along, holding him firmly by the arm. His head was down, and his eyes were half-closed, as if he was trying to sleep.

I felt enraged, ready to do battle with the witch herself. I tried to reach him but there were too many people between us, too many skirmishes. I stood there, feeling helpless, as they pulled him along, into the middle of the fray.

Then I lost him again, could only see people moving back and forth, swords rising and falling. Someone cried out. Should I grab a sword like Ben, join the woodsman's army, try to rescue him? I stood, horribly uncertain.

Finally some soldiers in front of me moved, and I saw Nick again, only a few feet from me, so close I could make out his expression. His face looked set, determined, fighting against his obvious exhaustion.

The man holding him jerked his arm. Nick moaned and pulled away, sinking toward the floor as though he wanted to lie down in the midst of the battle. The man shook him roughly, forcing him awake. I looked quickly for wounds, scars, but Nick seemed unharmed.

Unharmed, I thought. I remembered something I'd noticed before, that none of the soldiers ever died, not here and not in Leeanne's story. No one even seemed to win these fights; they only scurried back and forth in confusion. It wasn't a war, then, not really. It was something else.

Nell had said they were fighting, though. But Nell had lied about other things; I couldn't trust her.

What were they doing, then? They were keeping Nick awake, for one thing, tiring him out. Was that why they made him dance as well? But why? What did they want?

Suddenly I understood everything, all the ways they'd tricked us over the years. I spotted Ben and ran toward him. "Ben!" I shouted. "Stop! Stop fighting!"

He glanced around, looking puzzled. Of course—I was still wearing the damn cloak. I shrugged it off. "Ben!" I said.

"Kinda busy here!" Ben said.

"Listen—this is important. Over here—I have to talk to you. I figured something out."

He lowered his sword. His opponent lowered his, too. If I'd needed more proof for my theory here it was: it wasn't the battle they cared about.

Ben came toward me. "I need your help," I said.

"I'm busy, I said." He looked out at the confusion in front of him, clearly anxious to get back into it.

"No, look. Why are you fighting for them?"

He turned back to me, reluctantly. "Why? For the reward, obviously."

"What reward?"

"Oh, come on, you know how fairy tales work. I help them, they help me."

"That's not what's happening here, though. They don't need you to fight for them, not really. The fighting isn't important, it's just—"

"Of course it's important. Don't you get it? I'm helping them overthrow the queen. She doesn't want to give me her good luck—well, maybe I can take it from her."

"But that's just what she wants. She wants everyone to fight, wants to spread chaos. She's tiring Nick out—look at him, he's exhausted—"

"Nick? Is Nick here?"

"Yeah, back over there. You have to stop fighting and help me—"

He wasn't listening. He grabbed the cloak from my hands, threw it over his shoulders, and in a blink he was gone.

"Hey!" I said. "Give that back!"

No one answered. Now what? I looked out at the battle but nothing had changed, no invisible warrior fighting among the witch's guard.

Nick screamed. Some invisible force was pulling on his arm, trying to force him away from his captor. He hung between the two of them, stretched to his limit; another minute and he'd be torn in half.

Take his shackle off, Uncle Lem had said. Did I believe Uncle Lem, though?

I thought I did. "Ben!" I shouted. "Take his shackle off. The shackle!"

The shackle opened, then vanished. Nick's captor let him go, and he stood staring around him, uncertain.

"Nick!" I said. "Over here!"

He ran toward me. I put my arm around him, held him close.

When I looked up I saw Ben again; he'd taken off the cloak and was confronting the witch. "I have the shackle you put on Nick," he said. "Do you want it back? I'll trade it for the same bargain you made with the Feierabends. The one where I sleep for seven years, or someone in my family does, and everything I do prospers."

The fighting around us stopped. Everyone stood and watched the two of them, waiting.

The witch said nothing for a long moment. "All right," she said finally. "Give me the shackle and you can go. Go, and I'll grant you good fortune, you and all your family."

He grinned and started to hand her the shackle. "Wait!" I said. "What about us?"

"You?" the witch said. "You will stay here, you and your family."

"No, but wait," Ben said. "They come with me."

"Ah, but you didn't say that, my pet," the witch said. "You'll have to bargain better than that."

"All right, then. We all get to leave, *and* I get my good fortune, and then I give you the shackle back."

The witch laughed. "You mustn't overreach yourself, dearie. The shackle isn't that important to us. We'll give you the good fortune you want, but Nick has to stay here."

Livvy and Maddie had come out of their room and were watching him closely. What would he do now? I remembered how envious he'd always seemed, of me and my life, all the times he'd wished he'd had my luck. And I remembered how he'd been returned to the ballroom, and my question about why the other realm had thrust him out. Maybe some force had been working to protect us then, the Feierabends. Maybe the magic had known he would betray us, and had put him somewhere he couldn't do any harm.

"Great," Maddie said, echoing my thoughts. "It's all over—he'll sell us out. It's always been about him."

"Quickly now," the witch said. "I can't wait forever for you to decide. Give us the shackle or go."

He walked toward me, slowly, and handed me the shackle.

"What?" I said. "What do you—"

"Your turn, man," he said. "Do what you want with it."

I turned the shackle over and over in my hand. What *did* I want? I thought of Livvy at the hospital, how cold I'd felt, how I could never seem to get warm. I shuddered, overtaken by a memory of that coldness.

And I remembered my earlier thought, that leaving Nick here might not be so bad. That we would escape all of life's disasters, that Nick might even thank me. Who wouldn't want that control over the malign fates, over all the ill chances out in the world?

All I had to do was give the shackle back. We could walk away, everyone but Nick. Livvy and the rest of the family would understand; I couldn't have done anything else.

Except I could. I did know something that might get Nick back. But should I do it? We'd been protected for so long; it would be like taking a step in complete darkness. Would there even be ground beneath me, or was I about to walk off a cliff?

And what would Livvy and Maddie think? Maddie didn't even know Nick that well; would she care enough about him to let him go?

There wasn't enough time to ask them, though. I made my decision. Quickly, before I could change my mind, I turned to the witch and said, "All right—we're back where we started. Let all of us go, and I'll give you the shackle."

"Didn't you hear me, my little poppet? The shackle isn't important to us. I'll let you go free, but you'll have to leave Nick behind."

"I don't believe you. You need us—you've been taking us for years. And you need the shackle to keep us here."

"Nonsense. We take you because it amuses us, nothing more."

"That isn't true. I know what you're doing. I figured it all out. You're taking over places in our world—that hill that Wilhelm Grimm went into, and Lem's restaurant, and parts of Telegraph Avenue, and the farmhouse. You take someone for seven years, and you keep them busy fighting, busy dancing, because the more tired they are the easier it is for you to—to come into our world. To use them as a stepping stone. You take over their subconscious, somehow, you use their dreams. There isn't any fighting, not really. Both sides are the same—that's why there are never any dead left after a battle. It's all a—a play you're putting on."

For the first time I saw her look shaken. "All right," she said. "You're right—we do need the shackle. But I can't let Nick go—it's impossible."

"Why?"

"It would mean breaking the bargain, for one thing."

She was considering it, thinking about what would have to happen before she let us go. I might win after all. But there was no triumph in the thought—instead I felt uneasy, fearful of what I'd done.

"Well, but you broke it at least once, that I know of," I said. "There was a book that said you did, *Spiderweb and Candlelight*."

"That book didn't tell the whole story. Someone has to sleep out the whole seven years. And even so, the bargain will be broken immediately, your luck will run out the moment you leave our realm. When Livvy—when Livvy left us we bided our time, waiting for another sleeper. Then Nick came, and he took her place. One of you has to stay here, for whatever time is left. Six and a half years, now."

"I don't believe you. I took Livvy last time—why can't I take Nick now?"

"You were outside our realm when you took her. And now you're here, and you must abide by our rules. He won't be allowed to leave. Even if I tell my guards to let him go, the realm itself will keep him."

"I'll do it," Marya said suddenly. "I'll trade places with Nick, I'll sleep here for seven years. And I don't even want the family's good fortune—all I want is to stay here after I wake up."

"I can't do that," the witch said.

"Why not?"

The witch looked at her. I thought I saw sadness in her eyes, even sympathy—but no, it had to be a trick of the light on her spectacles. "Because there are a good many conditions. The most important is the glamour—the people we take have to have a sort of magic of their own. I'm sorry, my child."

"All right," Rose said. "I know what you're all thinking. I'll stay here."

Everyone spoke at once. "Rose!" "No!"

"Why not?" Rose said. She looked at her mother. "Isn't that what you wanted? You never had much time for me—it was always Maddie and Livvy, how smart they were, how talented. You always thought I'd be the bondmaid."

"You can't stay here, Rose," Ben said. "You have your whole life ahead of you. You're supposed to be a history professor, remember?"

"No I'm not. I'm supposed to do this. It's what they raised me to do, Sylvie and Hilbert." She looked at Sylvie again.

"All right," Sylvie said. "Maybe I did think that, a little. Anyone would. My daughters were so—so wonderful, so much more than I ever expected. And you were wonderful too, of course you were, but by the time you were born I couldn't bear to lose Maddie or Livvy. Hilbert was the same way—that's why he left, partly, because he felt so guilty about the way he treated you. And so did I—I felt guilty too." She raised her head. "All right. I'll stay here—you go and live your life."

"What?" Rose said.

"Sure. I can't make up for the way I treated you, I know that, but I can do this one thing. It's funny—this was what I was afraid of, all those years. Afraid that one of you would fall asleep. But it doesn't seem so bad, not really."

"But—" Livvy said. "But what about Hilbert? Didn't you say he's thinking of coming back?"

Sylvie nodded. "He wants us to get married again. Well, if he's really serious about it he'll wait for me, don't you think? I'll be—let's see, in six and a half years we'll both be sixty-four." She laughed.

"It's not as easy as that," the witch said. "You're breaking the bargain, remember. We won't take another bondmaid after Sylvie. All the good fortune we bring you will come to an end."

Sylvie looked at me. "All right," I said, quickly, before I could change my mind. I tightened my arm around my son.

"Very well, then," the witch said. "But one other thing will happen if we break the bargain. Our realm and yours will move further apart, and the places where they overlap will disappear. Our glamour will fade from your world, and magic will vanish. Your lives will be less exciting."

"Can't you just find another bondmaid?" Marya asked.

"Very good, my clever one," the witch said. "Yes, we might find a new family, and make a new bargain. But as I said, those who make the bargain are not so easy to come by. The people we take can't want too much, for one thing—they have to be content with what we give them. They have to come from a large family, of course, so we can choose one from every generation. And they have to live close to our realm, to believe in the possibility of it, to have their own magic. The Feierabends—you were the best we'd found, in all our long years of searching. We'll miss you."

I was startled, and I could see from the sisters' expressions that they felt the same way. The witch seemed to grow less and less malevolent the longer we stood there. Maybe, I thought, she was as bound to the story as we were. Maybe she had to act the part of the witch who kidnaps children, just as we had to be the children she kidnapped.

"Are you ready, Sylvie?" she said. She grew taller; she seemed as great as Mother Holle in Rose's story, or the giant in the cave.

She led Sylvie into a room, and showed her a bed. Sylvie went over to it and lay down. I wanted to ask her if she was sure she wanted to do this, but I was too afraid of what she'd say. Instead I gave the shackle to the witch, and she fastened it around Sylvie's wrist.

Sylvie's daughters leaned over her and kissed her. "Goodbye," I said.

"Goodbye," she said. She laughed again. "See you in six and a half years."

"You can leave now," the witch said to us. "The guards will let you go."

"Thank you," I said.

We went slowly, though, with a lot of backward looks at Sylvie. Once we were past all the soldiers we started hurrying, and then we ran through the castle corridors to the doorway.

"Rick rack ruck!" Maddie shouted as we pushed through the front door.

Nothing happened. We looked at each other nervously. "The frog told Fiona we had to stand at the border," Rose said.

"That's right, I did," the frog said. I hadn't realized he'd followed us.

"And were you telling us the truth?" I asked.

"I've never lied to you," he said.

That wasn't exactly an answer, but I remembered all too well what had happened the last time I hadn't taken his advice. "All right, then," I said. "Where's the border?"

"I tell three secrets only," the frog said.

I could see why Maddie had thrown him against the wall. "I think we have to get back to the beginning," Livvy said. "Where we came in."

I looked at the frog again, but he said nothing. "All right," I said.

We started walking across the castle lawn. Nick took my hand as we went, and looked up at me. "I was fighting, Dad," he said. "And there were lots of people, and horses, and, and dogs... And I liked it, at first, but then I got tired, and they wouldn't let me sleep. They never let me sleep, Dad."

His face twisted, but he managed to keep himself from crying. "It's okay," I said. I hugged him closer to me. "You'll never have to go back there, I promise. And when we get home you can sleep as long as you want to."

"Weeks?"

"Sure, if that's what you want."

"Hello!" someone called. It was Fiona. "Is that your son? And who's this?"

She was looking at the frog. "I'm Maddie's husband," the frog said.

"No he's not," Maddie said.

A man came running toward us, the tail of his frock coat flying. "Uncle Lem!" Livvy called. "What are you doing here?"

"I told you—I want to help," he said. "I was thinking about you going into the castle alone, facing that witch, and I had to come. Am I too late? What happened?"

"This is Nick," I said to Lem and Fiona. "You were right, Lem—I had to take the shackle off to free him. Thank you."

"So there's nothing more I can do?" He looked dejected; he seemed to want to redeem himself, to make up somehow for Nell's trickery.

I couldn't think of anything, though. Then suddenly I remembered the ferryman at the river. He wasn't part of our story, but if Lem could help him he might feel useful.

"Do you know why the ferryman has to carry people across the river?" I asked.

"I do, yes." He looked around at the others, and his eyes behind the half-moon glasses narrowed with suspicion. He didn't know Ben or Marya, Fiona or the frog.

He drew me aside. "Someone has to take the pole away from him," he whispered. "Then that person becomes the ferryman."

"Okay, thanks," I said. I had the beginning of an idea, but I wasn't sure if it would work.

Fiona studied us when we came back. "Uncle Lem?" she said. She seemed to be trying out the name. "How are you related to the family?"

"I'm Peter's son," Lem said.

"I was Peter's cousin. Fiona."

"Fiona," Lem said, looking amazed. "I remember your mother, my great-aunt. She never stopped mourning for you."

"Oh," Fiona said.

"And here you were, all this time. Why did I never meet you?"

"Oh," Fiona said again. "I was—well, I was in the shape of a dog. Rose freed me. Can you—maybe you can help me, show me around this realm. I didn't learn very much about it, while I was a dog."

"Of course I can," Lem said. "I'll take you home with me, introduce you to my wife Nell. We'll help you—of course we will."

"Be careful of Nell, though," Livvy said.

We began to walk away from the castle. "Now, Livvy," Lem said. "She's not as bad as that."

"Isn't she?"

Lem laughed. Clearly he didn't want to answer her.

We headed back along the path, away from the castle. Fiona was busy with Lem, asking him questions. I turned to Ben. "So why did you give me the shackle?" I asked.

"Yeah," Marya said. "Why did you? You could have given it to me instead."

Ben shrugged. "I don't know. Maybe it was because of what Maddie said, that all I cared about was myself. Maybe I just wanted to prove her wrong."

"Well, that's petty," Maddie said. I hadn't known she was listening.

"Come now, Maddie," the frog said. "That's no way for any wife of mine to behave."

Maddie turned toward him angrily, but Ben spoke before she could answer him. "I was kidding," he said. "You want to know why, really? Because friendship is stronger than greed."

I couldn't say anything. Ben couldn't either, I saw, and I knew I had to change the subject or we'd end up getting a lot mushier than either of us wanted.

Just then we came to the river, and the ferryman.

21

"I HAVE TO LEAVE YOU NOW," Lem said. "My house is this way."

"Fiona?" I said. "Are you coming?"

She shook her head. "I told you—I have to stay. I made a promise."

"We've broken other promises," I said.

"Not this one. I'm going with Lem."

Everyone hugged her, even the frog, and Rose told her to visit the farmhouse if she ever changed her mind. Then we all climbed on the boat, me and Nick and Livvy, Rose and Maddie, Ben and Marya and the frog. We watched the two of them walk away as the ferryman pushed off from the bank.

"Do you know why I have to carry people across the river?" the ferryman asked.

"I do, yes," I said. "It's because you're the only one in all the world who can do it. There isn't another person who can take this boat across the river."

"That can't be right," he said.

"No, it's ridiculous," the frog said. "I don't believe it."

"It's true, though," I said to the frog. "Uncle Lem told me. Go ahead—try it."

"All right, I will," the frog said. He grabbed the pole away from the ferryman and pushed the boat through the water. "There, see?"

The ferryman walked up and down the length of the boat. "Hey," he said. "I'm free. I'm free to go." He laughed and flung out his arms, then did a little dance on the deck. "I'm free! You got the frog to take over from me, and I'm free!"

"Wait," the frog said. "I'm not doing any such thing. Here." He tried to put the pole down, but it stuck to his hand. His pretty face twisted in horror. "Here—take this thing away from me. I'm not a ferryman—I have to marry Maddie!"

Maddie laughed. "I told you, that's not going to happen," she said.

"But the witch said—"

"Yeah, and other people said other things," I said. "Someone put a spell on the ferryman, and you broke it."

We reached the other bank and leapt off the boat. "This isn't over!" the frog shouted after us, jumping up and down. "I can break the spell too! You'll see!"

"He'll forget how to break the spell, just like I did," the ferryman said. He had gotten off the boat with us and was walking back and forth, as ungainly as a puppy. "Don't worry, he won't come after you."

"But what if someone else figures out how to break it?" Maddie asked.

"Well, they might," he said. "But I doubt if he'll be able to find you by then. You're going back to your own realm, aren't you?"

"Yeah."

"Listen," the ferryman said to me. "Thank you. If there's anything I can do for you—"

"Anything?" Marya asked, turning her strange flat eyes on me.

"Forget it," I said. "We've made enough bargains for one day. I just want to leave this place without getting into any more trouble."

"What about letting me stay here?" Marya asked the ferryman.

"That isn't up to me, I'm afraid," he said. "What else would you like?"

"Well, I'd like to find the border," I said.

"This way," he said, heading down a path. His gait was surer now. "But I meant something difficult, some way I can help you."

"All right," I said. "What *can* you do?"

"Well," he said. "Not much, now I come to think of it. All I really know is how to take someone from one place to another."

I got an idea then, something to do with the Blake poem I had once quoted to Rose. "Did you ever take Hans across the river?"

"Hans?"

"He works for Those People, the way I did. A short stout man, with a feather duster made out of peacock feathers."

"Yes, of course. I remember him."

"When he comes back here, could you take him somewhere?"

"Where?"

I'd forgotten the address, but Rose remembered it. I gave it to him, then said, "It's in the Mission District in San Francisco. A woman named Valerie lives there. If he could clean her house every so often, well, things might start going better for her."

"Sure," he said. "I can do that."

"Great."

Every few seconds I had looked around for Nick, and now I saw him a few feet behind me, walking with Livvy. I waited for him to catch up.

"Hey," he said. "That was funny, what you did to that guy in the boat."

I pulled him close. In just a year or two, or so people said, he was going to stop letting me hug him. I decided to take full advantage of it while I could.

We turned onto a familiar-looking road, one that would take us to the meadow. It hadn't been so close to the castle the last time, but I knew that things worked differently here.

We continued on through the meadow, past the red and orange and purple wildflowers. The path took a final turn and came out at the market. We made our way through the vendors hawking their wares, the acrobats, a group of people with beaks instead of mouths. A troupe of dancers wove ribbons around us; we brushed them off and went on.

Marya slowed, looking with longing at everything around us. "Did you see that?" she asked as someone passed us, herding a flock of possums. "Do you think I can, well, stay here?"

I didn't think so, not when they'd tried to push her out once before. It had to be heartbreaking: she loved this place, she fit in far better here than she ever had in our world. And yet for some reason the people in this realm didn't want her.

"I don't know," I said.

"They wouldn't even make a bargain with me," she said. "She was polite about it, that queen, but she sure let me know that my family isn't good enough. We don't have the right whatever-it-was. Glamour."

"Yeah, but she said that almost no one does. There aren't a lot of families like the Feierabends."

"Don't flatter yourself."

"I'm not. I wasn't born into the family—"

"Yeah, but they chose you. Listen—you're supposed to help me here. How the hell am I supposed to get on with my life after I've been, well, rejected? Rejected by all this?" She waved her arm at the market around us.

"I guess we'll work on it," I said. Maybe now, with all her hopes of making a bargain gone, she could learn to live in our world. "At your next session."

She said nothing, but I thought I saw her nod.

We came to the booths and stalls we'd seen when we first got here. "Are we all here?" I asked.

The ferryman had slipped away. I looked around for him and saw that he had caught hold of a ribbon and was dancing along with the rest of the troupe, winding the ribbons through the market.

I saw the rest of them, though—Livvy and Nick, Rose and Maddie, Ben and Marya. "All right," I said. I took a breath. "Rick rack ruck!"

Fog billowed up around us. I took hold of Nick's hand, then turned to look for Marya on my other side—and saw her running away blindly through the fog. I grabbed Livvy instead and we stepped forward.

The fog parted. We stood in the ballroom, the huge space echoing around us. "Wow," someone said.

"Yeah," I said.

Someone had fallen, halfway across the room. I went to help and saw that it was Marya. She couldn't stay after all; the other realm had thrust her out again.

She stood up cautiously, saying nothing. We left the room, each of us caught up in our own thoughts.

And that really is the end, though I can't say we lived happily ever after. We lived like most people, I guess, the good and the bad mixed together.

We didn't find Nick asleep in his bed, of course; he'd left the other realm with us. Sylvie was in her room, though; she seemed to be sleeping peacefully enough.

We also found that a roof had collapsed in one of the unused bedrooms. It wasn't exactly the Fall of the House of Usher, but we knew that it was the beginning, that other things would start to go wrong from now on. We couldn't take care of Sylvie in Napa, so Livvy and I brought her home with us.

A week after we came back Ben told me he was dating Rose, which surprised me at first and then seemed to have been inevitable all along. I realized that I'd thought she might be gay, though that had only been because she reminded me of Fiona, a stupid reason if ever there was one.

I did wonder if he was seeing her because he was still interested in the family's luck. But their luck had ended for good; he had to have realized that.

A year later Rose got a job at a college up north, and Ben moved up there to be with her. Around that time we had a family meeting to discuss selling the farmhouse, but Ben and Rose were against it; they said they wanted to live there someday. I didn't see how they could, with Rose's job hundreds of miles away, but Maddie, surprisingly, agreed with them; at least, she said, it should stay in the family. The mortgage had been paid off a long time ago, so we're hanging on and trying to fix as much as we can.

And Ben actually finished his novel, and got it published. I think he expected more to follow after that, movie deals, television appearances, who knows what. All that happened was that it got some good reviews and then disappeared—and that Ben realized he had to write another one. He's made a start, though.

Maddie keeps working, though every time she gets a part she's sure it'll be her last. But she's never said a word about the bargain to me, and I think she finally realizes how much the other realm had taken from her family. Maybe not, though—as I say, we don't talk about it.

Marya still comes to see me once a week. Sometimes I even think we're making progress.

And the bad? Well, that part isn't as easy to talk about. A year after we came back from the other realm, in 1987, Livvy got pregnant again, but our child was stillborn. It was a girl, beautiful, perfect. Was this the other realm reaching out, telling us that if they couldn't have a girl we couldn't either? Or was it just random bad luck, the kind of thing that could happen to anyone? One thing I do know—it would never have happened if we hadn't broken the bargain.

Even now, three years later, Livvy is still sometimes depressed. I don't think her family knows how to deal with hardship; everything has always gone so well for them. I tried to help, but in the end it was antidepressants that did the most for her. She's still not completely over it, though, not yet.

Ben and Rose just came to visit. We usually don't talk about the bargain, but a few days before their visit I thought of a question I'd never really had answered.

"You know what I was wondering?" I asked Ben after dinner. Livvy and Rose had gone off somewhere to talk. "What the hell was all that about the spider? 'Spinne am morgan,' whatever? Do you remember the whole thing?"

"Sure," he said. "It's a proverb, about what happens when you see a spider. 'Spinne am morgan bringt kummer und sorgen.' Spider in the morning brings sorrow and worry. 'Spinne am mittag bringt glück am dritten tag'—Spider at midday brings luck on the third day. 'Spinne am abend bringt glück und gaben'—Spider in the evening brings luck and gifts."

"But what does it mean? What does it have to do with the bargain, and the Feierabends? Why did they use it as a password in the other realm?"

"I think—well, it means that some people get luck and some people don't."

I thought about Valerie. I kept wanting to visit her, to find out if having a clean house had made any difference in her life, but I never did. Maybe I didn't really want to know. Anyway, Hans had been freed this year, fifty years after he'd started; I knew that because the farmhouse was looking worse and worse, dust piling up in the corners, spiderwebs (those spiders again) on the ceilings.

"Maybe," I said. "But maybe—well, the spider stays the same, all day. It's the luck that changes, from bad to good. Maybe they're saying—I don't know—that all luck is the same, that it all depends on how you think about it."

"You really believe that? That all luck is the same?"

"I don't know. I'd like to." I thought about Livvy again—sorrow and worry—and I tried to listen for her and Rose. Rose had strict instructions to cheer her up. "How are you and Rose doing?"

"Pretty good."

"The bargain's over, though, right?"

"Well, yeah. Sure." He thought a moment. "Wait a minute. You don't think—do you think that's why I married Rose? To get the family's luck?"

"No. Well, I did wonder about it for a while, after what you told me about Professor Rothapfel. But you were there, in the other realm—you saw what happened. You had to know that it was all over."

"I did, yeah." Another pause. "There's still something about that family, though. You know what I mean? That glamour the queen talked about. Rose has it, just like Maddie and Livvy. Even Sylvie, in her own way."

He stopped. We were both very much aware of Sylvie sleeping heavily in the bedroom upstairs. She would wake up in two and a half years—changed, of course, the way every bondmaid had been.

"I couldn't stay away," Ben went on. "Well, you saw me. I had to keep coming back, even though I knew Maddie hated me."

"She doesn't hate you."

"She doesn't like me a whole lot, though, does she?"

"Well, maybe not."

"That was a rhetorical question."

"Well, that was a rhetorical answer."

He laughed. Livvy and Rose came back just then, and the talk turned to other things.

And here I am, the day after their visit, trying to finish up this account. But there's something I keep coming back to, one final question. I thought I was writing this history to get everything straight in my head, to set it all down, but now I wonder if it was just so I could find an answer.

What was it the queen had said? "One other thing will happen if we break the bargain. Our realm and yours will move further apart, and the places where they overlap will disappear. Our glamour will fade from your world, and magic will vanish. Your lives will be less exciting."

I hadn't paid a lot of attention to that; I'd been too focused on getting Nick back, and then on leaving safely. Now, though, I sometimes think about nothing else.

It's true, our lives are less exciting. The thrills of our youth, when the four of us were together—I've never had anything like that again. There seems to be less fun in the world, less laughter; even the colors seem duller.

Or am I just a cranky old guy, complaining that everything is so different nowadays? Or, worse, just another aging hippie? But our time, when we were young—it really was special, even the history books are starting to say so. There never was music like that, never those intense discussions, never so many people so passionately committed to changing the world. It felt like the world was just about to crack open and show us something new, something brilliant.

I'm writing this in the epochal year 1990, right after the Berlin Wall came down. All week long we've been seeing celebrations on TV, the East Germans' and our own. "We won!" the people over here are shouting. "Hooray for capitalism! Greed is good!"

And of course the fall of the Berlin Wall is a terrific thing, I'm not saying it isn't. I never thought I'd live to see it. But what are people really saying here? That the only thing that works in this world is greed, the only thing that matters is coming out on top? Even if that's true, is it really something we want to celebrate?

And yet people seem to. Some of my patients spend hours talking about the things they want to buy, mansions, different kinds of mustard, books about getting ahead in business. They seem more superficial, though I'm trying hard not to believe that.

Just the other day one of them said, "Nothing surprises me anymore." He said it proudly, as if he'd reached some hard-won wisdom, some pinnacle of cool. And I thought of the days right after I met Livvy, when I'd felt stupefied with wonder, startled and delighted at every turn.

The eighties were like the fifties, Ben said yesterday, only in color.

What did I do, when I broke the bargain? Did I change the world that much, will magic and adventure and joy and beauty start to dwindle and fade away, will nothing be left but selfishness and greed? Was that the fourth thing the frog knew, the secret he wouldn't tell us?

No, I'm being ridiculous here, grandiose. One person can't really have this much power—at least I don't think so.

I still enjoy my life, of course I do. I love Livvy and Nick (though Nick is now fourteen, and spends all his time away from home; I hardly see him at all). I enjoy getting together with Ben and Rose, though they live too far away to see very often. I like my work, though it's getting a little repetitious, just a tiny bit boring.

If I had known that all this would happen, would I have chosen differently?